HERE LIES A VENGEFUL BITCH

HERE LIES A VENGEFUL BITCH

CODIE CROWLEY

HYPERION
Los Angeles   New York

First Edition, August 2024
10 9 8 7 6 5 4 3 2 1
FAC-004510-24165
Printed in the United States of America

This book is set in Horley Old Style MT Pro/Monotype
Designed by Zareen Johnson
Stock image: peach emoji 1073375483/Shutterstock

Library of Congress Cataloging-in-Publication Data
Names: Crowley, Codie, author.
Title: Here lies a vengeful bitch / by Codie Crowley.
Description: First edition. • Los Angeles : Hyperion, 2024. • Audience: Ages 14–18. • Audience: Grades 10–12. • Summary: Annie Lane was not doing much of anything with her young life, but now that she is dead she has a purpose—figure out who murdered her and make sure they can never kill anyone else.
Identifiers: LCCN 2023017700 • ISBN 9781368099905 (hardcover) • ISBN 9781368103480 (ebook)
Subjects: LCSH: Murder victims—Juvenile fiction. • Murderers—Juvenile fiction. • Revenge—Juvenile fiction. • Ghost stories. • CYAC: Mystery and detective stories. • Ghosts—Fiction. • Murder victims—Fiction. • Murderers—Fiction. • Revenge—Fiction. • LCGFT: Detective and mystery fiction. • Ghost stories.
Classification: LCC PZ7.1.C7725 He 2024 • DDC 813.6 [Fic]—dc23/eng/20231101
LC record available at https://lccn.loc.gov/2023017700

Reinforced binding

Visit www.HyperionTeens.com

SUSTAINABLE FORESTRY INITIATIVE

Certified Sourcing

www.forests.org
SFI-01681

Logo Applies to Text Stock Only

If you're so pissed off it feels like
the next man who mistakes you for a good time
is going to find out you're actually his worst nightmare—
this book is for you.

Author's Note

This book is, in some ways, an exorcism of my own lived experiences—and it touches on subjects that may be part of your experience, too. Please consider the following content guidance when deciding if it's the right time for you to read this story.

Here Lies a Vengeful Bitch contains depictions of:

- Violence and murder
- Emotional, verbal, and physical abuse
- Implied threats of sexual assault
- Sexual harassment
- Revenge porn/leaked nudes
- Drugs administered without consent
- Fire and burn injuries
- Gore, including blood and vomit
- Bullying
- Alcohol, tobacco, and drug use
- Death of a loved one

ONE

I HAVE REALLY out-fucked myself this time.

I mean, I know I'm already a champion screw-up, but if you were waiting for my gold medal moment—well, this is it.

My fingers claw at the earth. Cold dirt cakes my chipped red nails. The rushing current tugs at my frozen legs, pulling like hands around my ankles, dragging me back to the dark riverbed.

Back to where I just woke up, beneath the icy water.

I don't know how I got here. When I opened my eyes, I was already thrashing in the current. Daylight glares through golden leaves, which means I'm missing *a lot* of time—because the last thing I remember is the sweaty crush of kids crammed into the club where I was waiting for my ex-boyfriend's band to get onstage.

Now I'm *here*.

Crawling out of the river, hair tangled with leaves, cold water pouring from my mouth.

My hands find a tree root, and I wrap my muddy fingers around it. Stones along the bank scrape my legs, catching my frayed tights as I haul myself out of the churning cold.

With chattering teeth and shivering limbs, I squirm until I'm sitting up against a tree trunk. The bark pokes at my spine through my soaked black minidress. All I see are more trees around me, stretching on and on in every direction. I could be anywhere in the endless acres of state forest that surround my tiny hometown.

What *happened* last night?

Did I drink too much of the tequila stashed in my bag? Did Gun and his friends dump me out here as a joke? The last thing I remember is being with him, but tossing me in the river seems like kind of a sick joke, even for my narcissist ex and his butt-sucking bandmates.

No. Whatever happened last night, I doubt it was anyone's idea of a joke.

When I close my eyes I see the same forest, but it's dark and I'm running from something. Some*one*. I open my eyes and gasp, choking on something caught in my throat. I dig my fingers into my mouth and scrape mucky pine needles and twigs from my tongue.

What. The. Fuck?

I stare at the woodsy detritus slicking my fingers and gnaw on the remnants still stuck between my teeth.

My mind is sloshy, and my body feels as if it's made from the same stuff I just coughed up, needly and waterlogged. I wipe my fingers on my tights and look around again, blinking past the droplets caught in my lashes.

I might not know where I am, but I don't want to wait until whoever left me here comes back for me.

I have to get the hell out of here.

I stand, knees mushy, my boots flopping and squelching under my feet. I shiver against the breeze that blows on my damp skin and the dress that barely covers me. I don't know where my jacket is—or my purse, or my *phone*, for that matter. Maybe they're lost in the river I crawled out of, but I'm definitely not going back in there to look for them.

I wrap my arms around my stomach, pick a direction at random, and start walking.

My feet drag in the dead leaves like I'm trudging through snow. My whole body feels like room-temperature cherry soft serve, pink and runny in the cold dawn light. While I hike, the sun shifts higher in the sky, but its rays barely warm me through the browning canopy of leaves overhead.

I'm not sure how long I walk. My thoughts rush, the trees sway, the water on my skin never dries. Then, finally, a break in the trees—and beyond it, pale yellow siding and a moss-covered porch.

Civilization. Hopefully, I've found my way out of these woods . . . so I can get to figuring out how the fuck I wound up here in the first place.

My numb legs grow weaker with each step. I stumble past the tree line and collapse in the tall grass behind the house. I tip my face up toward the dawn and notice the cracks in the yellow siding, the variegated shimmer of the sun on broken windowpanes.

There's no one here who can help me.

There hasn't been anyone here for a long time.

My legs are liquid against the grass. I think they could melt right into the ground and trickle between the dirt and rocks, sinking into the clay. Maybe the rest of me could follow. I could water this little patch of grass, catch the sunlight on its blades, and fade away with the passing autumn. I think about it for a while, but then I get up again and stumble around the side of the house.

Across the parched lawn there's a dirt road that curves through the trees, lined with more long-deserted homes. A blue cottage faces the yellow house behind me. THE DEVIL WAS HERE is streaked on the door in stark black paint. I shiver and hurry past, hiking farther up the road.

At least now I know where I am.

"Hey!" someone shouts. "Where are you squirming to, worm?"

3

"Yeah. Wait up for the early birds!"

I spin around. Two boys stand on the road behind me. Their eyes are the same shiny copper as their hair, their sweaters are ill-fitting, and they have matching toothy grins on their identical faces. They can't be much younger than me, but they *are* much smaller. Their petite stature and gaunt limbs don't make me any less uneasy to find them here.

If I am where I think I am, *no one* should be here.

"I need help," I croak. "Do you have a phone?"

"A phone? Who would you call?" The boy on the right giggles.

"Lady, there's no hotline for *your* problem," says the one on the left.

The right one lifts his hand like he's picking up the receiver on an old telephone. The left one does the same.

"Operator," says the right.

In a falsetto impression of me, the other says, "Hello, Operator, I need help—"

"Whoa there, lady. What you need is an undertaker!"

"Leave her alone, brats," barks a third voice from behind me. A girl swoops in, drawing a knitted shawl off her shoulders to bundle around me. I grasp at the dry wool as the solemn-eyed girl who gave it to me chucks the plum she's holding at the boys in the road.

The boy on the left catches it and takes a bite. Bloodred juice dribbles from his teeth.

"She needs help," the boy on the right taunts, before he steals the plum from his mirror image.

"What the hell is your *problem*?" I snarl.

"Same as *yours*," he says like some kind of playground insult, sticking his hands on his hips.

The girl folds an arm around my shoulders and turns me away from them. "Beat it, you two, seriously," she says.

The two boys chitter behind us, but they don't follow as she leads me away. Once we make it around the bend in the road, she says, "They don't mean anything by all that. They think they're just playing around."

"Sure. They're hilarious."

"They're Hunt and Howl. I'm Fern," she tells me.

"Annabel," I say.

"All right, Annabel. You know where you are?"

Of course I do. The abandoned town at the top of Resurrection Peak is the stuff of local legend. I visited once with my big brother, Neil, who said that when the paper mill closed for good in the 1950s everyone just up and left for lack of work.

Maybe that's the truth, but it's not the only tale I've heard about why the town was abandoned.

As kids we used to whisper about it during slumber parties, breathless and hushed in the dark like the ghosts might creep down the mountain and snatch us from our sleeping bags. There was always something about a phantom killer who slaughtered half the town and drove the other half to flee, a sadistic demon who couldn't be caught and must roam the mountain still. Resurrection Peak was our nightmare fuel, our campfire story, our goose bump shivers and sleepless nights.

But it's just an urban legend. There's not *really* supposed to be anyone up here.

My sloshy legs buckle, and Fern seems prepared. The arm locked around my shoulders crushes me to her side to keep me up. Her downturned mouth presses tight, but she holds my weight and we keep walking. It's nice and all, but I have to wonder what she's doing up here at dawn, walking around an abandoned village in suede slippers with her hair wrapped in blue silk like *she* just woke up, too. And where is she *taking* me?

A stone obelisk at the corner says the road we're on is called He Is the Way. I'm so tired of walking. "I really need help," I whisper. "I think something happened to me last night...."

Fern's fingers knead at my shoulder through the shawl wrapped around me. "I know," she says. "We'll help you, okay? Can you tell me what happened?"

What happened...

What happened?

I drop my lids and images splash across my mind. I see headlights blinding my eyes. Broken glass beneath my boots. My face bent over a toilet seat in a pink bathroom stall. Trees turning sideways as I fall to the ground. Blood on my palms, glimmering black in the moonlight.

I shake my head and force my eyes open, staring up at the gates that guard the empty estate at the highest point of the peak. One of the wrought-iron doors is open, beckoning us on.

"No," I say. "I don't— I'm not sure—"

"Okay," Fern says as we pass through the gate. "It's okay. Let's just get you inside, all right?"

"Inside?" I repeat. "Do you live up here? I thought nobody *lived* up here...."

"Technically we don't," Fern says, and keeps leading me up the dusty drive.

The Gilded Age mansion at the top of the hill is a moldering testament to a time before this town's industry became obsolete.

Everyone back home calls this place Chapel House, probably on account of the cathedral-like touches to the mansion's grandiose Romanesque architecture.

Brittle ivy swaddles the wraparound porch. The brick has darkened to the color of old blood. There's a turret that looks like a church spire jutting up toward the yellow sky. I guess it's kind of a cool place to crash if you have nowhere better to go, but I still can't believe there's really anyone living all the way up here. The road to the top of Resurrection Peak is just an unkempt byway, the turnoff nearly hidden on the main highway that cuts through my hometown. It wouldn't be easy to get back and forth if you needed food or supplies—or help.

Fern leads me up the stairs to the darkened porch, supporting me as my boots flop on the parched wood. A scrawny blue-gray cat skitters through the porch posts and hides against an overgrown bush to watch from the shadows.

The double doors are inlaid with stained glass, one window depicting a lion with a gold halo and the other a serpent stabbed through with a dagger. The lion's eyes have been busted out of their lead frames, leaving vacant holes that whistle when Fern swings the door open to a high-ceilinged foyer.

"Sam?" she calls out, but there's no response.

We trudge through the foyer to a sweeping staircase with an elaborately carved handrail. I groan as we start climbing, and around when we hit the fifth or sixth step I slump out of Fern's grip. My butt hits the wood and my head thuds on the banister behind me. I cough up a little water and curl in on myself.

"Do you have a phone?" I mumble, too cold and exhausted to think of anything else. "I need help...."

Fern squats to rub her hands over my upper arms. She tucks the shawl she gave me more securely around my torso and says, "Just stay right here, okay? I'm gonna get help. Don't move. Stay here, Annabel."

I nod and my temple grinds against a swirl of carved wood filigree.

I close my eyes.

When I open them I'm not on the stairs anymore.

I'm not alone, either. A murmured conversation draws my gaze to two shadowy figures by the fireplace. I keep my lids low and watch them through my eyelashes.

I recognize Fern, but the boy she's talking to is a stranger. He looks like a remake of *Rebel Without a Cause*, with his hair brushed back, biker boots, and blue jeans.

I'm laid out on a couch in a wood-paneled drawing room, still soaked beneath Fern's wool shawl. The recessed ceiling above me is frescoed with some kind of abstract jungle scene. Fern and the boy are speaking quietly to each other as a small blaze sizzles on the fireplace grate.

"Did she say anything about being DOA?" the boy asks Fern.

"Not *exactly*," she admits. "But if we just tell her we're—"

"Cut the gas for a second, would ya?" he interrupts, holding his hand up between them. "You're gonna scare her right back into her grave. You don't want her to wind up like the townsfolk, do you?"

"She's not *like* them," Fern says, glancing over her shoulder at the window behind her. Through the warped glass I can see the houses of Resurrection Peak sinking into the overgrowth. Fern turns back to the boy and tells him, "She's like *us*."

The boy nods and takes a cigarette from behind his ear. He strikes a match on the fireplace and lights his smoke.

"You know what that means, don't you?" he says.

"Yeah, I know," Fern says. She twists at the braided bracelet on her wrist. "But I *saw* her holding herself together. She won't fade away."

"Still. Give her a little time to get her sea legs before you shove her overboard, all right?" he says.

"Oh, drop dead twice," Fern says. The boy smirks and a dimple sinks into one of his cheeks.

I've had enough of lying still.

I sit up and untangle one arm from Fern's shawl, stretching it out toward them, fingers beckoning.

"Can I have that?" I ask the boy. I watch him without the obstruction of my mascara-sticky lashes now. His brows rise above the round rims of his tortoiseshell glasses. His eyes are inkblot black, impossible to read. I have to rely on the upward twist at the corner of his mouth to know what he thinks of my abrupt demand. He flips the cigarette around and comes closer to place the butt between my fingers. I bring it to my lips and squint at him to keep the smoke out of my eyes as I inhale.

"Careful. There's nothing but exhaust in that pipe," he says.

I know what he means as soon as the smoke hits my lungs— there's no filter on his cigarette. My throat aches as I breathe out, but I don't cough. "Thanks," I murmur, like the cigarette doesn't suck. I shift my eyes from him to Fern. "Sorry I passed out on you."

"Honestly, you were getting kind of heavy anyhow," Fern says as she plants herself on the couch beside me. "That's Sam, by the way," she tells me. Before I can acknowledge him, she asks, "How do you feel?"

I groan and say, "Like I got lobotomized by a power drill."

"Yowch." Fern winces. "Do you . . . know what happened?"

This time I don't close my eyes when she asks that question, but I hear the water rushing in my ears anyway. The smoke from the cigarette toasts the riverbed muck in my throat. I swallow and say, "No. Not really."

"You must remember something," Fern says. "What's the *last* thing you remember?"

I glance over at Sam, whose black stare makes goose bumps prick across my arms. I drop my gaze to the burning cigarette between my fingers and shrug. "Last night I . . . was at a club in Newton with my ex. His band was playing. Was supposed to play. I don't . . . actually remember seeing them *play*, I just—" I lift my free hand and push my bangs back from my forehead. My palm is wet. *Why haven't I dried off yet?* "I, um . . . I remember getting there with him, but I don't . . . know what happened . . . I must have gotten too drunk or something. . . ."

That doesn't make sense and I know it. I had a bottle of tequila stashed in my purse, but I was only taking tiny sips between Gun's chugging mouthfuls. I was pacing myself on purpose, making sure I wouldn't wind up drunk enough to think hooking up with my ex might be a good idea. But the last thing I remember with any coherent clarity is Gun leaning in toward me, his jaw scraping my cheek as he yelled over the noise of the venue, telling me he was going outside to help his bandmates grab their gear. . . .

Everything that came after is muddled and blurry, like trying to glimpse the bottom of a river through rushing water.

I lift my stinging eyes to Fern's face and meet her gaze. "I don't know. The club is the last thing I remember."

Fern's eyes are steady on mine, searching for something that she clearly isn't finding. "Are you sure?" she says. "There's nothing else? Nothing at all?"

There *is* more.

I remember running through the trees.

Someone was chasing me.

Screams splitting my lungs. Blood slicking my palms. Cold water in my nose and mouth.

I gurgle up a mouthful of icy water. It pours over my chin and splashes onto my chest, soaking into the straw-colored shawl. For a moment my eyes roll up toward the ceiling, but I don't see the fresco overhead. I see black trees swaying against a violet sky. I see water splashing above my head. I see a shape, dark and angry, crouched above me—

Fern's hands clutch my shoulders and wrench me out from underwater. I gasp for air like I've been drowning. The cigarette drops into my lap, fizzing on my damp stockings. I cough up a little more water and curl forward, pressing my forehead to the curve of Fern's shoulder.

I shiver in her embrace as the lashing river fades from my ears.

"Oh, Annabel, I'm sorry. Don't—don't get lost there—in that moment—you're *here*. You're here, you're safe, it's okay. . . ."

My arms coil behind her, hands locking between her shoulders. I lift my face enough to see the boy by the fire, who is tense and still as he stares back at me.

I don't know why *he* looks so freaked out. *I'm* the one who keeps drowning on dry land.

"I don't know what happened," I whisper through chattering teeth. "I don't know what happened to me."

"It's okay," Fern says. She squeezes at my shoulders. "Did you, um . . . Do you still want to call someone?"

I chew on my jittering lip as I consider my options. I know I kept asking for a phone earlier, but now that I think about it . . . I don't even know *who* I'd call for help. Not my mom—this early, she's probably just getting off work and heading to her boyfriend's place to sleep off her overnight shift. I was supposed to be watching my younger brothers last night, and if I called my mom and she had to drive an hour on zero sleep to come get me I'm pretty sure she'd just kill me anyway.

There's my best friend, Maura, but I don't want to call her either. The last time I saw her we got in a huge fight about my kind of rekindled thing with Gun. I'd rather hike all the way home than deal with her I-told-you-so bullshit if she finds out that after going out with my sleazebag ex I woke up *in the river.* And I'm definitely not calling 911. I think these kids are squatting here and I doubt they'd want the police getting involved.

Besides . . . Maura's dad is the sheriff, and telling him where I was last night would suck even more than telling Maura or my mom. Sheriff Harker has always treated me like his surrogate daughter, but he might just cast off his last shred of paternal affection for me if he has to come pick me up hungover and drenched in my tightest black dress.

The fact is, I don't think there's anyone who would want to help me now.

"No," I rasp. "No, there's no one I can call."

Fern looks back at Sam. He slides his hands into the pockets of his jeans and heads to the arched doorway framed by gleaming wood. "Stick with us, then. Fern'll fix you up. Just keep it together, all right?" His black eyes shift from me to Fern. "I'm gonna go have a talk with those twins."

And then he's gone.

Fern helps me stand, her oval mouth fighting off a frown. As she guides me around the tea table toward the hall, she says, "No more sorrows, Annabel. You're safe and snug here with us."

And I believe her.

Maybe I should be creeped out by this old mansion and the ghost town that surrounds it, but I'm not.

I'm only afraid of what I see when I close my eyes.

TWO

THE WAY FERN was walking around Resurrection Peak in her slippers did give the impression that she's made herself at home here, but it didn't prepare me for *this*.

"Is that a freaking *ball gown?*" I demand, pulling off the rack what is, indeed, a freaking ball gown. And it's not alone—more tulle and glimmering beads surround it, accenting a row of extravagant formal dresses. It's not just the ball gowns, either. From the drawing room I woke up in, Fern has led me through a labyrinth of halls to her bedroom in Chapel House—and from her bedroom, into her *wardrobe*.

It's not the room itself that surprises me. This mansion is all shimmering glass and carved mahogany, so the opulence of the walk-in closet just vibes with everything else. But in here, the sunlight beams through an iridescent skylight to illuminate racks of clothes and buttercream shelves stocked with shoes and handbags, all arranged in neat, color-coded rows.

"Sure," Fern says as I stand there clutching one of her ball gowns. "You never know when you're gonna need to get chrome-plated."

"Where did you get all this stuff?" I ask as I hook the gown back in place and skim my fingers along the racks of clothes that line the walls of the wardrobe.

"Well, I made most of it myself." Fern shrugs.

"You *made* this stuff?" I look around the closet again and try to do the mental math, but nothing adds up. Where did she get the materials? Where did she get the *time?*

"Mm-hmm." Fern sighs. "Some of it's just existing pieces I reworked. Some's stitched from scratch. I always wanted to be a fashion designer, you know? Like an Elsa Schiaparelli for the McCardell age."

I have no idea who she's referencing, but there's something about the way she says it—past tense, so sad and wistful—that makes an uneasy chill creep through me. I frown as I push aside a speckled brown wiggle dress to eye a color-blocked skirt, dizzy with the sense that there's something I'm missing here. "I'd say you already *are* a fashion designer if all this is really yours. What can I wear?"

A laugh bubbles from Fern's mouth, and she leans her elbows on the marble-topped island in the center of the closet. "Whatever you want. If you're gonna be hanging around here, I need to get a sense for your taste."

"Oh. I hope this isn't a test," I say. I flip through the racks, gravitating toward the darker-colored pieces. I pull a black slip from its hanger and hold it up for Fern's approval. "How's this?"

"I mean, you can take more than underwear if you want." Fern laughs.

"Nah," I say. "Might as well be up front, I have bad taste."

"Beastly, baby," Fern says. She stands up straight again and lifts her arms, adjusting the silk wrapped around her hair. "Do you want to take a shower? And *don't*"—she interrupts me before I can even balk at her question—"go rotary over the dang waterworks. There's a pump house and a power station that runs off the river. Our handyman is aces. We even got electric in here."

"Your *handyman?*"

"Yeah, Dearborn. He's much beamy. You'll meet him later," Fern says. She crosses the wardrobe and opens the door opposite the one we came in through.

It leads to a bathroom with a black marble floor and gold-framed windows. There's a deep tub with rusty brass fixtures, half shrouded by a filmy shower curtain. A garden of wildflowers has been hand-painted on the emerald walls, with bees and butterflies scattered among the psychedelic blossoms. Everything seems old but carefully maintained.

I drop the slip onto a gold towel rack while Fern cranks the handles on the tub to get the water chugging.

"This place is wild," I say as I stare at the vivid florals on the wall. I turn to Fern, unraveling her shawl from my shoulders. "Thanks, by the way. For everything."

"Oh, no how," Fern says, waving her hand as if to brush off the gratitude. She takes a fluffy towel from a heavy oak cabinet by the tub and hands it to me. "I'm gonna run downstairs for a beat. Just wait in my room if you come out before I'm back, all right?"

I nod and hug the towel to my chest. Cool water trickles down my back from my still-soaked hair.

"Flippy. Great. I'll be back in no time, promise," Fern assures me. "Sorry about the water!"

"What's wrong with the water?" I murmur, but she's already closing the door behind her.

For a few still moments I listen to the sound of the water spewing from the shower head. I take a grounding breath and hook the towel on the rack.

I kick off my soggy boots and peel myself out of the dress I wore to Gun's dumb show last night. I roll my stockings down my legs and fling them onto the marble with a satisfying splat.

I search for bruises or injuries on my mud-streaked skin, but as far as I can tell there aren't any.

So . . . why can't I shake the image of my palms shining with blood in the moonlight last night?

I reach out and put my hand under the showerhead. The water is cold enough to sting my skin. I twist and pull at the handles for a bit, but the water never seems to get any warmer.

I step beneath the icy spray.

It's as cold as the water I woke up in, the rushing river I crawled out of this morning. As cold as the churning tide in my chest. Cold as if the house is coughing it up from the ancient rock beneath its foundation, cold like a knife in the gut.

I suck in a breath and press my hands beneath my ribs.

Blood on my palms . . .

Suddenly I feel like cotton candy in a rainstorm. Like the water moves *through* me rather than over me, dissolving me into the chilly tide that swirls around my feet. I grasp a handful of shower curtain, and when I fall into the tub's porcelain cradle, I pop a few of the brass loops it hangs from.

My back hits the wall of the tub. Cold water bubbles from my throat. I watch in horror as my legs drip away, flowing with the eddy that rolls toward the drain. My hands claw at the edge of the tub, and I hold on, baring my teeth as I kick against the pull.

I will not slip away.

My legs jerk up out of the seething water. Waves smack against the porcelain. I draw my knees up to my chest and knead my fingers down my shins, confirming that my legs are whole, solid, tangible.

My teeth chatter. The frigid water pounds against my shoulders. Maybe it would have been easier to just melt away. Instead I'm still here, digging my nails into my ankles, staring at the water as it circles the drain.

I'm still here.

What the hell happened to me last night?

I might not have any wounds, but I don't feel fine. And I don't think I'm just hungover. No amount of tequila has ever made my legs melt before.

I reach for a bar of soap on the edge of the tub and wring my hands around it. Crushed rose petals in milky suds coat my hands. As I rub away the muck that sticks to my skin, I wonder if I'm dreaming.

Maybe I'll wake up in my rumpled sheets, and I'll have to text Maura and apologize for being shitty yesterday just so I can tell her I dreamed about taking a bath in Chapel House. Maybe if I tell her how much it creeped me out, she'll let me sleep over tonight.

But if I was dreaming, I would never wonder if it was a dream.

I'm just about to start considering the other options when I hear something behind me.

It's a soft hiss, muffled through the curtain circling the tub. A little creak on the floorboards. Something scraping against the porcelain basin behind my back.

I turn, and I'm staring at a face through the filmy curtain.

At first it's just a blot of black through the fogged plastic, but as the face presses closer, I see charred skin stretched across smoldering bones. Blackened fingers creep over the edge of the tub.

"They're not going to tell you the truth," she whispers, her voice like sap steaming on firewood. Smoke wafts from the burning fissures in her face, and ash floats off her scorched dress like little flies

buzzing around her. *"They follow him. The king of lies. There is no truth in him."*

I want to scream, but my throat is too full of water.

Then I wrench the curtain aside and there's nothing there.

THREE

I'M STARING AT an empty bathroom—no sizzling shadow crouched by the edge of the tub, not even a dusting of ash where she once was. But I don't have to ask myself if she was really here. Mildewed smoke lingers, an odor like scorched wood that has been doused and left to rot.

"What the f—" I grip the edge of the tub, hauling myself up. I twist off the shower and stand there as the water runs down the drain, leaving whirls of pine needles and river muck around my feet.

Silence.

I don't think she's here anymore, but I'm not going to wait around to find out.

I trip out of the tub and grab the towel Fern gave me. I smack it across my chest and give my hair a cursory wring, but every second I'm alone in here feels too long.

I elbow my way into the black slip, pull my damp tights up my shivering legs, shove my feet into my boots, and then I'm *out* of there.

I exit the door opposite the one Fern led me in through, and I expect to be relieved once I'm out of the bathroom, but the hall I step into is even creepier. I stumble to a stop as I stare down the hallway, expecting to see a smoldering face somewhere in the gloom. But there's only empty shadows between the pockets of bright carved out by the sun trickling through the windows in the hall.

Once I'm sure I'm not headed straight into her ghostly clutches, I start running.

My boots echo on the floorboards as I dash past warped windows and doors with keyholes and shining glass knobs that lead to other rooms or hallways or god knows what. Chapel House *did* look huge from the outside, but now it seems positively fathomless.

And definitely freaking haunted.

I don't know where I'm going. I followed Fern to her room in a soggy-brained stupor, so I don't even know how we got there. But she said she was going downstairs, so when I find a flight of stairs, I rush down them. They're narrower and steeper than the grand staircase I collapsed on earlier, and they lead me down to a big, sunny kitchen with a cast-iron stove and checkerboard floor.

It all feels so homey and lived-in, nothing like the cold kitchen my mom never cooks in back in the blue shake house at the end of Quarry Road, and not at all the kind of place you'd expect to find a ghost. Windows framed by soft gray paint look out into a glass-walled solarium attached to the kitchen, and through the condensation I see plants overflowing from their pots. The stove smells like smoldering pine. An assortment of chipped mugs are drying on the rack next to the sink. A table sits on the far end of the kitchen, its surface stained with cup rings and burn marks. Bundles of dried herbs hang from a pot rack over the counter.

The coziness of it all wraps around me like a warm blanket, chasing away the shivers from the cold shower. I glance over my shoulder at the stairs I just came down, but no twisted spirit has followed me here.

My curiosity is caught by a glimpse of colors and shapes peeking through the crack in the triangle-shaped plank door beneath the staircase. As I ease it open, sunlight fills the tiny closet, illuminating walls covered in a collage of strange artwork made with vibrant watercolors and vintage magazine clippings. Little boys with butterfly wings run through psychedelic landscapes of spiky alien flowers and swirling multicolored skies. I'm fascinated by the trippy medley, but a distant giggle from somewhere beyond the kitchen snaps me back into focus.

I leave the mysterious cupboard behind and follow the echo of voices through a swinging door into a dining room with a long table and a stately fireplace, carved mahogany animals running up the mantel. Framed paintings have been meticulously defaced, likely by the same hands that created the artwork in the kitchen cupboard—scenes of wild hunts and rustic landscapes have been altered to include winged children and otherworldly plant life, the hunters on horseback scratched out and replaced by drooling black wolves with glowing white eyes.

"Only the squares end up as shades, and she's not a square."

Fern's velvet voice drifts in from the room beyond a pointed arch on the other side of the dining room.

"Baby Betsy wasn't a square," Sam says.

"She was a *kid*," Fern insists. "Betsy just couldn't brain it yet."

"I don't know why you're still arguing. They've clearly made up their minds," an unfamiliar male voice cuts in.

"It's not fair. The twins always vote with Sam," Fern continues in protest.

"Sam, Sam, he's our man," chimes one of the two fox-faced imps who found me this morning.

"If he won't tell her, no one can," the other singsongs.

I cross the room and step through the arch into a cavernous ballroom.

Below the cracking frescoed ceiling and ornate crystal chandelier, six people sit in a circle on the parquet floor. Immediately noteworthy is the fact that none of them are on fire—so whoever I saw in the bathroom, she's apparently not invited to this meeting, either.

I recognize Sam and Fern and the identical brats who were messing with me earlier, but the two other boys in attendance are strangers to me.

One is a frowning giant with sandy hair and ruddy cheeks.

The other boy has the look of a coiled-up snake, long-limbed and lithe with eyes bright as bites of lime and inky-black tattoos that peek through the loose knit of his sweater.

Most of them look surprised to see me, but Sam only raises his brows and readjusts his tortoiseshell glasses.

"All right, somebody tell me what the fuck is going on up here," I demand as I cross the ballroom.

"Well, don't *you* know how to make an entrance," purrs the snake-eyed boy. The twins scramble to their feet beside him, disturbing him only slightly when they trip over his legs in their headlong rush for the door.

"She's angry! Angry! Angry!" they chant as they vanish into the dining room.

"Ignore those germs," Sam says to me as he draws up a knee and leans his elbow against it. "What's ticking, baby? You look wound up as an eight-day clock."

"What's *ticking*?" I repeat, edging on shrill. "I'll tell you what the fuck is *ticking*, dude. I'm trying to figure out what the hell happened to me last night, and meanwhile you're all up here with your ball gowns and your creepy cabinet paintings like you own this place! I mean, I can't say I've ever seen a squat house before, but

I'm pretty sure most of them don't have a goddamn *herb garden*. Also, what was in that cigarette? Because I think I just saw a ghost."

By the time I'm done Sam's brows have traveled a little higher up his forehead, but otherwise his expression's unchanged. The same can't be said for his compatriots, whose looks range from concern (most notable on Fern and the freckled giant beside her) to outright amusement (an expression exclusive to the green-eyed snake boy). Sam sighs deeply, removes his glasses, and rubs at the red marks left on the bridge of his nose.

"Yeah. This place is full of ghosts," he says.

The weird thing is . . . for a second there, before that scorched bitch showed up, I was kind of wondering if these guys *were* ghosts. I mean, it seems about as likely as a bunch of kids getting away with squatting in this old house long enough to have a shoe collection. But here, in the bright of this grand ballroom, they all look so *alive*.

That burning shadow that crept up behind me in the tub—*that* was a ghost.

So I guess I'm back to the drawing board on whatever the hell *their* deal is.

"Shit. So this house really is haunted," I say.

Sam nods and sticks his glasses back on. He gestures to the empty space left by the twins. "C'mere, take a seat. I'll tell you *what the fuck is going on up here* best as I can."

I pause for dramatic effect, but eventually I stomp over and drop into the circle, the laces of my untied boots lashing the floor as I drape my long legs in front of me and cross them at the ankles. I arch my brows at Sam and wait for the explanation.

"Look . . . I know it seems bughouse to you, us all settling in like this roost is our very own, but we all got our reasons to wind up here, and none of 'em are fit for telling this early in the morning,"

Sam says. "You can get our sob stories some other time, but suffice to say . . . a house full of ghosts is a better home than the ones we've known before."

So they *are* runaways squatting here. I get it, I guess. I might have grown up in the blue shake house at the end of Quarry Road, but it'd be a stretch to call it home. To me, home is the feeling I have behind the wheel of my hearse-black Cutlass, gripping the shift knob in my fist as the big block roars and my boot stomps the gas.

But still. I have *questions*.

"What happens if you guys get caught?" I ask. "I've heard cops *and* park rangers patrol up here."

"Hm," Sam hums, tapping his fingers rhythmically on his knee. "I've never seen any prowl cars passing through. I think the pigs got enough slop in their pens, no need to come snorting through our streets."

"But people definitely come up here," I say. Everyone who grows up in Hagley visits the abandoned village at the top of Resurrection Peak at some point—on a spooky night drive, on a dare, or to take artsy photos of the ruins. It's a rite of passage in my backwoods hometown. *"No one's* ever found you guys?"

"Unwanted guests aren't much of a problem," the snake-boy says, a smile tucked in the curve of his lips. He has a face full of sharp angles, all cheekbones and jawline, and there's a darkened scar on the bridge of his nose like it's been broken once or twice. His low hiss of a voice adds, "After all, this place *is* haunted."

"What, do you all just pretend to be ghosts and scare them away?" I say.

"Mmm, we can *pretend* to be ghosts if you want," the snake returns in his swampy drawl. "We'll get under some sheets and rattle and moan—"

"Oh, break it off," Fern snaps, swatting the snake's arm with the back of her hand. He yelps and rubs at his arm as if Fern's little slap really wounded him, but she ignores his performance. "Annabel, don't worry about us. We get by up here just fine," Fern assures me. "You, um. You seem like you're doing a little better. Did you . . . remember anything else?"

Here we go again. I stretch my arms behind me and drop back on my hands, sighing up at the ceiling. My eyes narrow on the babies with butterfly wings and flower blooms painted over top of the celestial fresco. "No," I say, because that's the truth. Vague impressions are all I have.

The trees from underwater.

The blood on my palms.

The headlights in my eyes.

Bile in my throat. Glass under my boots. The shrill sound of Gun's friends laughing.

I think they were laughing at me.

I close my eyes and draw up my legs, wrapping my arms around them as I shiver. Wet droplets skitter across my skin. I press my chin against my knees and try to breathe through the rushing in my ears, but I feel myself going under like sinking into cold, cold water. . . .

A hand grips my shoulder.

I open my eyes and the snake-boy is there, offering me a jar of something that smells like sour candy. His tattooed fingers are stained the same deep plum color as the liquid in the jar. "Damn, you really are all loose threads," he says. "I'm Virgil. Here, drink this."

I lift a shaky hand and curl my fingers around the jar. The glass squeaks against my wet palm. I look down and Virgil's lime-bite eyes are reflected on the indigo mirror of the liquid in the jar.

"What is it?" I murmur.

"Virgil is something of a vigneron," Fern explains.

"A vigna-what?" I frown. I tip the jar against my lip, and the syrupy sour-sweet liquor that flows into my mouth tastes like biting into an overripe plum. It's surprisingly delicious, but what's even more impressive is the heat that follows it down my throat as I swallow. Whatever this shit is, it's *strong*.

I gulp another tart purple mouthful, sighing as Virgil's drink pours warmth into my icy belly. The suffocating terror starts to fade like water draining from my ears.

"Thanks," I say. I bite my lip and cut my eyes across the circle to the other boy, who hasn't said anything since I arrived—the broad-shouldered giant in grubby denim overalls with a stitch permanently etched into his brow. "You got a name, dude?" I ask him.

"Me?" says the giant, brown eyes bulging. He squares up his hunched shoulders like he's snapping to attention, a splotchy flush on the apples of his cheeks. "Uh, m'name's Dearborn, but Dear's just fine. You're Annabel, ain't you?"

"Yeah." I nod. "Annie Lane."

"Well, it's real sweet to meet ya, Miss Lane," Dearborn says. I recognize his accent. He must have grown up deep in the Jersey Pine Barrens, just like some of the truckers who stop along their routes at the diner where I work. I almost ask him about it, but Virgil interjects before I get a chance.

"Did somebody finally teach this golem some manners?" Virgil laughs at Dearborn. "What have you been doing in that man cave of yours lately, reading Emily Post?"

"Aw, pound off, ya old witch," Dearborn grunts, his cheeks going redder.

"Why don't we give Annabel a tour of the place?" Fern suggests, standing up in her velvet mules to smooth the pleats in her belted slacks. She steps forward and holds her hand out to me. "Come on, doll. Let's show you around."

I thread my fingers through Fern's. My legs don't feel like water-logged sticks anymore, but Fern's palm pressed to mine is welcome nonetheless. I keep the jar Virgil gave me in my other hand, taking a gulp to chase away the cold whenever I feel it returning to my chest.

But it seems like touring Chapel House is exactly the diversion I need to keep the watery panic away. Fern guides me by the hand while the others trail behind, adding their commentary.

I learn that they call the ballroom where I found them—which they seem to treat as a clubhouse of sorts—the Ark.

On the first floor they show me a massive mahogany library full of musty books and leather furniture. A billiard room where a man's portrait has been repurposed as a dartboard, the face blotted out entirely by dart holes in the canvas. A jade-green breakfast room with a wall of tall windows, the corner panels etched with verdant stained-glass vines. The kitchen and the lush solarium attached to it, which seems to be Virgil's dominion, judging by how guarded he gets about the place.

The tour is about to continue upstairs when the door below the staircase flies open.

The twins come barreling out of the decoupaged closet, bare feet slapping the wide floorboards as they rush to me. One of them is brandishing a folded piece of paper, the other gripping his mirror image by the shoulders as if to steer him.

"Annabel!" shouts one.

"Annab-*El!*" the other crows.

"Annab-Elle-Elle-Elle!" they sing together, a strange ululation as they crumple at my feet, one freckled hand waving the folded paper like a white flag atop their pile of tangled limbs.

"It is for you," one boy says, his face crushed to his twin's shoulder. I take the paper, eyeing the magazine clippings that peek beyond the folds, and unfurl it to reveal a watercolor background and a collage of vintage telephones clipped from catalogs and antiquated advertisements. The words *Sorry Worm* are spelled out with buttons and pebbles in paste that's still wet; a few of the heavier bits drop off when I fully unfold the message.

The twins detangle themselves, sitting on their knees as they look up at me with pleading copper eyes.

"We're sorry," one says. "It was an operator error."

"Oh yes, we should not have connected you to the spirit hotline," the other agrees.

"We should have connected you to the *friend* hotline."

Fern gives a big sigh and places a hand on the left boy's head. "This one's Hunt," she tells me, and her hand moves to the other. "This one's Howl."

I fold up their apology note and tuck it down the front of my slip, where my little right breast keeps it safe against the lace.

I'm sure they didn't mean the things they said this morning.

Maybe they just mistook me for one of the ghosts up here.

FOUR

BY NIGHTFALL, I am supremely drunk.

Virgil's black potion enfolds me in mellow heat, dulling the jabs of memory that needle my mind. With a belly full of plum wine and the spicy green soup Virgil prepared for dinner, I hardly remember that there's something I'm forgetting.

Just as long as I don't look up at the branches swaying overhead.

Or stare at the jar in my hand until the wine looks like blood.

Or focus on how the crunching leaves sound like shattered glass under my boots.

"Yow! Where do the chumps wind up?" Howl crows.

"Six feet deep in a wooden onesie, oh yup!" Hunt returns.

I look up from the drink in my hand, blinking in the hot firelight. Around the bonfire, the twins are shout-singing and stomping their feet to the clamoring beat Dear strums on his guitar. Sam's head bobs, his glasses shining with licks of flame as he pounds the rhythm on a worn bongo drum.

"Oh, where do the losers go?"

"To the morgue, oh, with a tag on the toe!"

"What's a square got when the worms come?"

"Nothing but bones when the rest is gone!"

The fire toasts my cheeks as I watch them from the red leather wingback chair I dragged out of a study to serve as my campfire throne. We're deep in the wild garden behind Chapel House, where statues lurk in the overgrowth and the charred basin of a stone fountain serves as a makeshift fire pit. Glittering embers drift up toward the sky, and the smell of smoke and dry leaves blows on the wind.

The twins, I've come to understand, speak in riddles and rhymes with messages that seem clear only to each other. This song probably comes from the same strange fever dream world as the artwork they've scattered all around Chapel House.

It's easy to get lost in the weirdness and forget about the things I want to avoid. I guess that's why I'm still here at Chapel House, feeling like the dangling note before a beat drop, pretending the black hole of last night's memory isn't a sucking void trying to pull me in. Pretending that I don't see an angry shadow crouched over me every time I close my eyes.

I sip Virgil's wine. Everything's fine.

But . . . I do wonder if anyone back home is looking for me.

I wonder if they sent out an alert to every phone in the county. Maybe Hagley is already plastered with missing posters, my scowling senior photo printed alongside something like, MISSING: ANNABEL LANE. AGE 17. BLACK HAIR, GREEN EYES, RESTING BITCH FACE. I picture Sheriff Harker, his red brow tight beneath his sweaty brown Stetson, questioning my ex and his crew of crusty chauvinists. I wonder if they'll eventually find me up here . . . or if they'll even bother to look that hard.

Maybe no one will look for me at all.

Maybe they're all glad I'm gone.

I tip my head back and look up at the empty mansion, the windows watching us like eyes. For a moment, a smoldering form sizzles behind a second-floor window, but then . . . it could have just been a lick of flame reflected in the warped glass.

I can't believe someone left this place here to rot.

That's the thing that always made the stories about Resurrection Peak seem so real. As kids, we couldn't see any other reason why a whole town would be left behind—it had to be cursed, or haunted, or a portal to hell, or whatever.

Now, with a basic understanding of economics, I get how a town could empty out. Hell, my stupid hometown is barely hanging on by a thread now that the primary job opportunities are antique-store clerk or farmhand; I can only imagine that if Hagley had been any more remote than it already is, it'd be a ghost town by now, too.

But even when my fearless big brother took me up here to show me the houses being swallowed by the forest, he didn't bring me inside any. He told me the town went under because the paper mill closed, but he still only pulled up to the gate of Chapel House and then turned the car around.

Even he knew that there's something weird about this place, a kind of energy that seems to simmer on my skin like the embers that drift off the bonfire and fall on the dead leaves around us.

"Hey," I say, shifting forward to catch Sam's attention. He's seated beside me in a bamboo lounge chair, the drum balanced between his knees as he lights a cigarette. I notice a tattoo on his wrist below the sleeve of his leather jacket, words faded and patchy but legible in the firelight.

Rage, rage against the dying of the light.

I swallow when he turns to me, his brows lifting above his glasses and his lips parting on a smoky exhale. "What gives?" he prompts.

"Um." I struggle, my mind suddenly feeling like driftwood in a swirling current. I scrape my nails on the jar in my hand and say, "Have you guys heard about . . . what happened up here?"

Sam pauses to take a drag on his cigarette, his eyes narrowing slightly as he watches me. Finally he says, "What've *you* heard about what happened up here?"

"Just—creepy stuff," I say, rolling my eyes like all those old campfire stories don't feel kind of real now that I'm up here. I cross my legs and lean in toward him, ready to dish. "Okay, so I've heard that this place was totally picturesque at first. There was the paper mill where the whole town worked, everyone went to church on Sunday, it was all, like, cottagecore utopia, you know?" I pause, Sam nods, and I reach over and pluck the cigarette from between his fingers. "But *then*, in the fifties, there was this fucked-up murder here. Some guy took an axe and slaughtered a bunch of schoolgirls. When the villagers caught the guy who did it, they hanged him before the lawmen from Hagley could arrest him. Which, I guess, was a big mistake."

"Hm." Sam nods. I pull on his cigarette, and when I pass it back to him there's a kiss of red from my lipstick.

I go on.

"Yeah, so *apparently*, after the villagers killed him, the axeman would return each night. He'd strike at random, hacking up entire families in their houses, with no one ever hearing a thing. He was like some kind of phantom, butchering people in the dead of night. And even if they did catch him in the act, they couldn't stop him. It was like this guy *couldn't be killed*. So . . . one night they'd had enough, and everyone just took off without even packing their shit or anything. Like, if you go into some of these houses, the tables are still set because they ran out in the middle of dinner."

Sam nods, the fire flickering amber on his messy brown pomp. He draws on the cigarette I passed back to him, ducking his head as he does. I watch him inhale, exhale, and rub his knuckles on his jaw. Eventually he says, "Do you believe that story?"

"Oh god, no." I laugh to hide my nerves. "Come on. The paper mill closed down and everyone left. All that shit, it's just a scary story."

"Huh. Speaking of stories, you got yours figured out yet?" Sam asks, hauling the drum from between his knees to set it aside.

"Does it *look* like I have anything figured out?" I say, throwing myself back against my chair again. I roll my eyes, but when I see the swaying branches of trees that stretch over the courtyard, I remember looking up through the thrashing water and I have to chug from the jar to swallow my panic.

Sam watches me with arched brows. "Not for lack of trying, I see," he says.

"The fuck's that supposed to mean?"

"Nothing, just . . . not sure getting embalmed on Virgil's coffin varnish is gonna help you get your head on straight." Sam shrugs.

My eyes narrow as I lift the jar of syrupy wine to empty it in one angry swallow. "Sorry," I say with venom. "I wasn't aware you were timing me."

"I'm *not*," Sam insists.

"You know, if you have a problem with me staying here, you could just say—"

"No, *no*, that's not it," Sam snaps. He scrapes his hand through his hair and leaves it messier than before, a curl escaping his pomp to brush his forehead. "I don't have a problem with you being here. Just your *reason* for being here."

"My *reason* for being here?" I repeat. "If this is about to get all existential, I'm out. I always thought Sartre was a total blowhard."

"I'm sure Sartre feels real clanked about that."

"Screw you," I snip. "Tell me what my *reason* for being here is, then, if you think you know."

"You know there's something that needs doing. You can feel it, can't you?"

"What is this, the most patronizing horoscope reading of all time?"

Sam hunches forward like he can make up the space as I pull away from him. "What I mean to say is . . . *I know*. I know it'd be easier just to leave it all forgotten. But sitting here belting the grape ain't gonna unsmog your noggin, and if you keep it up, you're gonna lose the glue that made you. You're here for a reason, baby. Don't forget *that*."

I'm here for a reason. . . .

I'm not sure how literally I should take that. Is he talking about the reason someone (probably my prick ex) dumped me out here with no phone and no way home?

Or does he mean something else entirely?

Water rushes in my ears, drowning out the sound of the crackling fire, the chanting twins, the strum of Dear's guitar. Cold hunger snarls in my guts. My fingers claw at the armrests of my chair, clammy palms grasping red leather.

What happened to me last night?

I drop my boots against the ground and stand, casting Sam in my shadow as I block out the fire. My nails graze his fingers as I reach down and take his cigarette from him again.

"Let's get one thing straight right now," I tell him, my voice as sour as my eyes. "Don't *ever* tell me what to do."

I turn away and march across the mossy pavers, cutting through the garden courtyard.

The sound of voices gets lost behind me.

I crash through the dark overgrowth, stomping my way back to the portico outside the Ark. I flick Sam's cigarette to the ground and stomp it out before I slip through the opal glass doors into the ballroom. Chapel House is empty and dark, the echo of my angry footsteps beneath the domed ceiling the only sound.

Honestly, Sam's beautiful, but he's a human canker sore. He could have kept his mouth shut and let me admire his jawline in peace, but *no*—he just *had* to bring it up.

What if I don't *want* to remember what happened last night?

Through the swinging doors in the ballroom, I step into the short servants' corridor leading directly to the kitchen. My palms feel wet and cold. I rub them on the satin slip I borrowed from Fern, but they just slick against the fabric.

I'm only a few steps down the shadowy hall when I stop.

The smell of mildew and smoke drifts through the windowless corridor.

I take a small step backward, suddenly regretting entering Chapel House alone.

Because . . . in here, I'm *not* alone.

A rattling, smoky breath drifts from the dark ahead of me. I retreat until my back hits the doorframe, my fingers grasping at it to anchor myself in reality. I peer into the formless black that swallows the hall, but my eyes are still adjusting after the raging firelight outside.

If she's in here with me, I can't see her.

But I smell her. And I hear her.

"Hello?" I call out, ragged and weak. "Um. Listen, I've had a super-shitty day, and you're actually really quite grotesque, so if you could *not* be terrifying right now, that'd be gr—"

I let out an involuntary shriek as a grating scrape resonates from the ceiling above me. A hot breeze blows back my hair as something falls from the ceiling, landing with a *thump* that seems thunderous in the tight space.

I stare at the shape on the floor, crumpled and still before the threshold to the kitchen.

A beam of moonlight streams in from the kitchen, shining across a heart-shaped enamel pin.

Cold water stings my throat as I creep forward, eyeing the red roses stitched to the lapel and the gunmetal spikes that glimmer in the narrow light. I reach down and close my fingers on the damp leather sleeve, pulling it up by one arm to reveal the clotted brown blooms that stain the red satin lining.

It's my jacket.

And I think it's covered in blood.

FIVE

I KNOW I WAS wearing my jacket last night. I remember the way the collar rubbed against the back of my sweaty neck while I waited for Werewolf Fetus to take the stage at Boondocks. But I don't know where it was when I woke up in the river, and I *definitely* don't know why it would be stained with blood.

I'm not exactly the forensics unit, but the stains really do look like blood to me. I brush my fingers over the dark sepia blotches, and they feel stiff against the fabric lining. The dagger patch I stitched on last winter is a brown-rot watercolor.

I lift the jacket and sniff one of the denser stains inside. I can still smell my candy-apple perfume on the fabric, but it's laced with a rancid sourness that turns my stomach. I gag and crumple the jacket in my fists, then burst through the swinging doors back into the ballroom.

Sam grabs me, stopping my momentum.

Steady hands clutch my arms. I shiver in his grip, my body as cold and wet as the jacket in my fists. I look up at him in the ballroom's blue glow, his eyes wide behind his glasses.

"What's that?" Sam whispers, noticing the jacket clutched to my chest. Pins and spikes scratch at my skin through the lace edge of Fern's slip.

"It's mine," I say. My trembling hands unfold the leather,

revealing the bloodstained lining. I look up at the frown on his mouth, the fathomless black of his wary eyes.

"That's blood," he says, confirming my suspicions.

"Yeah, but . . . it can't be *my* blood, can it?" I say. "This is . . . full-on laceration-level bleedage. I didn't even wake up with a paper cut."

"Hm," Sam grunts. His thumb rubs at the goose bumps on my skin. I know I was just annoyed with him, but shock has thoroughly chased away my anger. "If it's not your blood, whose is it?"

"I don't know," I whisper, my chest tight and watery. "None of this makes any sense. . . ."

"Annabel," Sam says, drawing me closer, crushing my bloody jacket between our chests. "I really slobbered a bibful, trying to talk to you out there. What I meant to say—what I *should* have said—was, we're *with* you. *I'm* with you. You don't have to be afraid of finding out what they did to you. It's *them* who should be afraid of *you*."

He's right. Rage rises in me, flooding up from my choppy guts. Sam might not have a specific *them* in mind, but I do.

I should have listened to Maura.

The fight we had yesterday was the culmination of months of tension, a thread of discord that had been tightening around the throat of our friendship ever since Maura started ditching me to work on her summer journalism program for stupid Princeton, leaving me to fend for myself under my mom's roof when I'd usually spend most of the summer sleeping over at her house.

But Maura's uncharacteristic aloofness wasn't the only issue brewing between us.

Though we hadn't talked about it, I knew what Maura thought

of the fact that I'd started talking to Gun again. She loathed him when we were together, and after the way we broke up, she probably could have disemboweled him with a look if he'd ever had the balls to face her. I knew she'd totally flip if I told her I'd started hanging out with him again—so I didn't, and it's not like she noticed anything was up. She'd chosen to investigate some unsolved murder from the nineties for her Princeton piece, and it seemed like she was always too busy to hang out with me anyway.

But once school started, I couldn't keep it a secret anymore. The first time she caught Gun and me together, laughing at my locker before lunch on the third day of school, I thought she'd totally go off. But she didn't say anything.

The distance between us just grew.

And yesterday morning, I had decided I was done waiting for the slow simmering pot of resentment to finally boil over.

I knew exactly what I was doing. As I raced my Cutlass down the winding highway through the center of Hagley, I started blasting Gun's band through the speakers. I bet she heard me coming as I pulled up the long dirt drive to the Harkers' secluded little farmhouse.

It was the same Saturday routine we've had for months: me arriving to pick Maura up fifteen minutes before our shift at the diner, with just enough time to smoke a joint and talk a little shit in the parking lot before we'd head inside to serve burgers and fries to ungrateful locals and skeezy truckers. But this time we veered away from routine.

Because as soon as I saw Maura's face, I knew we were finally going to have that fight.

"Isn't it a little early for Werewolf Fetus?" she asked as she climbed into the passenger seat, her voice searing with disdain.

"It's always go-fuck-yourself o'clock somewhere," I returned. I twisted the dial to turn up Gun's shrieks competing with the slamming instruments around him, and Maura scrunched her nose and stretched forward to turn it back down.

"I'm just saying—in this political climate, maybe we shouldn't be enjoying the music of blatant misogynists—"

"Shut up, Maura, your favorite movie is *The Shining* and Kubrick was a massive misogynist."

"I can separate the art from the artist, Annie. Don't try to tell me you're listening to Werewolf Fetus right now because you're just a *huge fan of the music.*"

"I *do* like the music," I said—a total lie. Gun's band is absolutely trash.

Maura threw herself back against the seat as she laughed at my bluff, her sweater bunching around her ribs to bare her freckled stomach. I knew exactly where to find the constellation of freckles by her belly button that vaguely resembles a ladybug, but even her stupid cute freckle-bug wasn't enough to blunt the sharp edge of my anger toward her.

"They're playing at Boondocks tonight," I told her.

"Are you *going?*"

"Of course I'm going."

"What do you mean, *of course?*"

"Well, it's not like I have any other plans," I said, petulant.

"Rabbit, I *told* you, APs this year are kicking my ass—"

"Yeah, whatever," I snapped, cutting her off. Maura has *always* been an overachiever in school, and it never stopped her from hanging out with me before. Even if she had hours of homework and studying to do, she'd still let me come over as long as I promised not to distract her too much.

What had changed?

Maura huffed, tipping her sunglasses down to stare at me over them. "You and him *aren't* getting back together."

"Wow, Maura, are you the boss of my sex life now?"

"Are you having *sex* with him?"

"I've *had* sex with him—"

"I know—I know that, but are you fucking him, like, currently?"

"*Currently?*" I repeated, jolting the Cutlass forward after clearing the pothole at the end of Maura's driveway. "Yes, M'ra, his cock is inside me right now."

"Jesus Christ, Rabbit, you've done some dumbass shit before, but this is literally *so dumb.*"

"You never even *asked* what's going on with me and him lately! What gives you the right to care *now?*"

"I don't have to *ask*, Annie, I have *eyes.*"

I hated to think I was so transparent, but then again—of course she knew.

We spent our whole shift at the diner yesterday refusing to speak to each other—which our boss Leo just *loved*, considering that if we did have to communicate, we'd go through him.

"Tell *her* that table six needs a refill."

"Tell *her* I'm not taking the church lady table; it's *her* turn!"

"Tell *her* to call her dad for a ride home."

"Tell *her* to have a miserable time tonight."

And I know our fight wasn't just about Gun—but the truth is, when it comes to him, Maura was absolutely right. I had no business going anywhere with Morgan fucking Donovan last night.

My nails bite at the damp leather in my hands. The missing pieces of my memory feel like punched-out teeth. I can run my tongue along the raw places where the details should be, the empty grooves tender and ragged. I look down into the stained lining of my jacket, the blooms of gore in clotted swirls seeped across the red satin.

"Sam . . ." I say, lifting my face to his, meeting the black of his eyes behind his tortoiseshell glasses. "I have to find out what my ex did to me last night."

"That's the spirit," Sam says, a faint smirk pulling the corner of his lips. He glances over his shoulder at the gold moon that hangs in the corner of the ballroom window, then asks me, "Where can you find him when the sun comes up?"

"Like, at sunrise? It'll be Monday, so . . . I guess he'll be going to school."

Sam nods, turning his face back to me. His hands are on my arms like he's ready to hold me together if I start to melt away. "All right. And you're ready to hear what he might tell you?"

"Yes," I tell Sam. "I'm ready."

And I hope it's not a lie.

SIX

I KNOW THERE'S something I'm missing, more than just my memories.

It reminds me of one of those Magic Eye pictures, the ones where you stare until you see the hidden image. Maura would always pick up right away on the shark or camel or butterfly hidden among the static neon splashes, while I'd stare *forever*, crossing and uncrossing my eyes, and half the time I'd never see anything at all. But even if Maura would point out the outline of the shape she saw in the spinning colors, I could never see what she did. Not until I found it for myself, anyway.

There's something hidden in the swirl of memories from last night, something I'm just not seeing.

I sit with everyone around the bonfire until sunrise, the mood somber. When I ask why we have to wait until dawn, Virgil tells me it's because Sam's afraid of the dark. It seems like a joke I'm not supposed to get.

I don't know where *they* all fit into this, but I think the kids in Chapel House are part of the spinning kaleidoscope that makes up the big picture.

When the sky turns wheat gold and Dear pulls a chugging old Chevy Blazer out from the carriage house behind the garden, I gather my bloodstained jacket from my armchair, and we load into the truck for the ride down the mountain.

I'm surprised they're all coming along, but I'm glad. It's like I'm returning with my own personal army, bumbling and chaotic as they are. The way they've accepted me into their pack is empowering and, even though I've only spent twenty-four hours with them, I feel like I *belong* in Chapel House now.

I never felt like I belonged in Hagley.

And I'd say the feeling is mutual.

I know what everyone back home thinks of me. I can see it on their faces everywhere I go. There are men whose condescension hardly hides the fact that they *would* if they *could*, teachers who anticipate my failure with perverse glee, hateful girls who demean me, and horny boys who degrade me. I guess I'm the most exciting thing in Hagley, because it always seems like *someone's* talking about me.

I wonder what they're saying now.

To be honest, I don't even know if anyone will have realized I'm gone. My big brother, Neil, used to try to keep track of me, but he left for Fort Bragg in July, so now I'm the oldest sibling in the house. My mom rarely comes home between her overnight shifts as a dispatcher for a trucking company—her boyfriend's place is closer—so me and my younger brothers are used to being on our own. Neither of them would blow my cover by telling Mom I haven't been home since Saturday, especially knowing they'd incite Mom's wrath by pestering her when she's busy popping Xans with her pill-head boyfriend on her off hours.

I didn't show up for work last night, but besides cursing me out under his breath while waiting tables in my stead, I doubt Leo really thought much of it.

I bet Maura noticed though.

We might have fought that morning, and I might be a hopeless screw-up in everyone else's eyes, but Maura and I have never gone this long without contact. Even when we're mad at each other, even if the only texts we send are angry ones, we still can't stand silence between us.

So . . . I *hope* Maura noticed. If she didn't, then things between us have gotten even worse than I realized.

The Blazer we're all crammed into has just as much character as the spaces these guys have claimed in Chapel House. There are plastic skeletons strung from the stained ceiling, butterfly-winged babies decoupaged on the wheel-well covers, mounds of candy wrappers and empty bottles on the floor. The wheels creak and the shocks clank over ruts in the dirt road as we descend the mountain, Dear in the driver's seat and Fern up front beside him.

I sit next to Sam on the tartan back seat, the jacket balled up on my bare thighs. The twins are both sprawled on their backs in the cargo space, cawing like baby birds as Virgil feeds them candy worms.

When we hit the bottom of the dirt byway, Dear pulls the Blazer out onto Route 15. The sallow autumn sun strains through the foliage lining the winding highway to the center of Hagley. Dear glances at me in the back seat, where I've been sitting silent the entire drive.

"Where to, darlin'?" he asks. "You're the captain of this ship."

"Keep going for now," I murmur. "I'll tell you when to turn."

The Blazer chugs through the only traffic light in town and crosses the bridge over the Paulinskill River. I have to close my eyes when I hear the trickling water through the open windows; the sound seems too familiar, and I feel my limbs all turning to liquid again. I wait until we're past the river to open my eyes.

"God, I hope nobody planned a candlelight vigil." I sigh.

"For you?" Virgil laughs, which ends on a hiss as Howl nips his finger while being fed a worm. "Child, a candlelight vigil for *you* would be a summoning circle."

"I'm just trying to mentally prepare for worst-case scenarios," I say. "Like all the kids from Jesus Club making prayer cards. Or Nancy Grace accusing my mom of selling me to human traffickers. Or the news using my tagged pictures instead of my selfies."

"Damn. You think they've been putting on the siren like that?" Sam says.

"Probably not," I admit, rubbing at the jacket in my lap. "Nobody puts on the siren for me."

"Oh, baby. That ain't true. I'm a red-light wail for you." Sam grins.

"Bite me," I say.

Outside the Blazer's windows, the boxy brick building that is J.P. Kleckner Regional High squats between the parking lot and football field.

As the Blazer eases around the horseshoe drive in front of the school, I spot Gun's grass-green Mustang parked in its usual spot at the edge of the lot. I scan for the retired Crown Vic Maura's dad gave her, but I don't see it anywhere.

Weird. It's not like Maura to screw up her perfect attendance. Maybe her dad drove her today.

I look to Sam, who's rubbing his glasses with the hem of his white T-shirt, ducking his head as he squints at the kids filtering through the open school doors.

"You got a plan worked out?" Sam asks. I like how he squints without his glasses, nose scrunched and brow furrowed, and I lick my red lips before I answer him.

"Plans tend to cramp my style," I say, reaching for the door handle. "I think I'll just make rash decisions until I get somewhere; that always seems to work for me."

"Annabel," Fern says, her faint brows arching high on her forehead. "You woke up *in the river* yesterday. Maybe it's time to put some powder on that rash and come up with a *plan*, baby."

"Ow, Fern," Sam says, sticking his glasses back on his nose, "that's talkin' turkey."

"I think you guys have spent too long in isolation. Anthropologists will study your language someday with no clue how to decode it," I say.

"Can the lip and listen up, nosebleed," Virgil drawls in his best imitation of Sam. His tattooed fingers, sticky with candy-worm sugar, grip the back of my seat as he leans over to pop his head between Sam and me. "I know you don't make the king's jive, so I'll be your Rosetta stone. Somebody down here has it in for you, and we're not leaving until we know what you mean to do about that."

I sigh, slumping low in my seat as I roll my eyes to the ceiling. I stare at the multicolored skeletons strung overhead, watching them sway with the thrum of the idling engine.

The thing is, when strategy is required, I'm not usually the mastermind. Maura is.

It was Maura who devised a plan to blackmail Mrs. Ballard into giving me the respectable C+ I earned, when the failing grade she tried to give me for breaching her moralistic "class conduct" clause nearly held me back sophomore year. Maura, who orchestrated a Pokémon card Ponzi scheme in fifth grade that resulted in us collecting nearly every holographic card owned by our classmates. Maura, who found a way for us to catch Gun in his lies once and for all.

Gun.

I know I'm here to find him. I didn't come to school to *go to class*, that's for sure—there's no way I'm sitting around at a desk while I feel this weird, dangling thread in my psyche. I came here to ask Gun what the hell he did to me, and that's exactly what I'm going to do.

"All right, well, I *know* my ex is here," I say, pointing across the lot at the emerald Mustang. "I'm gonna go in there and find out what I can, and you guys—you just wait out here, all right? If things get weird, I want to leave."

"Hold on. You don't want backup on this drip dragnet?" Sam asks.

I swing the door open with a shove from my shoulder. "No," I say, shaking my head. "Something tells me my ex would be too preoccupied to tell me shit if he saw *you* with me."

"Sure, sure." Sam nods. "We'll keep plant out here."

"Yeah, we'll wait for you," Fern promises. "Just . . . don't leave me alone with these germs too long. I've gotten used to having another gal around."

"Seriously. Tragic demographics you've been working with here." I smirk. "I'll see you soon."

My borrowed slip hitches up my thighs as I drop to the curb outside the Blazer.

I wave off chirping goodbyes from the twins as I head in through the open doors of J.P. High. A suit of armor for the school's mascot sits behind glass, fluorescent bulbs glowing in the display case. Some beige-bland PTA mom sits at a folding table taking names for the Hagley Harvest Candy Raffle.

At first no one notices me as I make my way down the hall to my locker.

And then it seems like literally everyone notices me at once.

Clusters of sleepy-eyed students freeze in the middle of their morning rituals. Sentences dangle unfinished as I pass by. I tip my chin up and glare right back at their stares, like I'm daring them to say something, but all of them wait until they're behind my back to start hissing their gossip.

I don't know what they're saying, but I guess my absence really *was* noticed.

My steps slow when I reach my locker. I spin out the combination and the door thunks open, revealing the stickers, notes, and photos decorating the inside. I shrug on a wrinkled old flannel to ward off the chill in the hall and tug my backpack from a precarious tower of textbooks and trash. A crushed soda can tumbles out with it, clattering to the tile by my feet. I stuff my bloody jacket into the backpack, and as I swing the door shut, my gaze lands on the words scrawled on the wall above my locker.

She spits acid through her cherry pout. We're not in love, but we're never out.

I remember when Gun stood there with a Sharpie, writing on the wall while I rifled through my locker on the third day of school, back when I thought that line was totally dreamy rather than totally ridiculous.

I remember the first time I heard the song it's from, too.

It was in August. I was sitting against the hood of his emerald Mustang, the bumper scorching the back of my thighs beneath the frayed hem of my shorts. I had resisted talking to Gun all summer, but that day he caught me on a munchie run at Village Market, the only grocery store in Hagley. He begged me to come to his car "for a minute." He said he had something for me, and I was hoping it would be the bong he never returned after we broke up, so I agreed.

I went to his car, but I wouldn't get in. I set myself there on the burning bumper, crossed my arms, and made it clear enough in my stance: He had a minute, but I wasn't getting into Morgan Donovan's car. Not after how things ended.

Still, my eyes were shameless while he leaned into his car. I studied the muscles roping his long arms, the bead of sweat that dashed from his hairline down his neck, the stubble on his jaw and the blond roots showing beneath his green hair. I stared at the tattoo he had gotten on his bicep over the summer, a red-eyed wizard smoking a joint. I hated how insipid it was, but most of all I hated how my heart was pounding while I waited to see what Gun had planned. I turned away when he emerged from the car, and stuck my eyes to the ants clustered around a wad of red candy on the ground.

"Listen to this," he said, dialing up the volume on his sound system. At first I didn't realize it was his band playing through the speakers—usually Werewolf Fetus plays raucous bullshit that can't decide if it's thrash metal or punk, but this was more like an overblown emo ballad. Soon the sound quality and the look on Gun's face alerted me that this was indeed a Morgan Donovan Original, and I narrowed my eyes as I listened.

As soon as I heard the lyrics, I knew exactly what he was doing.

He dropped against the hood beside me and showed me the Bandcamp page on his phone. The cover for their album was a photo of Gun with the carcass of a hulking black bear draped over his back like a cape.

"Gun, that's sick." I made sure to say it in such a way that he couldn't tell whether I thought the picture was disgusting-sick or cool-sick, but this was Morgan Donovan I was talking to. He never thought I might not mean it as a compliment.

"Awesome, right? Tre and I found it on Resurrection Peak," he said.

I scrolled down the track list and felt excitement spark in my chest at other titles that seemed to imply this wasn't the only one about our relationship. I wondered if he'd been waiting all summer for the chance to show me this, to prove he'd been suffering since we broke up. Gun thinks he's clever, but I've always seen through his ham-fisted attempts at manipulation. He can't manipulate me unless I let him.

The problem is, I always do.

He wanted those songs to draw me in. I knew that, but ... I *wanted* back in. I let those tortured lyrics hitch hooks under my ribs, and the rest of the summer turned into an awkward dance between us. We pretended to be friends. We went to the movies. We gorged ourselves on greasy diner food. We snuck through the woods with a joint and a bottle of vodka. We lay around Hagley Lake and read creepypasta out loud to each other off our phones.

I wanted him.

I didn't know what he wanted from me.

The bell shrieks and snaps me back to the present, and then I'm moving, boots pounding the drab tile as I cut down the hall.

I know exactly where to find Gun. This year we were both cursed by the Fates of Scheduling to first-period phys ed. He and his dickwad entourage are probably just about to stumble out of the locker room in sweat-reek shorts with big stoned grins on their faces.

The only way today would be any different is if he's already heard that I'm coming for him.

Voices filter through open classroom doorways as I go, voices that hiss and snap sentences in which my name is all my ears seem to catch. Annie Lane. Annie Lane. Annie Lane. I ignore them, focusing on the weight of the jacket in my bag as it bumps against the small of my back.

I push through the double doors into the echoey gym, where the air stinks of ammonia and BO. Clumps of kids gather for roll call—and there, waiting on the bleachers, is my idiot ex-boyfriend and his little shit-stain brigade.

I see him, green hair grubby as sidewalk moss beneath the fluorescent lights. His face is turned toward Trevor beside him, but his profile was always my favorite angle on him anyway. I remember when staring at the place where his throat curves to his jaw used to get me wet.

Now it makes my empty guts growl.

I stride across the glossy floor toward him as he giggles at his friends' stoned chatter, their voices too far off to reach my ears. The faces I pass stare at me with a mixture of shock and giddy intrigue, like they know shit's about to go down.

As the buzz of anticipation spreads across the room, he finally notices me.

I watch his face turn to me, all the bright washed out of his blue eyes by weed smoke haze. The smile falls off his face when he realizes I'm headed right for him.

And when he notices me, so do his friends.

Darren, Werewolf Fetus's big burly bassist, looks as slack-jawed as ever—though, maybe he might be looking a little *extra* confused by my rapid advance.

And then there's Trevor, sitting one bleacher above Gun like a little shitbird perched on his shoulder.

I have always wanted Trevor Aimes to die in a dumpster fire like the white trash piece of shit he is. He's a smug little sociopath with a pierced eyebrow and no chin, but for some reason Gun thinks Tre is the epitome of cool. Personally I think most of what needs to be said about Tre Aimes can be summed up by mentioning that he has a pair of truck nuts dangling from the back of his Toyota Hilux. He's *that* kind of asshole.

Currently that asshole is looking at me from across the gym with a big coyote smile spread across his jagged mouth.

The water's rising in my guts. The rot-green lights overhead snap and flicker. A snarling eddy flows so loud in my ears that when my name is called it sounds like a memory, like a passing dream.

"Annie?"

I blink. My steps falter.

"Holy shit, *Annie*."

My boots skid to a stop. I turn, thumb hooking in the strap of my backpack as I face the person calling my name beneath the crackling lights. My brother. Owen.

He's frozen, gawking at me, a carousel of emotion spinning across his eyes.

Surprise. Relief. Hurt. *Anger.*

"What the *hell*, Annie? Where *were* you?"

The lightbulb above us sizzles like a splatter of water on a pan. "You wouldn't believe me if I told you."

"This is so weird," Owen says. And then his eyes scan the trajectory of my charge, tracing the dotted line straight up the bleachers to Gun.

When his gaze comes back to me, I know which feeling has won out.

Owen is barely a year younger than me—he'll turn seventeen in March, just a month before I'll turn eighteen—but we look about as close to twins as siblings can get. We have the same slender leggy build. The same wild black hair, his shoulder length now, nearly as long as mine. The same acerbic-green eyes.

We also have the same dad, the only two of Dawn Lane's four children who share that distinction.

And when he speaks, I have to admit we also have the same ability to cop the absolute *shittiest* tone.

"Oh. I see. You just couldn't stay away from your beloved."

"Ew," I say, my voice thin as a raindrop. "He's not— I'm here to kick his ass, Owen."

"For what? Not taking the bait? Did you *really* think he'd care if you went missing?"

Ouch. I don't know what the hell he means about bait, but I'm not used to him turning this attitude on *me*. Even at my worst, Owen's always accepted that I am what I am, his affections unchanged by what a consummate pain in the ass I can be.

But right now, I don't see any love in his glare at all.

He's looking at me like he looks at Mom.

"Owen—what are you talking about?" I say.

"He couldn't give a single fuck, for the record." Owen shrugs, crossing his long arms over his stomach.

"I have *no idea what you're talking about*. I don't even remember what happened the other night!"

"Blacking out isn't a good excuse, Annie; that's, like, a *Mom* excuse—"

"Owendigo, please," I say, hoping the nickname will soften him to me, but my brother is looking more *done* with me by the second.

"I really hate you for roping me into all this," he says as he turns away from me.

Desperation clutches at my chest and I feel the water in me surge like a cresting tide, and then—

As if propelled by some unseen current, I slip toward him, my boots dragging rippling puddles across the gym floor.

It's faster than I could even run. In the blink of an eye, I'm in front of him. But I don't remember moving my feet at all. I'm just *here*, cold wet hands clawing into his arms.

"Owen—" I whisper. "Owen, I'm not . . . There's something wrong with me—"

"*Annie Lane!*"

I hear boots drumming the floor and a duty belt jangling, and I know exactly who has come for me.

I don't turn around, and Owen isn't looking at the sheriff behind me either. "Annie . . ." Owen says as boots close in on us. "What did they do to you?"

That's what I'd like to know, but I'm not going to get to ask them now.

Grady Harker is here.

SEVEN

"ANNIE."

A hand hooks my arm and pulls me away from Owen.

I turn a hostile glare on Sheriff Harker, whose look is one of utter bewilderment, the shadow of his Stetson deepening the bags under his basset-hound eyes. His freckled hand closes all the way around my forearm.

"What are you *doing* here?" he asks me, his voice tight as his fist around my arm.

"*Ow*, Grady—" I hiss, and his grip instantly loosens.

"*See?*" Principal Arroyo gloats. "I *told* you she was here."

Grady Harker hasn't come alone—he's flanked by J.P. High's fascist principal, Mr. Arroyo, and the overbearingly compassionate school counselor, Ms. Sand.

Grady is still staring at me with his droopy eyes all wide. Ignoring Arroyo, he asks, "What's going on, Annie?"

"That's what *I'm* trying to figure out," I grumble, glancing back at Gun on the bleachers.

He flinches when I look at him.

The lights simmer overhead.

"Sheriff, she says she doesn't remember anything." Owen's voice stills the rushing in my skull. I drop my sour stare from Gun and look to my brother.

Principal Arroyo scoffs, tossing his sport coat back to stick his hands on his hips. He's a cell-phone-belt-clip kind of guy. Unashamed of his utter nimroddery, he says, "Faking amnesia won't shield you from repercussions, Miss Lane."

"She's not faking," Owen snaps at Arroyo. "I'd know if she was faking it."

Grady nods a few times too many, like he's shaking all the conclusions around in his head to see which one pours out. Finally he gives a gentle tug on my arm, pulling me away from Owen.

"Come on, Annie. Let's talk," Grady says.

As he starts to guide me across the gym, Arroyo follows close behind. Probably doesn't want to miss anything. Meanwhile, Ms. Sand closes in on my brother. She has to reach up to pat his shoulder, and he jerks away from her hand.

"Owen, remember what we talked about. Your sister is not your burden," Ms. Sand says in a stage whisper. Like she *honestly* thinks I won't hear it.

Did Owen tell the school counselor I was a *burden?*

Finally I notice things I was too worked up to clock before: his unwashed hair, the hollows beneath his eyes, the fact that he's wearing my Skating Polly T-shirt.

Maybe I kind of *am* his burden.

And the worst part is, as much as I'd like to explain everything and plead for his forgiveness, I really just wish he hadn't gotten in my way. Because I still see Gun on the bleachers behind him, staring down at me with wide pool-water eyes.

Grady pulls me through the doors.

His voice is thin, like the breath is being pressed from his chest, when he says, "You're all right? You're not hurt at all?"

"I'm really not sure," I answer.

"We can take her to the nurse if you'd like to administer a drug test, Sheriff," Arroyo offers.

Arroyo has tried that one before. I bet he thinks he'll finally be successful this time, with the sheriff's blessing. I laugh, twisting to shoot him my mocking smile. "I'll piss on your grave before I piss in a cup, Hector," I say.

"Annie, cut it out," Grady growls, giving my arm a warning yank.

"I don't know what everyone is so mad about, if I'm such a *burden* you all should be happy I gave you a little vacation—"

Ms. Sand, who's finally caught up to us, says, "Oh, Annie. You weren't supposed to hear that. The discussions I have with your brother are private—"

"Maybe you should've shut your mouth, then," I say.

Grady huffs in exasperation, and I ignore the little gasp from Ms. Sand behind me.

Grady perp-walks me all the way to the door of the main office and releases me only after we pass the reception desk where the secretaries sit staring. Arroyo leads the way into his office, marching around his desk like a captain taking the helm, and I pray for the strength not to roll my eyes.

Wary as a lion tamer, Ms. Sand pats the back of one of the Pepto-pink chairs that face Arroyo's desk. "Why don't you take a seat, sweetheart?" she says.

My resentful stare tracks from her to the chair and then to Principal Arroyo. "I'm good," I say.

"Annie. Sit down, please." Grady sighs.

I comply with an irritated grunt, dropping into the chair to look up at my oppressors from a vantage point I know well. This is not the first time I've been asked to "take a seat" across from Arroyo's desk. The woolen upholstery bites at the back of my thighs and I fidget, shifting my legs against the fabric.

Ms. Sand posts up by the door like she's there to block any escape attempts while Sheriff Harker leans against the desk to my left. His receding red hairline is hidden by his Stetson, which is as familiar to me as the mentholated musk of his aftershave and the way his brows wing like two rusty fishhooks over his eyes.

Grady has always treated me like a second daughter, even though he hardly needed to add my problem-child antics to his single-father burden. If Maura got a new coat, I got a new coat. If I needed a permission slip signed or an extra couple bucks for school store day, I always asked Grady instead of my mom. It's always been Grady who knows my shoe size, how I like my pancakes soaked in syrup, that my favorite color is bright rose red, and that I only chew my nails when I'm trying not to cry.

And it's always been just him. Maura's mom ran off when she was only three, but it never seemed to matter that her mom wasn't around. Grady takes care of everything, protective as a father and doting as I imagine a mother should be—though I have nothing but fiction to base that on, considering what a total bitch my own mother is.

Sometimes people don't even realize that I'm not really Grady's daughter, confusing me and Maura for twins even though she is all auburn glow and I'm just scowls and snarled black hair.

Maybe it's the way Grady looks at me that convinces them, because his droopy brown eyes always regard me with all the weary love of a father, no matter how my wild ways press his patience.

But right now, he's watching me like I'm a hurricane at his front door.

Behind his desk, Arroyo clears his throat. "Miss Lane, I hope you can explain yourself, because this is a new low even for you."

"Really? But I thought you said I could go no lower when I spray-painted a dick on Riley Cassidy's locker," I say.

Ms. Sand makes a panicky little sound and interjects, "Annabel, it's clear to us that your actions are a cry for help. Sweetheart, we know you're in pain. And though there *are* going to be consequences for your actions, more than anything we want to focus on getting you the help you need."

"A cry for help?" I repeat, venom rising.

"Well, Annabel, it's . . . I mean, the fights, the truancy, the vandalism—"

Arroyo interrupts her to say, "Miss Lane, you're lucky I never turned you over to the sheriff, or a file with your name on it would be in the prosecutor's office instead of my filing cabinet."

"Really?" I laugh. "You think Grady would have arrested me?"

"Why do you think he's here now?" Arroyo says. "What you did was cruel and uncaring, but more than that, it might constitute a felony."

Arroyo means to drop a bombshell, and I'm sorry to give him the satisfaction. I gape for a second and then shake my head, my nails scraping at the woolly fabric of the seat beneath me.

"What are you talking about?" I say. I look to Grady like he's the only life preserver in the sea, my eyes wide and desperate. "*What did I do?*"

"Annie . . ." The sheriff winces, shifting his hip off the edge of the desk to draw his phone from his pocket. He taps through the lock screen and then drops it on the desk, screen up, for me to see.

It's the kitchen at my mom's house . . . but it's a *total* wreck. The back door is open. The fruit bowl is smashed, shards of clay scattered across the floor. One of the cabinet doors is hanging by a single hinge, partially ripped from its frame. Some of the glasses inside have been knocked down and lie cracked or broken on the counter and floor.

Ruddy-brown droplets speckle the linoleum in front of the sink.

Water fills my throat, and when I close my eyes, the droplets on the floor morph into the bloodstains on my jacket in the dark behind my eyelids.

My eyes fly open, and I look up at Grady. As I shake my head wordlessly, he says, "The county detectives believe this scene was staged, Annie."

"By *who?*" I ask, picking up his phone, zooming in on the details. The glass on the counter. Owen's shoes by the back door. The droplets of blood on the yellowed floor. One smeared handprint on the busted cabinet door, bloody fingerprints dragging down.

"By *you,*" Grady says. His hand covers the screen as he takes the phone back from me.

"I didn't do this . . ." I say, but I'm looking down at my hands, trying to remember the swirls in the rust-red fingerprints on the cabinet like I could compare them to my own.

Could I have done it?

Once I saw Gun tickling some random girl in the hall at school, so I punched a bathroom mirror and cracked the glass. I threw a plate at the wall like a Frisbee when one of my mom's old boyfriends tried to order me to make him dinner. I kicked a post out of the banister on Bryan Long's staircase at his house party the night Gun and I broke up.

So I guess it's *possible* that I trashed my kitchen in a rage—but if I did, then *why?*

I shake my head and look up at him. "How do they know I did this?"

"Well . . . the county detectives said there wasn't enough damage to indicate a genuine struggle," Grady says. "Plus, Donovan had a real convincing story about you wanting to get his attention. . . ."

"They think I set up a fake crime scene to get Morgan fucking Donovan's attention? Like I'm not already living rent free in his pathetic little gerbil brain? Why were they even there in the first place—did *you* call for county backup?"

"No," Grady says. His face is flushing, red blotches forming on his cheeks. Maura and I used to call them his worry spots, and when they darken on his skin, I know he's realizing that there's something seriously wrong with all this. "They came because Owen called nine-one-one. Because . . . Because apparently, that's what Maura told him to do."

"Maura?" I dig my nails into my thighs. "Why would Maura tell my brother to call nine-one-one?"

"I'd love to ask her, Annie, but I haven't seen her since Saturday," Grady says. "Though I'm pretty sure *you* have."

A trickle of cold water traces down my temple. "Wait, didn't you pick her up from the di—"

"You know, enough of this act," Arroyo says. "We all know what you did, and we all know why you did it. The only thing I can't figure out is, how did you get Maura to go along with this?"

"I wasn't even *with* her," I insist, soft and watery.

"Well, if she's not with you, then where is she, Miss Lane?" Arroyo says.

"I don't know," I whisper. "I don't know where she is—"

I feel like a leaf in a stream. Someone is knocking on the door.

Everything is muffled like the room has suddenly been submerged in water.

Between the splashing in my ears, I hear Arroyo say, "What if the police had implicated Mr. Donovan in your fake disappearance? You could have ruined that young man's life."

Ms. Sand whispers, "Her mother is here."

And that does it.

I double over and stick my head between my knees. The splash of my vomit hitting the grubby carpet seems too loud in the sudden quiet of the room.

Everyone is staring at me. I can feel their gazes on my bowed head. Someone thrusts a small wastebasket into my hands, and I clutch it under my face as I gag on another wave of nausea.

My esophagus floods again. It's cold in my chest, cold in my throat, cold in my mouth. Instead of the hot liquor stew that should be pouring from my belly I spit out another chilly mouthful.

I open my eyes and look through the blur of tears into the trash can.

It's just water.

There's no trace of the purple wine I guzzled last night, only a bucket of cold water mucked by a few wads of algae and soggy pine needles. I wipe my mouth on my wrist and lift my eyes.

Everyone is frozen, staring at me with some mix of disgust and horror on their faces. At some point my mom came in and now she's standing there with her peroxide hair in a frazzled swoop over her forehead and her sweater on backward. The whites are showing all around her eyes, which means she's basically just a breath away from shrieking hysteria.

Another mouthful of water gurgles up my throat, and I spit it into the bin in my hands.

"*Annabel,*" says Dawn Lane, the bane of my existence. "What is *wrong* with you?"

"Maybe you should take Annabel to the restroom, Ms. Lane," Ms. Sand suggests. My mom's bugged-out eyes whip Ms. Sand's way and I cringe instinctively, but the look is a warning shot. She doesn't tell the school counselor off just yet. Instead she brings those frantic eyes back to me, jabbing me with pinprick pupils that swim in choppy blue irises.

"You better stop puking and start talking. *Now,*" she says.

I scrape the back of my wrist across my wet chin and gesture to Principal Arroyo. "Why don't you ask him?" I croak. "He seems to have it *all* figured out."

"I'm asking *you,* you vile brat," Dawn Lane snarls at me.

"Hey, Dawn," Grady interrupts, brow screwed like my mom's already giving him a headache. He steps forward, hand out like he might be able to lower the volume on my mother's manic energy. "Come on, that's not necessary—"

"Shut up, Grady," Dawn says without looking at him. She keeps at me, saying, "Where the hell have you been? Do you have *any idea* what you've put me through? The cops interrogating me and your brothers, the police in and out of our house, the whole town asking questions—and now *here* you are, safe and sound!"

For a long second I just stare at her as I pick through the shrapnel of her words. The kitchen. The blood. My jacket. A crime scene. *Maura.*

The trees from underwater.

The cold current filling my throat.

I spit more water into the wastebasket and snarl at my mother, "Wow. You really have a way of making that sound like bad news."

"Sorry, if it's either my daughter's dead or she's a liar, I think I know what I'd pick," Dawn says.

"Jesus Christ, Dawn," Grady snaps, stepping up into the space between my mom and me. "That's *enough*."

"I thought you wanted me to be more strict with her?" my mom says.

I grind my teeth, crushing pine needles in my molars.

"I wanted you to *parent* her, not stand around and scream at her after the damage is already done," Grady says.

I've always loved the way Grady handles my mother. For the most part, Dawn Lane steamrolls everyone in her path, using shrill belligerence to get her way. But Grady is a rock against her battering force, solid and immovable, the contrast with his calm revealing her chaos.

He's doing it now, looking at my mom from under his Stetson with such a cold stare that even my mom's fury is somewhat chilled.

"She's practically an adult, I shouldn't have to *parent* her anymore," Dawn says.

"You can't retire from a job you never started," Grady says.

"Dawn, maybe you should think about filing a PINS petition and letting the state take over Annabel's care," Principal Arroyo suggests, jostling the mouse on his desk to dismiss the aquarium screen saver, like he's ready to print the relevant paperwork right here and now. "There's no shame in admitting you need help."

"Yes, especially with the legal ramifications of what Annie's done—I'm sure the court would see the need to intervene," Ms. Sand agrees.

"Oh. *Well*. Considering how well *this* government agency has handled the situation, I think I'll pass," my mom says through gnashing teeth. I wonder if the symptoms of her withdrawal seem as obvious to everyone else as they do to me.

Dawn strides forward on her yellowed sneakers and snatches my arm in her skinny hand. I barely manage to place the garbage bin on the floor before she hauls me up, narrowly avoiding a lapful of water.

"If you're done here, I'm taking her home," my mom announces.

"Dawn, hold on," Grady starts.

"Wait—Annabel has already missed quite a bit of school this year—" Ms. Sand protests, cutting him off as I step over the puddle I left on Arroyo's floor.

"Oh, *get real*," Dawn snaps, yanking the door handle. The ladies behind the desk in the main office stare as my mom swings me through the doorway. "She's not gonna graduate, and she's sure as shit not going to college next year. What's the point? Just give it up already, spare yourself the headache."

I turn back, mouthing a watery "please" at Grady over my mom's shoulder. He's got the look of a threadbare blanket, worn and tired, his stubble overgrown from days-old neglect, and his eyes bloodshot from sleep deprivation.

But the way he's looking at me reminds me of something.

I know I saw that look when I fell off the trampoline he bought for Maura and me when we were in second grade. A rock on the lawn gouged my knee so deep I needed stitches, and when Grady picked me up out of the grass, blood pouring down my leg, he was looking at me like this.

There's something safe about it. Something that makes me want to run and hide behind him. I wish he'd stop my mom. Even if he actually arrested me, it would be better than having to leave with her. But he just shakes his head and rubs at the cinnamon overgrowth on his cheeks.

Arroyo calls from his desk, "There needs to be *consequences* for her behavior, Dawn!"

Before she slams the door, my mom smiles and says, "I can handle that."

EIGHT

"SERIOUSLY, ANNABEL, you are so fucked up," my mom says as she shoves me through the doors into the parking lot.

I try to pull my arm from her grip, but her bony claws tighten on my bicep. Her junky Cherokee is parked in the fire lane, one wheel up on the curb. Talk about *fucked up*.

"At least I know how to park," I say.

Past my mom's truck, the Blazer is pulled into one of the parking spaces reserved for faculty. Through the open windows, I see them—Dear leaning an elbow on the steering wheel as he frowns at me, Fern's oval face peering out from under his arm. Virgil assessing my mom with a critical glare. The twins peeking from the back, crouched beneath the window like cats watching birds.

And Sam, head tipped back against the window frame, brow furrowed behind his glasses. The breeze blows the curl on his forehead as he exaggeratedly collapses forward, crossing his arms on the window and resting his chin on them as he watches me getting towed to the car.

But there's a smirk on his lips, and when he turns his head forward and says something to Dear, the Blazer starts up with a guttural roar that throbs on the pavement.

I look to my mom, expecting to see a reaction, but she's way too focused on unlocking the car. And I know she's always pretty oblivious, but still I wonder . . . would she even be able to see them?

I glance at the Blazer again, which seems real enough . . . but maybe I *am* losing it.

I climb into my mom's Cherokee and look across the console at her as she flings herself into her seat and jams her key in the ignition. It's not like mental illness doesn't run in my family. Sometimes, deep in her beer-and-benzo benders, my mom might see bugs that aren't there or yell at us for sounds we didn't make. But even when she's not actively hallucinating, Dawn Lane is *not* sane.

Maybe I'm not, either.

My mom's car smells like cigarettes and some coconut air freshener that reminds me of morning-after-Malibu-Rum vomit. The entire ride home I struggle to contain the cold nausea still bubbling in my throat. It makes it hard to focus on what she's saying, but I get the gist: I'm a selfish bitch, my brothers are traumatized for life, she nearly lost her job because of me, and I'll never be allowed out of the house again.

Honestly it's nothing I haven't heard before.

Occasionally I glance in the rearview mirror, just to check that the Blazer is still behind us. When she turns her car onto our street and I see the blue shake house at the end of Quarry Road, it's like a reoccurring nightmare.

It's exactly how I left it. The lawn hasn't been cut since Neil left. The leather ottoman my littlest brother, Cooper, set on fire six months ago is sitting at the top of the driveway with mushrooms growing from its seat. The Christmas lights Neil put up last winter are nearly seasonally appropriate again, but right now the cracked plastic snowman tipped over in the bushes paints a pretty bleak picture of the kind of house Dawn Lane keeps here.

Fact is, my mom just can't get her shit together.

I know what that must sound like coming from me. Maybe I seem like a hot mess, but I'm just a lukewarm splash compared to the cataclysmic spill of volcanic ash that is my mother. She's Vesuvius, and this house and everyone in it is her Pompeii.

She parks the car at a crooked angle halfway down the driveway. "Are you even listening to me, Annabel?" she asks, but I'm not. I open the door and plant my boots on the cracked asphalt.

"I know you like hurting me," she goes on once she exits the car. "You should have heard the doctors when I was in labor with you—even *they* said you were torturing me."

"Jesus Christ," I groan. She *loves* to bring this up—how I made her sick for nine months straight and then nearly killed her coming out. You'd think the doctors might have wanted to study me, the first baby ever to *intentionally* get stuck in the birth canal.

"I'm just saying. You've always wanted to hurt me, but what about your brothers? And Maura? What were you even *thinking* when you got *them* involved in this shit?" she says as she starts to rummage through her purse for her house keys, which for reasons entirely illogical to me, she keeps separate from her car keys. "It's like you keep getting *worse*."

I roll my eyes and reach into the pot of sunburned ivy hanging off the awning for the spare key hidden there. I unlock the back door and step into the brown enclave of the wood-paneled kitchen, my mom still going on behind me.

"Paul says it's that birth control you're on," she says, tossing her purse on the counter. "All those hormones they put in those things. It's just not natural."

I've heard this before, too. Her boyfriend, *Paul*, blames my blatant animosity toward him on the "artificial hormones" he claims my birth control is pumping into me. One time, after I called him a fucking creep, he even fished my pills out of my bag and tossed them in the garbage disposal.

"It's not the pills," I tell her. "I'm just a bitch."

"Oh, I *know* that." My mom laughs, as if she's the one who made the joke. "At least Maura gets to leave for Princeton soon. We're stuck with you."

I lean my hip against the counter as she yanks the dishwasher open and starts loading it. "You must have been so disappointed when they told you this wasn't a real crime scene, huh?"

Speaking of that "crime scene," the cabinet door that was hanging off its hinges in Grady's photo is just gone now. The only other indication that something happened here is the missing ceramic bowl that sat on the island for over a decade, a relic from when my mom still had her pottery business and most of her mind.

Maybe it's symbolic that it's gone now because it really seems like she is, too.

"Disappointed in you?" Dawn scoffs, totally missing my point. "I'd have to have some respect left for you in order to be *disappointed*, Annabel."

"Jesus Christ. Is my phone here?"

"No. Don't *you* have it?" she says. I shake my head and she goes on, "Well, maybe the cops have it, then."

"Why would the cops have it?"

"It could be evidence."

"Evidence of what?" I say. "I thought they said nothing happened to me."

I watch her slam plates into the dishwasher. She doesn't rinse any of them; most will come out just as crusty as they went in. "You'll probably never get it back. And you know what else? You can forget about that car, too." She bangs a ketchup-clotted plate into the dish rack. "I'm sending that thing to the salvage yard. They can crush it like a tin can."

"What the fuck, Mom, that's *my car*," I snap, pushing off the counter.

Dawn huffs and drops the last plate into the washer like the blade of a guillotine. "We'll see how much *you* like getting hurt," she taunts.

"You can't take my car," I grind out, stepping toward her with fury flaring in my eyes. "It's *mine*. *I* pay for it. If you took it, you'd be *stealing* it."

"Shut up, Annie. I *made* you." My mom laughs, sweeping back her bleach-scorched hair. "I can't steal from you. Your things are *mine*. Your *life* is mine."

"You're absolutely insane," I declare, shaking my head. "Where are my keys?"

"You're not gonna find them," Dawn singsongs, laughing again as she shuts the dishwasher.

"Where the hell are my *keys*, Dawn?" I repeat, rage rising like water filling a glass, ready to spill over.

"It doesn't matter. You're not getting them, and you're not going anywhere."

"Excuse me?" I say, brows shooting up under my tangled bangs. "I am *not* staying *here*."

"Annabel," Dawn says, her manic smile dropping abruptly. "The free and easy life is over for you. No more running around, doing whatever you want, smoking whatever you want, fucking whoever you want. That car is going, and that's *final*."

My fury feels electric. It trembles seismically through my body and rumbles out from my hands. The counter thrums beneath my palms and then—*crack*.

A fissure shatters the yellow laminate and exposes the particleboard beneath. Tiny cracks web out, spreading toward my fingertips. Dusty white drifts down from above. My mom looks up, and I follow her gaze to a crack in the ceiling, directly above the split in the counter.

"What the hell," Dawn whispers.

The crack in the ceiling widens with an earsplitting snap. I duck to avoid the dry plaster that falls like crackling hail to the linoleum.

My mom is screaming something, but I'm not listening.

Crouched low, I notice something tossed beneath the kitchen table, glinting in the shadows.

I crawl toward it, stretching my arm under the table, snagging the cool metal.

I know what it is even before I bring it out from the dark.

Maura and I have worn these matching rings every day since we bought them at a little shop in the Adirondacks where Grady takes us camping every summer. On two silver bands, two half-circles make a whole when stacked together—one etched with a sun, the other a crescent moon downturned like a frown.

I'm still wearing the moon.

So why the fuck is Maura's sun under my kitchen table?

I know she was wearing it at the diner. No matter how mad I was at her, I would have noticed if she'd taken it off.

I slide the ring on my finger, matching up the two halves, then stare at them, water in my eyes, river muck in my throat.

Maura was here. Sometime after the diner, after the last time I remember seeing her.

But if Grady hasn't seen her since Saturday . . . where is she now?

"Annie!" my mom shouts to get my attention. "Annie, what is going on?"

I grab the edge of the table, stand on soggy legs, and glare at my mom across the settled dust, where she's still standing directly below the crack in the ceiling.

I could never tell her what's really going on. I can't tell her where I woke up yesterday, that I'm missing chunks of my memory, that I think something terrible happened to me.

I can't tell her that I'm afraid that if Maura was with me, something terrible might have happened to *her*, too.

So instead I say, "I'm leaving. And if you want to send Grady after me, tell him maybe he should be looking for Maura instead."

I turn around and stalk out of the kitchen. As I pass the front door, I glance out the dusty window at the Blazer pulled up to the curb. The old glass distorts their faces slightly, but my new friends are waiting there for me like a pack of loyal dogs. I won't be long.

But I have to check my room first.

I don't remember making it back to my house the other night, but I guess I must have been here at some point. Maybe I left something in my room—some clue that can tell me why I trashed the kitchen, or how Maura's ring wound up under the table.

Something that will make all this make sense.

The beaded necklaces on my doorknob jangle as I ease the door open. Whatever police search was conducted here didn't disturb my room by much. Wondering how thorough it even was, I cross the black shag rug and pick up the stuffed rabbit flopped against my pillow.

Maura and I each have one of these button-eyed stuffed bunnies, though hers is white and mine is brown. Grady gave them to us on Easter morning when we were six years old, and while the rabbits used to be a treasured reminder of egg hunts and cinnamon bun breakfasts, these days Maura and I both use them for the same thing.

I press my thumb against a seam and find the tear. My finger hooks the plastic pill bottle hidden in the stuffing, and I draw it out to inspect its contents. Sure enough—a half-smoked blunt and three ashy nugs are still there waiting for me.

Some crack detectives they sent. Didn't even find my stash.

My room is the only okay place in this house. I don't spend much time here—I'm always at school, or at work, or out with friends, and in all I've probably slept more nights at the Harker house than at my own, but . . . my room is all right. I painted the walls red and put a string of star-shaped lights over my bed. I pinned blacklight posters and hung my favorite paintings on the walls and filled a bookcase with creepy dolls. I thrifted the perfect painting desk. I melted a patch of the black shag rug in a small fire caused by an unattended hair straightener. I made this room my own as much as I could, but in the end I've never felt completely at home anywhere in the blue shake house at the end of Quarry Road.

Not like how I feel behind the wheel of my Cutlass.

Not like how I felt at Chapel House.

I drop the rabbit and swing my backpack off my shoulder. As I pick a few wrinkled metal shirts and old flannels off the floor to stuff into my backpack, I hunt for clues. Is my purse here? The bottle of tequila I brought to Gun's gig? My phone? No, no, and no.

I zip my backpack, toss it over my shoulder, and cross toward my bed and the window.

I climb across my bed, boots dragging Resurrection Peak mud on my twisted Monster High comforter. (Grady got Maura the same one for Christmas eleven years ago, but she's long since upgraded to something cool and bohemian that she found on Etsy. Not me. New comforters aren't really in the budget around here.)

I shove the window open and swing my legs out onto the roof, stockings snagging on the rough shingles. It's not the first time I've snuck out this way, but it's not ideal. It's usually easier to wait until my mom's pilled up, when she won't even notice me leaving at all.

I crawl to the edge of the roof and eye the drop down to the autumn-blond yard.

Someone whistles at me, and I look to the side of the house, where Sam stands with his hands cupped around his mouth. He drops his hands and a dimple-crease smile spreads across his face as he trots over to stand below the overhang I'm crouched on.

"Hey. I gotta get out of here," I say, already kicking one leg down from the gutter.

"Well, you really pour on the coal, don't you?" Sam says.

I dangle my other leg off the roof and start to slide down, expecting Sam to help me out. When I feel his hands grasp my waist, I release the gutter and let him guide me to the ground.

His fingers dig in below my ribs.

My boots thump against the dead grass.

I twist to face him, and he releases me, but he's still standing close. The water in my chest turns to hot steam. "Thanks," I murmur. I glance at the driveway over my shoulder, then back at him. "Where's the Blazer?"

"It's on the street," Sam says. His eyes are intent on mine, like he's searching for something. "Did you get what you came for?"

"*No,*" I scoff. "I didn't even get to talk to my ex, and apparently everyone thinks I tried to fake my own death or something."

"Well, that's a gas," Sam says.

"Yeah, *and* my mom stole my car keys." I take a step back, because standing so close to him is starting to make me feel like I might evaporate. "Can you guys get me out of here?"

"Sure, but don't you want your chariot?"

"I don't have the *keys*, dickweed."

"We don't need keys to clout a heap," he says.

I press my lips together, wavering for only a moment before I lead Sam around to the garage. I grasp the handle and haul the garage door up over my head.

Inside, my hard-earned Cutlass awaits, black paint still shining in the dull light. I skim my fingers along the trunk as I enter the musty garage, Sam following behind me. When I reach the door on the driver's side, I pull the handle and it creaks open.

"All that and she didn't even lock it," I marvel.

"Parents are so unsophisticated," Sam says as he wanders over to the workbench to sort through the tools. Some of them are Neil's, but most of them are artifacts from when this garage was my grandpa's dominion.

I toss my bag in the back and slide into the driver's seat. The broken-in red velvet feels like a warm embrace. I give a glad sigh as Sam makes his way to the passenger side, then I pull my door shut, run my hands along the steering wheel, and turn to him.

"All right. How do we do this?"

"Unhook your ears, baby doll. Let me pad your skull," Sam says, spinning a screwdriver in his fingers like a drumstick. I watch him closely, but not because I want to see how he'll start the car.

I really don't know anything about him at all.

I don't know why he knows how to start a car this way. I don't know how old he is, where he's from, or how he wound up hidden away on Resurrection Peak. I don't know why I trust him. I don't even know his last name. It occurs to me that I should probably slow down a little, but then he leans in toward me.

I can smell him when he comes close. It's a smell that reminds me of pool halls and poker games and the wind through the window of a racing car. It's his leather jacket, his cigarette smoke, the musky evergreen of the pomade in his hair. I study the angle of his jaw as he reaches for the ignition, his arms grazing the tops of my thighs.

Oh well. I've never liked going slow.

I press my foot down on the clutch. Movement wisps across the rearview mirror.

"God damn it," I say. Sam follows my eyes to the mirror, then twists around to look out the back window as my mom steps through the open door to the garage.

"Hey. Look alive," Sam says. He jams the screwdriver into the ignition and twists the handle. The engine turns over with a gurgling snarl, hungry and mean. Black Sabbath kicks on through the speakers in the middle of "Sabbra Cadabra."

"Let's go, baby," Sam says. "Ball the jack."

I wrench the shifter.

My foot eases off the clutch as I bear down on the gas and send Bathory flying in reverse out of the garage. I veer sharply to the right to avoid my mother, then jerk the wheel to careen around the Jeep in the driveway. The Cutlass sweeps onto the sloping lawn, tearing up the overgrown grass. The car swings onto the street, where the Blazer is idling against the curb.

As I shift into first, Sam hangs out the window to call to the others, "We'll meet you up top by sundown."

And then I stomp the gas and fly away from the blue shake house at the end of Quarry Road.

NINE

THE SHIFT KNOB gripped hard in my palm, I race the Cutlass down the couple blocks of suburban sprawl around Route 15. I'm gnawing my lip until Sam lights a cigarette, which I steal from him—though sucking down smoke does nothing to calm my roiling mind.

Maura's ring flashes on my finger as I twist the steering wheel. Cold water lurches in my guts.

"You're lookin' a little windy, baby," Sam says, eyeing me from the passenger seat. "You all right?"

"*No*, I'm not *all right*," I say, jamming harder on the gas as Bathory bucks onto Route 15. "Everything is *so fucked* right now!"

Sam lights another cigarette for himself. After he takes a drag, he blows out smoke and says, "Look, I know I'm nobody, but you can talk to me about it. If you want."

The truth is, I don't know if I can even *say* what I'm thinking out loud.

But . . . what if *I* did something to Maura?

What if it was *her* blood in the kitchen, *her* blood on my jacket? Her blood on my hands in the moonlight?

The idea that I might have hurt her seems unfathomable and yet . . . *not*. After all, I treat every argument like a fight to the death, turning simple spats into verbal nuclear war.

But our arguments have never gotten *physical* before, and the longer I try to imagine a scenario in which a fight with Maura could lead to bloodshed, the more I realize it's impossible.

No. *I* didn't hurt Maura. But that doesn't mean she's safe.

I know, from the sharp edges of my fragmented memories, that something terrible happened to me. I've known it since the moment I dragged myself out of the river, frozen cold as cemetery stone in my little black dress. I know it was no prank, no drunken misadventure, no accident that landed me there beneath the icy water, alone, stranded on Resurrection Peak.

Someone *put* me there.

And if Maura really was with me, something terrible might have happened to her, too.

Why else would her ring be there at the "crime scene" in my kitchen? She *had* to have been there. But where was she when I woke up underwater? Where is she *now*?

I push Bathory faster along the winding highway and pull so hard on the cigarette that the cherry burns my lips.

The Sabbath tape ends and the radio clicks over to blaring static.

I know this stretch of road. It's the last curve before the dirt byway that cuts up to Resurrection Peak. I know it because I've driven Route 15 a trillion times in Bathory, alone, forget the seventeen prior years I sat as a passenger on these same roads.

But I know it from that night, too.

The radio set in the cherrywood dashboard flickers. The dial ticks through stations. The static sounds like rushing water in my ears. I part my lips and cold water dribbles over my chin.

"Hey—Annie—" Sam says, but he sounds muffled and far away through the thrashing tide in my skull.

Then I hear my own voice in the static on the radio.

"Please . . . just take me home."

I yank the wheel and pound the brake. Bathory's tires carve through the mud on the shoulder, and we slide to a messy stop. I shove my shoulder against the door and fly from the car, panic surging out of my throat as I double over and cough up icy water and soggy pine needles. Squinting through tears, I watch the water pool in the treads of the tire tracks beneath me.

"Annabel!" Sam shouts, clambering out behind me. "Baby, don't you lose it on me—"

I don't answer him.

I straighten up and back away from the car. I rub my sleeve across my eyes and snort up the water clogging my nostrils. I stare at the tire tracks on the shoulder. They arc at a sharp angle and continue right into the steep incline where the base of the mountain meets the road. My gaze follows the trajectory of the tracks to where Bathory's tires have left their own imprints, running beside and then crossing over the older tracks in the mud.

"*Annabel,*" Sam says again, sharper this time.

"Look," I choke out, pointing to the tracks.

They're older, but the tracks that crash into the embankment are the same as the fresh ones behind Bathory's tires. The tread is identical, crosshatched on the edges and pebbled with diamond shapes down the center. The longer I stare at the veering course of the old tracks crossing my fresh ones, the more tenuous my grasp on reality feels. I don't remember *ever* pulling off the road here.

I look over at Sam. My voice is watery and faint. "Did you hear that? On the radio?"

"Yeah. I heard it. Sounded an awful lot like you," Sam murmurs. He's standing close to me, head bent toward mine, eyes black and inscrutable.

I grab on to Sam's arm, grasping just below the elbow, digging my nails into the leather of his jacket. "Sam. That night. I think . . . I think someone tried to *kill me*."

Sam's jaw flexes as he struggles with something for a moment. Then he finally asks, "Who? What kind of cubistic dim-light cruiser would try to cut you down?"

"It has to be them," I say. "My ex and his friends. And if they did something to me . . . they might have done something to my friend, too."

"So, let's go catch those cretins," Sam says, nodding back toward the car.

"I'm *not* going back to school. I won't get anything out of them there, anyway—the principal will be back on my ass *so fast*." The tide of panic is starting to recede, replaced by a sharpening rage. I narrow my eyes as anger focuses me, drying the water on my skin. "But . . . the orchard does this haunted-corn-maze thing. Pumpkin picking and stuff. We were supposed to go tonight."

Together.

I'm such a fucking sucker.

Sam glances up at the sky, still gold with autumn sun. "Tonight?" he says.

"What, do you have other plans?"

Sam chuckles and drops his eyes back to mine. "Oh yeah, I got a date with a cobweb on the porch rails," he says.

"Well, you can't miss that," I say with dry humor, twisting like I'm going to step away from him, even though I don't. "I'll go without you. Give her my best."

Sam's free arm tucks against my waist, turning me back to him. A car passes down the highway, blowing the leaves on the shoulder around our ankles as he pulls me in. I look up at him, my nails gnawing at his leather jacket, the splashy unease totally evaporated from my guts in the heat of his arms.

"There ain't a cobweb in the world creepier than you, baby," he says. "I'm with you."

I nod and bite my lip, the urge to press closer to him overwhelming my resolve. "We have some time to kill," I point out, and wonder if he'll get the hint. I could really use a distraction.

His fingers squeeze at my waist. I part my lips, chin tipping up. But he doesn't bend to meet me—instead his arms unwind from me as he says, "Well, I don't know about you, but I'm hungrier than a moth in a nudist colony. Let's find a spot to knock a scarf."

Cold chills through my limbs as he pulls away.

I shrug off my disappointment as I head back to the Cutlass. "Yeah," I agree. "I could eat."

We climb into Bathory, still chugging away on the muddy shoulder, and I rewind the Sabbath tape and hit play before I jerk the car back onto the highway. We fly past the speed limit until we reach Hagley's single square mile of suburbia again.

The center of Hagley is basically a trap.

It has charmed many a passerby on Route 15 into stopping to browse the oh-so-quaint antique shops that comprise the bulk of Hagley's most prominent businesses. The main drag of town stretches for only a mile, but the historic houses and repurposed mill buildings beckon invitingly, porches heavy with pretty, old junk piles.

We drive past the decommissioned gristmill that settled this town in the 1780s, which these days is repurposed as a giant antique mall. An old general store across the parking lot now houses Hagley

Café, a little restaurant that has been serving breakfast scrambles to the after-church crowd since 1924. The Paulinskill River runs alongside it all, flowing down from Resurrection Peak to cross beneath the bridge we blast over as I run the only traffic light in town.

We "park the hot boiler" in the lot behind a string of Victorian rowhouses down the street from the old gristmill. The car can't be seen from the road there, and the lot has the added bonus of belonging to Nicolo's, the better of the two pizzerias in town.

When we pass through the swinging glass door into the terracotta pizzeria, I'm not sure what to expect. I mean, so far nobody's talked to the kids from Chapel House but me. For all I know, I'm about to sit at a booth and have a chat with thin air. I'm about fifty-fifty on whether that means that Sam's an actual ghost only I can see or a figment of my imagination.

I'm also not sure which of those two options I'd prefer.

It's a relief when we approach the counter and the girl posted at the register gives Sam an inconspicuous once-over, eyeing him from head to toe. Finally—proof that he's *not* just something my horny-for-bad-boys brain conjured up to distract from the trauma or whatever.

I recognize the girl at the counter as Maribeth Conway (or was it Meredith?), a girl a grade above me who graduated from J.P. last year. From the look she gives me after she's done ogling Sam, I guess she recognizes me, too.

I suggest a buffalo chicken pie, but Sam pulls a face and orders the veggie lover instead. I watch him when he pays the tab with bills pulled from a wallet in his back pocket. I can't really think of anything less metaphysical than carrying cold hard cash.

Still. He might not be some kind of 3-D wet dream of mine, but I'm not ready to say he's totally *normal*, either.

After all, *I* don't feel normal. But unless Hagley holds the world record for most psychic mediums per capita, I don't think we can be ghosts—people can definitely see us, as evidenced by the scene I made in school earlier. Besides, I'm not sure ghosts drive crummy cars or carry wallets full of cash.

We could be vampires, maybe—definitely the corny-cool eighties teen-sleaze type, like from *Near Dark* or *The Lost Boys*. But unless Virgil's wine has a secret ingredient I'm not aware of, I've never seen any of them drink blood. And I'm not sure that this hollow hunger inside of me can be sated with anything so simple as a few swigs of AB positive.

I fill my soda cup with cherry cola and pick a booth while Sam waits on our pizza. Nicolo's is all wood paneling, terra-cotta floors, and red glass lanterns—a true retro relic, not a detail changed since the day it opened in 1972. I jam a straw into the plastic lid of my soda and drum my fingers against the table, idly examining the chipped red polish on my nails.

The same red that's probably still on Maura's nails, wherever she is.

We painted them together the Thursday before our fight. It was the first time Maura had agreed to let me sleep over in weeks, which I think she only did because I'd told her that my mom brought Paul home. She knows if I spend the night in the same house as my mom's boyfriend, I might commit a homicide.

And though my resentment about her weird aloofness, and *her* resentment about my rekindled thing with Gun, hung somewhere on the horizon, we didn't acknowledge it.

Instead we spent the night watching horror movies and painting each other's nails in the Evil Dead Shed, our little clubhouse in the woods behind her house.

I remember how I sat with my foot in her lap as she coated my toenails in glossy red lacquer while the wind rattled the rickety old windows of our shed-turned-clubhouse. Maura's laptop was open on the futon beside us, playing *Night of the Demons*. Even in the dark Maura's nail-polish application was neat and precise, a far cry from the mess I'd left around her cuticles.

As demon-possessed Angela danced to Bauhaus on the screen, Maura abruptly asked me, "So you're not even going to apply to Sussex County?"

She'd been bugging me about college for two years, but I thought I'd made it pretty clear that I have no interest in higher education. I don't know what made her decide to bring up my college plans—or lack thereof—yet again, much less in the middle of her favorite scene in one of our favorite movies, but when my eyes snapped to her face, she wasn't looking at me. Her freckled eyelids were lowered, her gaze on my toes in her lap.

I snorted dismissively and said, "Dude, the *last* place I'd ever go is SCC."

"Well, what are you going to *do*, then?" she said, thrusting the brush into the bottle to pick up more polish. "Just stay here? Hagley is a cultural wasteland. There are more churches than restaurants in this dumbass town."

"Not if you pretend the churches are restaurants, too," I said. "Personally I really like the all-you-can-eat communion wafers at Saint Joseph's."

"I'm being serious, Rabbit," Maura said, pausing her handiwork to lift her eyes to mine. "Rutgers has an art program. And it's only twenty minutes from Princeton."

"You want me to go into debt for *art school?*" I laughed.

To be honest, I wasn't surprised Maura had researched schools for me. It's not like she has any of her own college searching to do. She pretty much had her pick after an article she wrote went viral, exposing how a lauded male artist stole most of "his" work from unknown female painters. I thought she was going to choose Columbia, but at the last minute she went with Princeton, and now that that's settled—well, I guess she has nothing better to do than plan *my* future.

But I'm not like Maura, and there's nothing college can do about my oppositional defiance to being taught anything.

"I just don't want you to stay here," Maura said. "Face it. You're going to be miserable in this shithole without me."

"I think you're going to be miserable at Princeton without *me*," I said.

"Which is why *you* should go to Rutgers, so we can get a place in between together," Maura said as she resumed painting. "Imagine all the brand-new fights we can have as roommates. Like, we've never fought over what size garbage can to buy or how to organize a utensil drawer before."

"I don't have to go to Rutgers for us to get a place together," I pointed out. "But now I *really* wish you'd picked Columbia, because a place in the city would be way cooler than one in *Princeton.*"

"Princeton is total dark academia vibes," Maura said. But I watched her, the frustrated furrow of her auburn brow and the curl of cinnamon hair brushing her cheek, and I wiggled my toes in her lap just to get her to look up at me again.

"Don't *do* that," she chastised, but when her dark eyes met mine, I held them.

"Is that what you want?" I asked her. "You wanna be roomies next year?"

She rested a hand on my ankle. She nodded and her fingers wrapped behind my heel, red nails pressing, gripping tight.

"All right," I said. "But if you think the superior utensil-drawer order isn't spoons, knives, forks, I'm gonna need a garbage can big enough to fit your body in."

Her laugh poured like warm sand from her lips, sifting soft and gravelly as her tense brow unwound.

I can still hear it humming in my ears when Sam drops into the booth across from me.

"Sorry I didn't bite on the dead-bird topping," he says. "You are what you eat, and I ain't no chicken."

"Hm. I hope she didn't spit on this," I say, reaching for a slice.

"Who? That plain-Jane pie pusher?" Sam says as he takes a slice and folds the crust in half. "She gave you a heck of a dirty eyeball, didn't she?"

"Yeah. I'm kind of controversial around here."

"Controversy looks good on you."

"Sure." I shrug. "Until the villagers start gathering their pitchforks."

"You know, you still haven't given me the whole story of what happened this morning, and I got a lot of room in my ears yet."

I roll my eyes and tear off a bite of pizza, chewing as I try to figure out where to even start. "Well, I didn't get to talk to my ex because the *sheriff* apprehended me first."

"Damn. They sent the sheriff? What's a gal got to do to wind up on the head honcho hog's most-wanted list?"

"Don't get too excited," I say, catching the shine of admiration in Sam's dark eyes. "He's the sheriff, but he's also Maura's dad, and, like, probably the only actual parent I have at all."

"Ah, he's your U-Thor," Sam says, and when my blank stare goes on for several beats, he adds, "Jed of Manatos, father figure to A-Kor, who challenges the jeddak that imprisons him. *The Chessmen of Mars?*"

"Is this a Star Wars thing?" I ask, and now *his* stare goes blank. I wave my hand, moving on.

As we polish off the whole grease-puddled pizza together, I tell Sam about the "crime scene" in my kitchen, and how the county police apparently decided it was fake thanks in part to whatever my ex-boyfriend told them. I tell him how everyone thought Maura was with *me*, but she wasn't with me, or maybe she *was* with me. . . . And then I end up telling him all about the fight Maura and me had earlier that day, and how much Maura disapproved of my rekindled crush on my insufferable fuckboy ex, and about Gun, and how our relationship came to a catastrophic end. . . .

We talk until the light through the windows turns dusky blue. Sam glances at the watch on his wrist and tells me, "I better call the others before we head out."

"Call them?" I repeat, glancing around us at the total lack of a cell phone. "How?"

"The counter girl's got a phone for taking orders, doesn't she? I bet she'll lend me the line as long as you don't make her too frosty."

"Okay, but—what phone are you calling? I didn't see any of you with a phone."

"We have a phone. The one in the kitchen," Sam says with a shrug. He gets up, and even though my presence probably won't help him sweet talk Maribeth (Meredith?) Conway into letting him use the pizzeria's phone, I follow him.

"Sam. Are you telling me there's a *working telephone* connected to an *active phone line* in that house?"

"I didn't say all that, but you've clearly got a knack for inferences," Sam says. He steps up to the counter and smiles at Maribeth. "Hey, could I dial out on that horn real quick?"

She looks confused for a second, but her gaze follows his gesture to the landline on the counter, which she turns toward him a bit tentatively.

"Uh, sure," she says, like she's not *entirely* sure he's talking about the phone. But he grabs the receiver and I lean forward, peering around his shoulder to watch the number he dials.

1-5-2-1.

He puts the phone to his ear as I protest. "What the fuck, that's not even a real phone number!"

But after a moment, it's apparent he's talking to *someone*. He says into the telephone, "Yeah, sorry we're late. The mission's still on." A pause, and then, "No. Not yet."

I strain closer, and faintly I hear the tones of Fern's voice through the receiver pressed to Sam's cheek, though I can't make out what she's saying.

Sam responds to her. "Actually, we're not. We got a couple crabs to boil. At the orchard. No, you don't— Well. Yes. Sounded. Yes, ma'am. Gotcha. See you soon."

He hangs up and turns to me, looking slightly sheepish, like Fern might have told him off. "Looks like they'll be meeting us there," he tells me.

"Fine," I say, turning away from him. I snatch my backpack out of the booth and dig a Sharpie out of the front pocket, uncapping it with my teeth. I scrawl the numbers 1521 on the inside of my wrist, just in case. I show it to him and ask around the cap in my mouth, "That's the number? For real?"

"That's the one," Sam says.

As we leave Nicolo's, Sam stops at the gumball machines next to the door. I always thought there were only two—one with plastic rings, the other with sticky slap-hands—but there's a third one on the end, the glass strange and iridescent. Sam dumps some change from his pocket into the machine and twists the dial. The machine coughs a handful of rubber insects into Sam's palm, and he pockets them as we step out into the breezy twilight.

Maybe it was the food, but I feel better now—sharper, quicker, less watery and muddled. I notice everything. The hum from a TV playing a Lon Chaney movie through someone's living room window. The cheesecloth ghosts hanging in a tree, twisting in the wind. The flickering faces of pumpkins on porches, dry leaves skittering across the sidewalk, the distant yowl of a barking dog.

We turn up the driveway to the lot behind Nicolo's, where my car is parked. I look over at Sam, his face streaked with orange and violet from the candy-colored lights strung between the buildings. "Why do you believe me?" I ask him.

"What's not to believe?"

"You just met me, like, yesterday. For all you know I really am crazy."

"Oh, I know you're crazy." Sam chuckles. His laugh sounds like it's been rubbed over with sandpaper one too many times, gritty and quiet. "The only people for me are the mad ones."

"I mean crazy enough to stage a crime scene for attention."

"No. You're definitely not that kind of crazy," Sam says.

I pause at the driver's side door, cracking it open but looking over the top of the car at him. "Is this even a good idea? It's a big maze. We might not find them in there."

"We'll find them," Sam says, before he drops into the passenger seat.

I guess he's right.

At this point I'm so pissed off, there's nowhere Gun could hide from me.

TEN

MY BOOTS SCUFF the gravel as I climb out of Bathory, the sky over the farm pumpkin orange with the last splash of sunset. The air smells like popcorn, diesel fuel, and damp dirt.

As I slam my door, I glance around the parking lot, mist wafting between the cars from the fog machines in the corn maze. My sour gaze turns to acid when it lands on the emerald-green Mustang parked at the edge of the lot.

Gun's here.

And he's not alone.

I spot Tre's truck, too, chrome ball sack dangling from the bumper. Just in case the truck nuts weren't enough to tip you off, the inane collection of stickers plastered across the back window make sure you're aware that the car is owned by a total shitstain of a human. There's no way someone with a sticker that reads I'LL PUT MY CARBON FOOTPRINT UP YOUR ASS! could *not* be a blight on society.

I twist Maura's ring on my finger, spinning the sun above my moon. One of them better be able to tell me where she is.

Headlights flash behind Sam and me, and I twist to watch the Blazer barrel into the lot, tires spinning dusty earth as it jerks into an empty spot opposite my Cutlass. Before it even comes to a complete stop, the back doors fly open and the twins roll out like tumbling jesters, cartwheeling across the gravel.

"What a couple of hubcaps," Sam grumbles, a smirk on his lips.

Howl crashes into a silver Camry hard enough to dent the back door. Virgil climbs out of the driver's seat of the Blazer, his laugh like a diamondback rattle hissing through the smoky air.

Fern and Dear follow the others, Dear looking stiff and surly, Fern patting his arm as if to comfort him. As Sam and I step away from the Cutlass to join them, Fern falls into step beside me. She looks festive in a cream turtleneck with spiderweb embroidery across the chest, a pair of black pants belted tight on her little waist. I smile at her, grateful for her presence. If I have to listen to what Gun might say tonight, I'm glad they're here with me.

"What's up with him?" I ask Fern as we walk, nodding toward Dear, whose tense shoulders and bunched brow are even more pronounced than usual.

"Virgil's driving just twists him out of shape," Fern says, tossing back her curls in exasperation.

I eye Virgil, who is bending his long body to check his reflection in the dark windshield of the Camry that Howl crashed into. He licks his plum-stained thumb and smooths back a shock of black hair escaping his slick undercut.

"No kidding. I bet he learned to drive from a crocodile," I say.

Fern giggles and hooks her arm with mine. She looks over at me, her eyes bright rubies, her dappled cheeks dabbed with shimmering blush.

"You still don't remember what happened?" she asks, and when I shake my head, she squeezes my arm tight and puffs out a sigh.

Sam pays for our tickets to the maze and tells the lady he likes her hat. It's just a basic-ass witch hat, but she's so charmed she gives him a candy apple. He hands it to me as we walk on through the pumpkin patch.

I rip away the spiderwebbed cellophane and sink my teeth into sticky caramel and sour apple. But when I look up the hill at the corn maze on the horizon, the caramel curdles on my tongue.

Green hair glints in the torchlight as Gun leads the way up the path toward the mouth of the maze.

He's flanked by Trevor with his coyote smile. The rest of their usual gang isn't far behind—the bassist, Darren; their friends Kunal and Hogan, who are in a band called Sneeze Police; a dude named Jordy who everyone calls Horny for reasons I'd rather not know.

There are girls with them, too—Hogan's girlfriend, Aubrey; a violet-haired girl from Newton who I only know by her Instagram handle; and a pretty girl wearing mom jeans and wire-rimmed glasses who puts her hands over her ears as they approach the entrance to the maze.

And then there's Riley Cassidy.

Riley Cassidy has a few claims to fame. She's Werewolf Fetus's number one fangirl. She's violated the dress code so many times that her name has become a verb used to describe the act of getting sent home from school for inappropriate attire. Last year she shaved her head in the locker room and then spent a week in a psych ward. She once seriously argued in class that Australia could have warned everyone about 9/11 because they're fourteen hours ahead of us.

Oh, and she also stole my boyfriend.

For as long as I've been involved with Morgan Donovan, Riley Cassidy has been a thorn in my side. Gun always swore there was nothing between them, that Riley's just a "real fan of the music," but I never bought it.

It drove me nuts that Riley kept her Instagram private, but one night Maura made a decoy account and added Riley to snoop on her profile. Finally we unlocked a treasure trove of evidence that

Gun was spending a lot of the time he claimed to be at "band practice" hanging out with Riley, and when I confronted him about it at Bryan Long's house party two days later, he called me a crazy bitch in front of all his friends.

So I dumped him.

Why I was ever dumb enough to think he deserved a second chance is beyond me now.

"That's them up there," I say. "My ex is the one with the green hair."

"What a creature feature," Sam scoffs.

I watch them disappear through the painted wooden skull that marks the entrance of the maze. Scattered popcorn and dry leaves crackle under my boots as we hike up the path.

The twins rush ahead through the mouth of the skull into the darkened corn maze. Virgil reaches out to stroke one of the skull's jagged wooden teeth before he takes chase after them. The path through the corn is lit by tiki torches and bright blue moonlight. Energy snaps against my skin like grease on a skillet while the theme from *Halloween* plays from a speaker somewhere in the corn. I don't see or hear Gun's crew at all anymore.

Around a bend in the path, an animatronic skeleton lunges out of the corn, and my shriek pierces the night. Sam laughs and I try to stomp on his foot, but he hooks his arm around my shoulders and tugs me against his side.

"Come on, Crazy, let's go dig up some maggots," he says near my ear.

Chills crawl up my spine as the warm leather of his jacket presses against the back of my neck. We turn down a fork in the path, breaking off from the rest of our group.

His arm is around me, but he's not the one steering us. I am.

I know Gun isn't far.

Boy sweat and body spray, weed smoke, a splash of cheap beer. I bet he chugged a forty in the parking lot. I bet his car stereo was blasting some jockstrap metal band the whole time. I bet he didn't offer Riley any of his beer. I bet she still laughed at all his jokes anyway.

I bet he has no idea I'm coming for him.

As we prowl down the trail, I say to Sam, "You don't have to do this with me, you know."

"Are you telling me to get lost?" Sam says.

"No, I just want to give you a chance to bow out before shit gets messy."

"I told you, I ain't no chicken," Sam says. His hand tucks down the collar of my flannel, his fingertips graze my skin. "Besides, I'm with you, remember?"

I shiver, lips parting, his hot fingers tracing the dip below my collarbone—just as we come around a bend in the maze and step *directly* into Gun's path.

He's looking at Trevor, saying, "Nah, no way. The game is rigged, dude. You're gonna tell me Princess fucking Peach outranks my man Cloud Strife?"

Trevor shakes his head beside Gun. "It's some feminazi bullshit, man."

"Right? The game is called *Super Smash* BROTHERS—"

And then, in the middle of this enlightened debate, Morgan Donavan chokes on his words.

The moment when his blue icepick gaze falls on me seems to tick by in slow motion. I watch the widening of his eyes, the raise of his brows, the slack O his shocked mouth forms. And then, before he can recover from his shock, I ask him:

"Morgan. What. Did. You. *Do?*"

"Jesus, Annie, what is this?" Gun says, his voice cracking on my name. Then his eyes shift from me, to Sam, to Sam's hand under the collar of my shirt. Sam's fingers skim a little lower, leaving goose bumps in their wake. Gun's eyes narrow sharply. "And who the hell are *you*?"

Sam is all cool indifference when he responds, "What's it to you, drip?"

"*Morgan*," I snap, pulling his attention back to me. "You need to tell me what the fuck happened. Why was there a crime scene in my kitchen?"

"Annie, you *know* that wasn't actually a crime scene," Gun says. "I don't know how the hell the cops even got involved; there was barely any blood—"

"Barely any blood?" I repeat, fast and shrill. "I found my jacket, assface. It literally looks like someone *died* in it."

"Wait, *what?*" Gun frowns.

"Why is my jacket covered in *blood*, Morgan?"

"Probably because they don't make tampons big enough to deal with your permanent PMS," Trevor says.

And Gun fucking *laughs*.

Sam's arm tenses on my shoulders. His jaw is grinding as he stares at Trevor and Gun, his eyes sparking like flames beneath a black sky. His voice a low snarl, he says, "I get that you all barely evolved beyond the primordial pool, but the lady asked you a question. Now, are you gonna answer it or what?"

"I'm serious, who the fuck *are* you?" Gun says, taking a step closer to Sam.

"Oh." Sam smiles coldly. "I go by many names."

"Morgan," I say, demanding his attention yet again. "What *happened* the other night?"

"Do you seriously not remember *any* of it?" Gun says.

"Of course she doesn't. I *told* you it would work," Trevor says as he steps up beside Gun. His nasally voice pierces through the screams and sound effects of the corn maze around us.

Darren and Jordy are closing in, too, but when I scan past them, I'm surprised to see that Gun's other friends don't seem to want any part in this drama. Even Riley Cassidy, who normally hangs on Gun's every word, looks uninterested. Riley and her violet-haired friend have their heads bowed over a phone, both of them watching something on the cracked screen and murmuring quietly to each other.

I squint at them for a moment, but they're too far down the path for me to see well, and their huddled bodies mostly obscure the phone they're holding between them.

From Gun's side Trevor goes on: "You wanna know what happened, Annie? You got *fucked up*. I mean like, you got so drunk you forgot how to work a hamburger."

"*When?*" I demand, eyes slitted on Trevor. If they have something to hide, I vote Gun's punch-dumb best friend Most Likely to Slip Up and Say Something Incriminating. "At the show? What happened after?"

Trevor sneers at Sam and asks, "Does this bitch have dementia or something?"

"You can keep barking if you want to get carried out of here by the handles," Sam says, arm dropping away from my shoulders as he takes a step toward Trevor.

"You know, I could ask some questions, too," Gun announces, as if to remind us all of our roles as side characters in the Morgan Donovan show. "Like, why'd you have to go and put that video back up? I thought we had a deal. You fuck with me, I'm gonna have to fuck with you."

Leering, Trevor says, "Yeah, tit for tat, bi—"

But before his crooked lips finish the last disparaging word, Sam draws his fist from his jacket pocket and flings a handful of hissing black-brown bugs directly into Trevor's face.

One pings against his teeth and gets caught between his closing lips while others fall and alight on his shirt, serrated legs skittering as they crawl across Trevor's chest. Trevor retches as he spits the bug from his mouth, but he gives an outright scream when one darts out of his hair and scampers across his forehead. He jumps and thrashes and scrapes his hands back and forth through his scab-brown hair, shaking out a few more squirming black bugs.

"What the shit!" Gun shouts as he and Trevor both reel back, but when they look down at the bugs on the ground, they realize something at the same time I do.

The bugs aren't real.

A bunch of rubber insects lie still on the dusty path at our feet. I recognize them as the toy bugs Sam got from the iridescent gumball machine in Nicolo's, but I don't know why it seemed like they were *moving* a second ago. I'm still staring when Gun steps over the rubber bugs and closes in on Sam.

"That's it. You're done, man. You're *done*," Gun snarls.

"Whoa, whoa, whoa," Kunal calls from where he stands with Hogan and the girls. "Dude, hold up. You're not gonna fight here, this is a family establishment."

"Yeah, come on," Hogan says, putting his hand on Aubrey's shoulder. "Just tell her to delete the video and fuck off. This isn't worth it, man."

"She's just trying to make you jealous," the girl with the wire-framed glasses says. I think she's here with Aubrey, or maybe she's supposed to be Kunal's date. Either way, I don't know how she presumes to know anything about me, because I'm positive I've never met her before.

"I'm not jealous." Gun laughs. "Why should I be jealous that someone's been picking through my trash?"

"Morgan, *you're* the trash—*I* dumped *you*, remember?"

Gun ignores me. His eyes flick away like I'm insignificant, his focus shifting to Sam. "I'm serious, man," he says. "You better get this crazy bitch out of my sight before she makes me lose it."

That's when I drop my candy apple and punch Morgan Donovan in the face.

My right hook swings so fast that my fist connects with Gun's nostrils before the apple even hits the ground. My knuckles crush cartilage against bone, and Gun's head snaps back with the force.

And as blood blooms from Gun's nostrils and he stares at me with a slack jaw and dazed eyes, I can't help it—I *laugh*.

Sam turns admiring eyes on me, his smirk sinking a dimple into his cheek. I revel in his smitten stare, but of *course* Gun steals this moment from me. He charges Sam and plows him into the ground in a knot of thumping fists and rabid grunts.

"Gun! Stop!" I yell, rushing in to snatch at Gun's arm. Trevor grabs me by the back of my shirt and pulls hard enough to pop a button on my flannel.

"Skank, don't *even*—"

A howl from the corn cuts him off. The twins burst from the dry stalks and pounce on Trevor with a war-cry screech. Darren and Jordy seem ready to jump in, too, but Virgil slinks out of the corn just behind the twins with a wicked grin curling his viper mouth. Gun's would-be defenders back off while the members of Sneeze Police grab their girls and book it down the path with Riley and her friend.

While the twins claw at Trevor, I throw myself into the fray of Gun versus Sam.

"Are you serious, Morgan? *I'm* the one who hit you!" I scream as I land with my elbow jammed into Gun's spleen.

"You know—*first* you try to get me accused of kidnapping you, then you repost that fucking video anyway?" Gun yowls, his voice thin as I press him into the dirt. "What did I ever do to you?"

I laugh, slamming my fist against his ribs as I shove him away from me. "I don't know, Morgan, what *did* you do to me? What did you do to *Maura*?"

"You're the one who brought her into this," Gun huffs. I freeze, tangled on the ground with him as the struggle between Trevor and the twins blows torch smoke across my face, stirring my wild hair.

"Morgan. Where is she?" I ask. "Where is Maura?"

"How the hell should I know? Sheriff said she was with *you*—"

A sneaker collides with the small of my back so hard that I think my spine might launch through my gut. I shout and roll forward. Trevor's clunky skate shoe stomps on my back, full weight pressing down while he grabs Gun by the wrists and drags him to his feet.

"Let's *go*, man, let's go!" Trevor is screaming. They trip over me and rush into the corn.

I roll over on the disheveled stretch of trail. Sam's pushing off the ground, but everyone else has already gone, leaving nothing but kicked-up dirt and scattered candy. Sam reaches to help me up.

"Sam—"

"Come on," he says. I set my feet against the ground, and he hauls me up and starts to pull me into the corn.

"Sam, hold on," I say.

He grinds to a halt and turns to face me. "What's wrong? Do you want to stop?" he asks.

I think about that night.

I think about running through the trees, my breath hitching with sobs. I hear Trevor's hacksaw laugh and taste Gun's tequila breath in my mouth. I feel cold water choking my lungs. I remember the pain. I remember being so afraid.

Now I want *them* to be afraid.

"No," I murmur. "I don't want to stop."

Sam turns forward and keeps moving through the corn.

I hear someone on the path ahead, and Sam lets go of my hand as we break into a run. Trevor and Gun are sprinting away from us, but before they disappear around the corner Gun looks back and sees me on the path behind him. His eyes are wide and terrified. A smile splits my red lips.

My boots chew up the dirt. I run faster than the pop-hiss of the animatronics as they lunge out behind me. The torches lining the path blow smoke across my eyes.

I charge into the corn just as Trevor and Gun do, following the crash of snapping stalks to stay on their heels. When their paths diverge in the corn, I choose one at random and Sam splits off to follow the other trail.

By the time I reach the boy pushing through the field I'm moving too fast to stop. I drive him into the ground and land on his back, my knees digging into his shoulders and my hands fisting in his hair.

It's Trevor.

I twist his head up by his hair and pull his face out of the dirt. Wet earth sticks to the bloody scratches on his cheek while he chokes on a mouthful of mud.

I don't feel bad for him.

Once I heard him bragging to Gun that he drugged some girl's drink after a Werewolf Fetus show. A few weeks ago, I saw him spit on a Science Club kid who tripped in the hall at school. He told everyone Jessica Lesak gives shitty blowjobs after she refused to accept a ride home from him over the summer. I sat in the back seat of his truck last November, screaming at the top of my lungs as he stomped on the gas and sped toward a fox crossing the road. He cheered when he crushed it under his tires.

I could never feel bad for him.

"Trevor. Tell me what happened."

"Let me go," he coughs out.

I'm not very heavy or exceptionally strong. Trevor should be able to throw me, but his arms strain uselessly as he tries to push off the ground. He can't get any leverage beneath me.

"Let me *go!*"

"No," I hiss, bowing in toward his ear. "Tell me what happened."

"Bitch, get *off* me!"

"Tell me what you did!"

My voice surges out of my mouth, booming into Trevor's ear and stirring the stalks of corn around us. He flinches into the ground while my hands snarl forward on his head. I want to dig my nails into his skull, but when I curl my fingers in, they don't scratch. They sink.

I look down at my fingers as they disappear under the surface of Trevor's scalp.

Then I look up and see my driveway.

But I am not looking out of my own eyes anymore.

"Is that her?" Darren whispers.

"Shh, chill out." Trevor's voice.

I'm inside Trevor's head, seeing my driveway through his eyes. He's peering around the side of my house at a car pulling in—a white Crown Vic, the retired cruiser Grady bought for Maura for her seventeenth birthday.

Trevor dashes to the back patio and joins Gun and Darren by the door. I hear two car doors open and slam shut, followed by the sound of two sets of shoes plodding up the driveway.

A gravelly laugh echoes through the dark, but she's still out of sight.

"You really think it'll work?" Gun asks.

"Just shut up," Trevor says. "Of course it works."

"It needs to, dude, because I can't deal with her—"

"It'll work, just shut up!"

I see myself from behind my Trevor-goggles. I come around the side of my house wearing the same tight black dress and spiky leather jacket I wore to the Werewolf Fetus show that night. I look like I've been crying. Tears slick my makeup across my eyelids and trail mascara down my cheeks.

Maura is there beside me.

She's looking at me, saying something in her husky amber voice, but I'm frozen in place. She finally turns her head to see what I'm seeing, and the withering stare she gives the boys clustered on the patio is clearly inherited from her father.

"What the hell are you doing here?" she demands.

"I'm here to see my girl," Gun snaps back at her.

Maura laughs and steps up onto the patio. The silver sun circling her finger shines beneath the patio light as she tucks her red hair behind her ear and says to Gun, "You're genuinely deluded if you think she's your *anything.*"

"Come on, Annie. I just want to talk," Gun urges, shifting closer to me when I step onto the patio behind Maura.

"I *saw* you with her, Morgan. There's literally nothing to talk about," I growl at him. I reach into the ivy pot for the keys. Trevor eyes the stripe of skin above the lace of my stockings when the hem of my dress lifts up, but he looks away once I drop back onto my heels.

"Just— You need to know— Riley *knows* what'll happen as soon as we get back together," Gun insists.

I croak out a laugh as I push the key into the door.

"C'mon. Just have a drink with your boy for old time's sake," Trevor says. "Can't you see he's sorry?"

"Get bent, fuckface," I say. I twist the key in the lock.

Trevor smacks his hand against the top of the door, pushing it open so I can't close them out.

"Tre, cut it out," Gun says.

But Trevor is already shoving me into the kitchen.

"Stop!"

I crash to the ground. When I open my eyes, I'm back inside my own head, staring up at Trevor as he twists his hands around my wrists. He must have pried my fingers from his head and now he has me pinned to the dirt. I try to buck him off, but he only tightens his grip on my arms. He laughs when I fight, the sound shrill against my ear.

"Not so tough now, are you?" he sneers.

My stomach gives a quick hitch, and I spit a mouthful of murky water at his smirking face. He chokes in surprise, river puke dripping into his mouth. He lets go of my wrists to scrub at his face with his sleeves, and I writhe and kick against the ground as he grabs a fistful of my hair.

"What the hell is your problem?" he screams.

I ram my boot into his shin, and he yanks me up by the hair. I clench my teeth and wait for him to crack my head against the ground, but he never does.

"Let her go."

I open my eyes and look up at Sam, who is standing behind Trevor with a bone-handled knife to Trevor's throat. The blade slices shallowly at Trevor's skin.

"Back off, bro," Trevor says, fingers flexing in my hair. "Put the goddamn knife away and—"

"No." Sam's hand moves fast, drawing a line across Trevor's throat. The cut isn't deep, but it bleeds. Sam's knife is snug against Trevor's pulse again an instant later, before he can even process that Sam hasn't actually slit his throat. "Let's try that again. *Let her go.*"

Trevor's fist untangles from my hair and lifts to join his other hand, held up in surrender. I see his throat strain against the blade as he swallows. I push out from under him, scrambling across the trail until I'm out of his reach.

"Listen to me because I promise you're going to die tonight if you don't. You understand?" Sam says, and Trevor nods. "Good. Now tell her what you did."

"I—I didn't—" Trevor looks at me, his breath rapid and shallow. "It was *his* idea. It wasn't supposed to be such a huge mess—"

"What did you do?" My voice is a dry hiss in my throat. "Trevor, what did you do?"

He opens his mouth, but if he says anything, I don't hear it.

Something jumps out of the corn with a snarl that rumbles the dirt beneath my palms. All I see is ink-black fur and *teeth*—big, sharp teeth that gleam as they snap in my face.

I skitter backward across the ground.

I hear Sam yelling my name. There's a half-instant where I think it's an animatronic or something, but this is no cheesy prop I'm looking at.

What *am* I looking at?

A hunched back arches toward the moon over the corn, shoulders high as a bear. Jagged black fur spikes down a sloped spine. A thick tail sweeps across the dirt. Wet nostrils flare at the end of a wolflike snout. A pair of eyes shine in the dark, coruscating like white quartz. There are no pupils, but I know it can see me.

And it's not alone.

I hear another coming through the corn between the chiming bells of the *Exorcist* theme playing through a speaker nearby.

Snapping stalks, hungry snarls, panting breaths.

The beast lunges for me again, teeth bared in a rot-gray mouth, long tongue like a black eel dripping glistening saliva. I scream, but the sound gets punched from my chest when Sam comes in like a bullet and hooks his arms around my ribs to drag me off the ground.

Sam narrowly dodges the pouncing monster by jumping behind Trevor. Tre, still on his knees among the broken cornstalks, seems dazed and bewildered—but not nearly as horrified as he should be, considering the massive wolf-beast whose open, snarling mouth is mere inches from his face.

It's like he doesn't see it.

It's like it's only here for us.

Below the guttural breaths of the monster pacing nearer, I hear Trevor ask, "What the hell are you guys?"

Before Sam drags me into the corn, he mutters, "To define is to limit."

ELEVEN

I CAN HEAR them chasing us as we run through the corn.

Their toothy snarls aren't far behind, cornstalks snapping with the force of their massive bodies. Sam grips my hand as if he's prepared to drag me from their jaws if they catch me.

I hear the twins howling at the sky, and when we burst through the corn, I see them running ahead of us toward a picnic table where Fern and Dear are waiting. Everyone seems to get the signal, and Virgil pushes off the snack stand to join them in the rush toward the Blazer, flicking one of his black cigarettes into a pile of dry hay.

And as we run down the hill away from the maze, I know they're right behind us. I can smell them, reeking of sulfur and rot, their breath wet against our backs.

"What the fuck, what the *fuck*," I whine as my boots pound faster across the pumpkin patch.

When we reach the parking lot, the others are already piling into the Blazer. I throw myself against Bathory and wrench the door open. I fall into the driver's seat, hand grasping for the screwdriver in the ignition. A toothy snarl sounds from the crack in Sam's door just before he slams it shut. I shriek as the beasts close in against Bathory's windows, jamming the clutch and starting the car. The Cutlass snarls awake, the engine sounding like crashing rapids. I twist my hand on the shifter and we tear out of the parking lot after the Blazer, fishtailing briefly as my tires spin into second gear.

I recover and we shoot down Route 15 as I push Bathory over the speed limit.

"What the hell *were* those things?" I ask aloud, glancing at the rearview, searching for glowing white eyes in the dark behind us.

I've lived in this middle-of-nowhere town my whole life. I know we have wildlife out here. At night there are more deer than cars on the roads. I've seen coyotes and bears and box-faced bobcats the size of a mini fridge.

I know for a fact that those weren't anything I've ever seen or even *heard of* before.

"Should we call someone?" I say. I glance at Sam, who's frowning at the rear window of the Cutlass like he expects to see glowing eyes behind us, too.

"*Sam,*" I snap, and he turns back to me. "Shouldn't we call animal control or, like, Area Fifty-One or something? They were chasing us! They could hurt somebody!"

"I don't know," Sam says. He settles back into his seat and swipes off his glasses with one hand while the other rubs at his brow. "I don't think the extant are on the menu for those things."

I think of Trevor, trembling in fear of us while remaining blissfully unaware of the drooling monster in front of him.

He didn't see it. It was after *us.*

And I think I know why.

While we follow the Blazer up the dirt road to Resurrection Peak, I don't say anything. I swerve around the ditches in the road, my headlights shining on the thick trees and the empty houses that crouch in the overgrowth.

Only they don't seem empty anymore.

A face against glass, watching us go by. A wisp of smoke on a porch. A sizzle of gospel music through a broken window, lost fast in our dust.

And then we pull up to Chapel House.

I can hear the twins sing-shouting a strange rhyme as I climb out of the Cutlass, the two of them leading the charge into the Ark as they bellow,

"The flesh will crack, the bones will dry."

"The worms will squirm from eye to eye."

"The belly bloats, the guts turn up."

"The teeth fall out and turn to mush!"

"When all men die, as all men do."

"Except, that is, for me and you!"

Behind me, I hear Sam say my name, but I ignore him. The watery panic is strangling me, clogging my ears with river muck, rushing in my skull like charging rapids.

How could I not have known before?

Or did I know all along?

Water drips from my fingertips as I march across the amber leaves. I slip through the doors into the arched ballroom, which is decorated with paper lanterns and festive bunting, the floor scattered with half-carved pumpkins and tangled streamers. The others are there already, the twins lighting candles around the ballroom with sparking matches, and as I take them all in, I know for sure.

They're all dead.

And so am I.

It seems absurd, but the Occam's razor of recent events has sliced on the supernatural side. There's no rational explanation anymore—at this point, denying what I've seen seems like the *irra-tional* choice.

But it's not just about what I've *seen*.

It's how I've *felt* ever since I woke up in that river.

The fact is, I feel like a watery wraith, scrambled and wrong, the vengeful wrath stitching me together all that keeps me in the shape of a girl.

Sam stumbles into the ballroom, and I turn to face him. With his roughly swept pomp and vintage leather jacket, he doesn't even *look* like a part of the modern era. He's outdated, anachronistic; he's a *fucking antique*.

"So. When were you planning on telling me the truth?" I shout—to him, and to everyone else in the ballroom.

They all freeze like a record scratch, turning their eyes on me. The only one who looks unaffected is Virgil, who takes a seat on the edge of the bandstand like he's ready for a show. He draws on his black cigarette and then blows out a puff of slithering smoke, "You already *know* the truth, don't you?"

"Is this some kind of sick joke to you?" I say. "Just waiting to see how long it takes me to figure it out?"

"We would have told you if we could," Fern says, shifting in her velvet loafers.

"Well, why the hell couldn't you? Because *he* told you not to?" I snap, shooting a pointed glare in Sam's direction.

"Whoa. When did I become persona non grata?" Sam says, adjusting his glasses like my accusation knocked them askew.

"Nobody told us *not to*," Dear says, grumbly and impatient. "Last time we broke the news to someone, it didn't end so well. Seemed best we should just help you come to it when you're ready."

"Yeah? And do I seem *ready* now?" I snap.

"Not really." Virgil sighs. "You still haven't said it. For all we know, you think you're a mermaid."

"You're an asshole," I declare, pacing forward to glower at them, putting Sam behind my back because I don't even want to *look* at him right now. "Just *tell me the truth*. What were those things back there?"

Twisting at the braided bracelet on her wrist, Fern says, "We call them hellhounds."

"*Hellhounds?* Jesus, you can't be serious." I laugh. "Okay. And why would they be after *us?*"

Behind me, Sam says, "Because we're not supposed to be here. Not anymore." I hear him take a step closer to me, boots cautious on the creaky floor. "I know you know. You're claws sharp, Crazy. You got it now, right?"

I spin back to him and snap, "You're a condescending prick. Shove your self-help life-coach bullshit up your ass, Sam. You should have told me the truth."

"I'm sorry," he says. "I would have told you if I thought I could."

"Why *couldn't* you?" I ask.

Sam stares at me through the candlelight flicker on his glasses. His voice low, he admits, "Because I didn't want to lose you."

"Well, it's a little late for that," I hiss. "Since I'm already *dead*."

My stomping footsteps are the only sound in the cavernous ballroom as I make my exit. Sam's black gaze follows me, and my eyes don't leave his, either, not until I pass him and shove through the tall glass doors onto the portico.

I trudge through the overgrown garden and up the driveway to my car without looking back.

Who the hell do they think they are, anyway? Why do they get to decide what I can and can't handle? It's so insulting, I'm half tempted to turn back and tell them what I really think of their little pact to keep me clueless about my own fucking *death*, but instead I throw myself into Bathory's scarlet interior, stomp my foot on the clutch, and wrench the screwdriver jammed in the ignition. The wheels kick up dirt and dry leaves as I lurch into motion.

I speed all the way down the mountain, letting the Black Sabbath tape stuck in the stereo set my pace. When Bathory hits the highway at the bottom of the dirt road, I bear down on the gas and try to outrun my racing mind.

Route 15 is always good for that—I could follow it up until it turns to 206 and crosses a long stretch of state forest into Pennsylvania, or I could go down to Route 46 in Dover and hit I-80 from there. Either way I've got at least two lanes and infrequent traffic lights, so there's not much to slow me down.

My car cuts through the fog that floats above the slick black pavement. The dead leaves on the road stir as I drive, caught in Bathory's momentum. I run the red light at the center of town and blast over the bridge that crosses the Paulinskill.

My mind and the Cutlass are both moving so fast that I don't notice anything strange until I pass through the center of town a second time. That's when I realize that I've somehow gone in a circle without making a single turn.

The realization brings a watery roiling in my stomach. I know I turned left when I hit Route 15 at the bottom of Resurrection Peak. That should have sent me south through Hagley and on into the next town. How did I wind up back downtown? I roll down the window. There's static ringing in my ears that distorts the twanging synth in "Who Are You?"

I step harder on the gas. This time I focus on where I'm going—I charge the Cutlass south on Route 15, past the gristmill and Hagley Café, over the bridge and out to where the houses drop off and the wilderness closes in. I follow the curve of the highway as it winds around the base of the mountain. I recognize the landmarks I'm passing. I *know* I'm heading south.

The static in my ears shrieks like a dental drill from hell. I flick off the radio, but it doesn't stop. I pinch my nose and blow like I'm trying to pop my ears. The keening tone keeps jabbing into my skull.

I blink out like a bad signal.

I open my eyes on the other side of town.

To someone else, it might not look that different. There are still trees on either side of the highway, broken occasionally by sequestered homes on the outskirts of town. I'm heading south still, but I'm about fifteen miles north of where I was just a second ago. I pass the painted wooden signs advertising the corn maze at Decker Orchards and the farmer's market with a display of gourds and pumpkins out front. I take the bend toward the flat field where the high school stands, squat and drab in the center of a dark empty parking lot.

Soon I'm passing Hagley Café and the bridge again, cutting once more through the center of town.

I've had nightmares like this before, where I'm stuck in Hagley forever, unable to leave my bullshit middle-of-nowhere backwoods trash-heap hick town ever again. But this isn't a dream. This is just another symptom of *what I am now*, like the water in my chest and the hellhounds that hunt me and the hunger that never goes away.

I guess that leads to another question, doesn't it?

If I'm not alive, what does that make me? What *am* I? People can see me, talk to me, touch me—and I can touch them.

Will it always be that way?

Or will I fade away eventually, like the girl made of smoke who visited me when I first came to Chapel House?

My hands are wet and shaky on the steering wheel. A familiar pink glow shines across my windshield and I slow the Cutlass down.

I pull into the parking lot of the diner. The hand-painted sign propped up on the stainless-steel roof says YAYA'S KITCHEN, but nobody calls it that. Two of the letters are burned out on the giant neon DINER sign at the edge of the lot, and anyone passing on Route 15 just sees a great big DI E glowing in the night. So all the locals call this place the Die.

It's just as well, because I have no freaking clue who Yaya is supposed to be. The only person in the kitchen here is Leo.

I pull into the spot where I always park for my shifts, the one that faces the trees at the edge of the parking lot. My hands are wet and shaking, cool water slicking my palms. I dry them on my flannel, which still has a patch of mud on it from the corn maze. I sink back against my seat, tipping my chin up to stare at the velvet-lined roof over my head.

I'm still trying to get a grip when I hear a low snarl outside my window.

I look up, scanning the parking lot and the highway beyond. On the other side of the road, shadows with spiky black fur and hooked haunches are rising up from the patchy grass. I can't tell if they were prowling low along the shoulder, or . . . if they're climbing up out of the ground.

I shove the door open. As soon as my boots hit the asphalt, they raise their massive black heads, milky eyes shining in the dark. With a wet snarl, they tear into motion, clearing the two-lane highway in seconds.

I push against the side of my car and run for the diner. I can hear them right behind me, teeth snapping and breath ragged. They're getting closer and closer, and one lunges at my leg. Teeth long as fillet knives nearly sink into my shin, but I slam my boot against the top of the dog's head before it closes its jaws on me.

My fingertips catch the handle of the door, and I swing it open.

I jump through the threshold and shove the door shut.

Both hands against the oval of glass, I stare out into the parking lot.

The beasts that were bearing down on me a second ago are nowhere to be seen.

I crack the door open and peek out. Cold October air brushes against my face, but the breeze is the only thing I find.

There's nothing else there.

TWELVE

I GUESS I FREAKED Leo out when I burst through the door like I was being chased by Leatherface. He's asked me if I'm all right five times since I came in, and he keeps staring at me like my hair is made of serpents. Still, he sat me down at a booth in the corner and poured me a cup of coffee.

I'm surprised to see my boss waiting tables. Usually Leo sticks to the kitchen, but it doesn't look like there are any waitresses on duty tonight.

As far as bosses go, Leo isn't half bad. Maura and I have referred to him as "a total DILF," but as far as I know he doesn't actually have any kids. He's one of those guys in his early forties who still acts and kind of looks like he's in his twenties, but the immaturity is somehow charming on him. On slow nights he'd pour shots for Maura and me in the kitchen or share a joint with us in the woods behind the diner and let us play with the deep fryer. He only put his foot down once, when we tried to deep fry his boom box because he wouldn't stop playing the same Alice in Chains tape over and over again.

"You hungry, Cherry?" Leo asks me when he stops by to top off my cup.

"Huh?" I grunt. I glance over when he speaks to me, but then my gaze goes back to the window.

"Is there something out there?" Leo leans forward to see past his own reflection in the glass.

"No," I say, shaking my head. I stretch my legs out under the table and swipe a hand across my forehead, brushing back my damp bangs. "Sorry. What were you saying?"

"You sure you're okay, Cherry? You in some kind of trouble?" Leo frowns.

The question makes me laugh. The sound is sudden and harsh, and it attracts the attention of a group of girls sitting at a table across the diner. I know them from school, but I don't really *know* them, so I ignore their dirty looks.

"Annie," Leo says. He sets the coffee carafe down on the scuffed laminate table and drops into the booth across from me. "What's going on?"

I shake my head and rub the heel of my palm against my temple. I certainly can't tell him the truth—that I'm dead. That I don't know how I'm *here*, let alone how I *died*. I drop my hand to the hot cup of coffee in front of me and pick it up to take a gulp.

"I'm just . . . going through some shit right now, all right?" I say, looking at Leo over the cup. The flecks of gray in his blond hair shine under the lamp that dangles above our table.

"All right." Leo nods. He picks up the overturned cup across from me, filling it up for himself. He takes a drink and asks, "Anything I can help you with?"

"Actually . . ." I narrow my eyes at him, then set my elbows on the table and lean across to ask, "When's the last time you saw Maura?"

"Red Hot?" Leo says, brows winging up. "I haven't seen her since— What was it, Saturday? When you two were playing catty telephone through lunch rush."

Across the diner the girls from school are laughing. There's something about the tone of their laughter that catches my attention and curdles my stomach.

"She *posted* that?" one of the girls exclaims. I glance over and see they're all watching something on a phone, but I can't make it out from here.

Another girl laughs. "Like, talk about toxic, am I right?"

"They are *so* gross together."

"Wait, so *this* is why he posted her nu—"

"Shh!"

One of them shushes the rest, gesturing in my direction. The whole table has the most indiscreet reaction when they realize I'm watching them—they dive forward, crowding in over the table to stifle their giggles.

My nostrils flare. My nails scrape against the coffee cup. I swing my eyes back to Leo as he says, "It's good to see you two made up, anyway. I hate when my girls fight."

"How do you know we made up?" I ask. "I thought you said the last time you saw us, we were fighting."

"Oh, well, yeah, but . . . Red Hot posted that picture. . . ."

"*What* picture?"

"You know, that picture of you guys together."

"No, Leo, I *don't* know. I don't have my phone."

Leo shakes his head and pulls his phone from the pocket of his apron. He swipes at the screen a few times, then turns it toward me. Through the grease streaks on the glass I see Maura's Instagram. I take the phone out of his hand, staring down at the most recent post.

It was posted this morning, but that's not when the photo was taken.

The photo is from sometime in July, when Maura and I went to a Stevie Nicks–themed drag show in New York City. Maura snapped the selfie of us chilling on a bench in the hours before the show. The backdrop of the photo is decidedly *New York*, and I scroll down to see the caption beneath it: *check my rabbit.*

The fist that has been squeezed around my heart since this morning loosens slightly. If Maura is posting on Instagram, she must be safe somewhere—particularly comforting since Trevor's memory confirmed that she *was* with me at some point that night. But the cryptic caption makes my guts feel cold and choppy, and I shake my head.

"Leo, this picture . . . We took this *months* ago," I tell him.

"Huh." Leo shrugs. "Throwback."

"And this *caption* is weird," I add.

"I mean, that's what she calls you, right? Rabbit?"

"Yeah," I murmur. Ever since we were little, Maura and Grady have lovingly teased me about my big front teeth. As I stare at the photo, I say to Leo, "I didn't know you followed us on Instagram."

"Oh. Yeah, well . . . I didn't want you guys to think I'm some kind of creep. . . ."

Trepidation crawls down the back of my neck. I tap the home button on his Instagram app. The first photo that comes up in his feed is a girl who's got to be closer to my age than his, standing on her tiptoes to snap a pic of her tie-dye shorts in the mirror. The shorts are cute, and so is she, but holding his grease-grimed phone, I can't help but imagine what *Leo* sees when he looks at this picture.

Cold water turns in my guts.

I scroll down a little more as Leo protests. "All right, Cherry, come on, I gotta get back to work—"

Girl after girl after girl, flashing by on the screen as I scroll. Some of them tag locations nearby, some far, far away, but there's one thing that never changes: If any of them are older than twenty, they don't look it.

Leo finally snatches the phone from my hands, leaving me clutching the air as I watch him stuff his phone back into the pocket of his apron. "Man, you really don't listen, do you?" he grunts.

"Maybe my eardrums just don't register the sound of someone dumber than me talking," I say.

"That must be why you can stand to hang around that dumbass boyfriend of yours." Leo pushes up from the booth and swipes the coffee carafe off the table. When I look past him, the table full of J.P. High bitches are all staring at me again.

I wash down the muck in my throat with the last swig of coffee just as the girl who passed her phone around the table gets up and heads to the bathroom. I don't really know her, but I know she's on the field hockey team with the other girls. I think she's the one who Gun calls Xbox, because apparently one of the guys in Sneeze Police hooked up with her and said she has a square vagina, whatever *that* means. Her name might be Grace or Hope or something like that. I don't really care. I just want to know what she has on her phone.

"Are you coming to work this week, or what?" Leo asks.

"Don't hold your breath," I tell Leo as I slide out of my seat and walk past him. My boots clip across the checkered floor, and I glance at the other girls as I pass them. I recognize one of them from my photography class. She's notable to me because she is so surgically attached to her phone that the teachers don't even bother saying anything to her about it anymore, not even when she takes it out in the darkroom and screws all the pictures up.

She looks up as if she feels my eyes on her, and I hiss at her like an angry alley cat.

It's not a sound I should be able to make, but I know I didn't imagine it. Every girl at the table turns to look at me. I smile at them before I disappear down the hall to the bathrooms.

I reach out and drag my hands along the walls as I walk down the narrow hall. My fingertips leave wet streaks on the floral wallpaper.

The light inside the bathroom is squalid and dull. It dims further when I step through the doorway, as if the hungry hollow feeling inside of me swallows up the light.

My feet are silent on the tile. There is only one stall occupied, and I can hear her moving around inside—fussing over her clothes, bracelets jingling loudly while she adjusts and tucks.

I lean against the sink across from her stall and when Grace-or-Hope-or-Whatever opens the door to find me standing there, she jerks back in surprise. Unease tightens her shoulders, but she slides past me to the next sink without saying a word.

"Why don't you show me what's on your phone, Grace?" I ask.

"It's Faith," she says.

"I don't care. What's on your phone?"

"Leave me alone," she says, turning off the faucet. She's nervous. Instead of searching for the paper towel dispenser on the wall, she dries her hands on her sweater and heads for the door.

I get there first.

It's like what happened in the gym this morning, only this time I know for sure that I didn't walk. I feel myself slide, warp, shift. I blink, and between the drop and rise of my eyelids I go from standing at the sink to standing in front of the door. Faith stumbles short of walking right into me, her eyes wide and terrified.

My hands fly up to shove her away from the door. I expect her to stumble back a couple steps, but instead my push throws her against the wall. I wrap my hands around her upper arms and pin her to the pink tile. She flinches away from me, turning her cheek like she doesn't want to look at me.

"Stop! Annie!"

"Give me the phone."

"*No*, god, what's wrong with you? What's happening to your *eyes—*"

"*Give me the phone!*" I yell. The room vibrates with the sound of my voice. The mirrors rattle, the sinks rumble on their mounts, the stall doors squeak and sway back and forth. Faith shrinks against the wall. She chokes out a frightened sob and digs into her pocket for her phone. Her hands are shaking as she punches in the passcode, and I snatch the phone from her.

On the screen I see my Instagram profile. The last post is a video, and the thumbnail shows Gun's busted Vans standing on a floor tiled with pennies. I recognize the sticky copper floor and the graffiti-covered red walls from the cramped single-person bathroom at Boondocks, the venue where Werewolf Fetus played that night. Gun's sneakers are pointed at my boots in the frozen frame. I tap on the video and turn up the volume.

Gun's laugh clamors through the speaker. "Dude. You fucked with me," he says.

"You fucked yourself," I say. My voice is cool and cutting, but he chuckles again like I'm joking around and takes a step toward me. I warn him, "If you touch me, I'll make a candy dish out of your occipital bone."

"All right, what's your deal? Why'd you come here with me if you're just gonna act like this?"

"I don't know. I guess you should have just brought Riley," I say.

"Are you really still worried about Riley?" Gun scoffs. "Come on. Riley's not a problem if you want to be with me. She is *not* your competition. I'd *obviously* rather have you."

"Yeah?" I hear myself say. "Beg me, then."

"*What?*"

"Beg me to forgive you, if you really mean it."

"Annie, come on. I *love* you. Riley doesn't matter. Nobody else matters. If you want me to be sorry, I'm sorry. Whatever you want, all right?"

"That's not *begging*, Morgan."

"Are you serious? Annie—"

"If you don't get on your knees right now, you'll never touch me again."

There's a moment of hesitation. Gun's sneakers shift on the copper floor. The club throbs in the background. And then, finally—he gets down on his knees on the sticky penny tile, and his face drops into the camera's view.

"Annie," he says, his brow screwed up in a melodramatic display of sincerity. "Please. *Please* give me another chance. For real this time. Babe, please. You're all I fucking want, you know that? You're—you're like, the love of my life, dude, I'm serious. Everything has been *shit* since we broke up. I'm so sick of it. I just want you *back*. I can't take it anymore. I swear I won't fuck it up again. Please. Let me show you."

"Nah," I say. "I think I've seen enough."

The video cuts out and jumps back to the start. I grip the phone in my hand as I lift my eyes to Faith's.

"Annie," she whispers. "Your eyes."

I turn toward the mirror. The lights overhead are flickering and dim, but my gaze settles on my own reflection. It's dark, but I can see them. My eyes.

My eyes are completely black.

THIRTEEN

IT'S NOT JUST the green of my iris that's blotted out—my eyes are entirely liquid black, flooded from edge to edge. The tracery of veins on my eyelids looks like inky spiderwebs drawn across my skin. I stare into my reflection and brush my fingertips against a vein pulsing under the corner of my eye. My head is a whirlpool of soggy, swirling confusion.

I double over the edge of the sink and cough up cold water. Faith slides off the wall and escapes without her phone. Pine needles and river muck tickle my throat on the way up and splash into the pink sink. I gag on one breath and cough out a sob on another.

I remember what happened at Boondocks now.

We'd only been at the club half an hour, and I was glowing from the tequila stashed in my purse when Gun leaned in and told me that he had to go meet up with Trevor and Darren to unload their gear. I was pissed he was ditching me so early, but I wasn't about to act like I cared. I shrugged, told him I'd catch him later, and took out my phone so I could thumb through my notifications while he left me alone in the crowd.

It wasn't long before I grew tired of the band onstage, which consisted of two boys rapping and singing over shitty beats played from a laptop. I made a break for the door and slipped outside.

A cool breeze rustled my tangled hair, drying some of the sweat on my neck as I stepped out into the parking lot. It was filled with cars, but the forest loomed beyond the black square of pavement. My eyes fell on a guy wearing a Napalm Death shirt who was dragging on a cigarette a few feet away from the door.

"Hey, can I bum one of those?"

He looked over at me. He was definitely older—probably somewhere in his twenties—but I liked his pierced septum and full mouth, and when he smiled at me, I smiled back. He held out a cigarette and a pink plastic lighter.

"Hope you don't mind menthol," he said as I lit up.

I shrugged as I took a drag of cool mint smoke. "Whatever. Thanks. I'm Annie."

"Eric," he returned.

"Where are you from?"

"Nowhere you've ever heard of," he assured me. "Small town in Bucks County. You?"

"Not far," I said. "Hagley. Which *you've* probably never heard of."

"No, I know it. You go to Sussex County?"

"College? No." I laughed. "I'm still in high school."

"Freaky."

"Is it?"

"You don't look like you're in high school."

I shrugged, red lips curving behind the cigarette as I took another drag. "Is that a compliment?" I asked him.

"Definitely." Eric laughed, stepping a little closer to me. I kept my eyes on the parking lot and thought about telling him I had a boyfriend. I wasn't done deciding when my gaze fell on the Mustang parked a few rows down from where I was standing.

A chill rushed through my veins like the menthol filling my lungs.

The interior light was on over the back seat, and I could see movement inside through the haze on the windows. Eric said something else to me, but I didn't hear him.

I stepped out into the parking lot. The Mustang creaked, shifting on its shocks. My pulse was drumming so hard in my throat that my tongue was throbbing, and I couldn't swallow the puff of smoke in my mouth. I let it slip out through my lips as I reached the window and peered inside.

Riley's head was jammed against the door, the panel rubbing a knot into the back of her bleached bob. He's done it to me, too— thrusting away between my legs, drilling my skull into the door. Her skirt was hiked up over her hips and her face was turned away from his. I lifted my fist to announce my presence with a punch to the window, but a phantom pain at the back of my head stopped me.

No, I thought. *Better her head banging against his door than mine.*

I threw my red-kissed cigarette down on the pavement outside the Mustang and turned around. Eric was still standing by the doors, brow furrowed in annoyance, and I said nothing to him as I breezed past him into the crowded club.

I locked myself inside the little red bathroom at the back of Boondocks, and with makeup dribbling down my cheeks from yet *another* crying session over Morgan Fucking Donovan, I gulped tequila until the pink faded from my eyes.

I heard Werewolf Fetus go on and play their whole set while I sat in the bathroom. Gun didn't text me until the next band started up, and by then I was drunk and furious.

I wanted to humiliate him.

So when he texted, *Heyyy where's my girl?* I responded with, *Meet me in the bathroom.*

When he showed up, I filmed my little revenge video. I posted it to Instagram while I walked away from Boondocks, hiking up the dark wooded road beyond the venue. I guess I called Maura after that, asking her to rescue me from the crisis I'd created.

And of course she came, even though we were fighting. Even though she had no idea of the danger she was walking into.

I comfort myself with the reminder that Maura posted that selfie of us just this morning, so whatever happened that night, she *must* have made it out alive. I blink through watery eyes at Faith's phone as the video starts all over again, and I notice that there are dozens of comments. I scan through them, wondering what people really had to say about Gun's bullshit apology.

> Lol is this why they leaked her nudes?
>
> What a bitch her next boyfriend will probably abuse her
>
> I have a justice boner lol where the nudes?
>
> Small tits who cares
>
> As an ass man, I care
>
> @tit4tatbitch @tit4tatbitch @tit4tatbitch

My thumb taps on the tagged username. When the thumbnails appear, I choke on a watery sob. Flashes of my skin are tiled across the screen—pale arms, long legs, pinched waist. My knees bend as I stare at all the thumbnails of my exposed body, and I sink to the floor with the phone clutched in my hand, mopping water from my lips with the sleeve of my flannel.

These are all pictures I sent to Gun when we were together.

Crumpled on the pink tile with tears running cold down my cheeks, I stare at the screen. For a while it's all I can do, but eventually I manage to open one of the photos and check when it was posted.

131

I find that the account is only about an hour old, which is probably the only reason it still exists. I can't imagine it will last long without getting shut down—but it only needs a couple hours to do its job. By then, everyone in school will have screenshots of my nudes.

Let's not even get into the fact that Gun and Trevor are committing a crime here, and not just of the revenge-porn variety. I'm underage *now*, and I wasn't even seventeen yet in some of the photos they posted. But to be honest, I don't give a fuck about it being *illegal*—what really bothers me is the hundreds of followers, the endless scroll of comments, the astronomical numbers beside each little heart. A pitiless mob hidden behind a screen, all laughing as they throw stones at *me*.

My violation is their entertainment.

I've known these kids my entire life—we all grew up in a claustrophobic cluster, sitting in classes together every single day since kindergarten. And still, not one of them shows me any compassion. They attend my public execution with keen delight, like they'd swing the axe themselves if they could.

Nobody's on my side.

Nobody cares about me at all.

With trembling hands and hitching breath, I thumb away from Instagram and pull up the keypad. I yank on my sleeve to reveal the strange number I wrote on my arm earlier, then type it in and curl forward, pressing the phone to my ear as I wait.

One ring. Two. And then someone picks up.

I lift my head in surprise as I hear a breath on the other end of the line, but nothing more.

"Hello?" I say. "It's me."

Nothing.

"Hello?" I repeat. "Please, I need—"

"You're in the water."

The voice is a whisper, a breath through the static. I think I might recognize it.

"Wh-what?"

Nothing. More static cracks against my ear. I squeeze my eyes shut as if that might help me hear more clearly.

"Hello? Is anyone there?"

There's a pause, and then: *"Come and see."*

"See? See what?"

"The body."

"My body?"

There's nothing but static in response again. I stay on the line. I don't know who I'm talking to. I don't know *what* I'm talking to. "Hello? Who *are* you? Hello?"

Two familiar voices suddenly chime across the line, "This is your operator speaking!"

"How may we direct your call?"

I know who it is, but still I ask: "Hunt? Howl?"

"No," one of them says. "Just a ghost in the machine."

"What *was* that?" I ask.

"That was *not* a friend." Their responses are quick, and I can't tell whether they are speaking in unison or if there's an echo on the line.

"Who—who was it, then?" I say.

"Well, of course there are *others,*" one of them scoffs.

Chills prick across my skin. I swallow past the tightness in my throat. "Other . . . what? What *are* we?"

"We *are,*" says one.

"We are, we are, we *are,*" says the other.

"We are your otherworld operators!"

"Welcome to the afterlife help hotline."

"If you know your party's extension, you may dial it at any time."

"If you are experiencing a spectral crisis, press one now."

"For haunting advice from our expert poltergeists, press two."

"If you are being exorcised, purged, saged, cleansed, or trapped inside an amulet, press three."

"Cut it out," I command. "Where's Sam? Can you put him on?"

"Sam, Sam, he's our man."

"If he can't tell you, no one can!"

I grunt in frustration, kicking my boot against the frame of the stall across from me, then draw the phone away from my face and hang up the call. I drag myself off the floor and pocket Faith's phone as I head out of the bathroom.

The girls are gone when I come out. Leo is hovering just outside in the hall, concern stitched across his brow.

"Cherry? Hey, Cherry, what the hell happened—"

"Fuck off, Leo," I mumble as I blow past him.

"Annie! Hold on—" Leo grabs my arm to stop my momentum. His grip makes my skin crawl, flashes of his lecherous Instagram feed scrolling behind my eyes.

"Don't touch me!" I twist to face him, and he releases me fast, but it's not because I told him to. Horror is what makes him recoil from me.

"Annie," he whispers. "What's wrong with—"

I don't wait for him to finish his question. I turn around. In the reflection on the glass door, my eyes are full black. I push it open and storm through, but as soon as my boots hit the parking lot, I hear them.

The dogs are back.

They blast out from either side of the diner, the glow from the windows highlighting the sticky slime glimmer on their black fur. They snarl and snap behind me as I take off toward Bathory. It seems like they get closer every time my feet touch the ground, until finally I collide with the side of my car, grapple with the handle, and throw myself into the driver's seat.

I haul the door shut on a toothy maw, trapping the dog's muzzle just a few inches short of my leg. It fights to push its head inside, and I hold on to the door while my right hand twists at the screwdriver in the ignition. It takes two tries for me to get the Cutlass to roar to life, my clutch foot dangerously close to the snapping mouth of the beast.

The dog's teeth rip into my calf just as the car lurches into motion. Fangs slice through muscle and skin as I jerk my leg from its maw. The car fishtails and stalls. I grit my teeth and slam my boot down on the beast's nose as hard as I can.

"I swear to god, PETA will put you on a billboard when I'm done with you!" I yell, smashing my boot a few more times against the dog's chomping snout before I pound my foot on the clutch again and twist the screwdriver.

My tires spin and I steer Bathory toward the highway while I slip through the gears.

By the time I hit the curb, I'm flying. The dog stuck in my door yowls and whines and finally wrenches its head free to tumble across the road. I yank the door shut and grip the wheel, straightening out the car's zigzag trajectory as I rip down Route 15 toward Resurrection Peak.

I avoid the potholes as I speed up the mountain, and cold liquid runs down my leg from the dog's bite, soaking the back of my ankle and slicking my heel.

After I've pulled Bathory up the dirt drive and parked by Chapel

House's wild garden, I switch on the interior light and prop my boot up on the dashboard.

I stare at the spot where the dog bit me, but there's nothing there.

My tights are torn where the beast's teeth snagged in them, but the skin underneath is only wet with cool clear water. There's no blood and no bite, and when I press my fingers to my leg, I can't even find a bruise.

So, it's not their bite that everyone's afraid of.

What happens if they catch us, then?

I get out of the car and hike through the overgrown garden to the ballroom. Though I expect to find them all there where I left them, the dance hall is eerily empty. Half-carved pumpkins and jugs of cider are scattered all around. Pumpkin seeds and crunchy candies crack under my boots as I cross the parquet floor, moving between slices of moonlight coming through the windows.

I step into the little corridor that leads to the kitchen. Then I stop.

There's something shifting in the dark here.

The smell hits me immediately, like charred wood left to molder. The mildewy scorch-stink seems to drip down from above, where something is scraping gently against the dried plaster of the ceiling. I squint at the slant of shadow at the end of the hall. Something crouched there takes a breath that rattles and crackles like wet wood on fire.

"H-hello?" I call out. There's no response. I step deeper into the hall. "Are you here?"

"*Yes.*"

The response comes on a smoky exhale. I stumble back and press my spine against the frame of the doorway. "Wh-who are you?" I ask her again.

"Come and see."

"What did you mean? When you said I was in the water, what did you mean?"

"Come and see," she whispers again.

"Show me, then," I say. "I'm here. I want to see."

Silence stretches on. Everything is still except for the cool breeze blowing from the other end of the hall.

Then she comes scratching across the ceiling toward me.

Brittle limbs scrabble down the wall. I finally see her when she reaches the top of the doorway above my head, crawling into the light bleeding through the dance hall.

Char-cracked skin stretches over black bones. Her form is twisted and skeletal, made of shadow and smoldering ash. Her ragged hair hangs down like black cobwebs. Putrid smoke burns my nostrils and I take a stumbling step back into the ballroom.

"Jesusfuckingchrist," I gasp while the shadow stretches and elongates. Her feet dangle down from the doorway, and she drops with a thud to stand in front of me. Drifts of ash float off her skin and scorched dress. She stands still and looks at me with eye sockets empty and black.

We stare at each other for a long time.

Then she snaps forward and touches her fingertips to the ground. With her back folded she crawls on her toes and fingers, scuttling through the hall. I hesitate for only a moment before I follow her. If no one besides this barbecued bride of the Crypt Keeper will be straight with me, I'll take what I can get.

She crawls across the Ark and gusts through the doors onto the portico. I run out after her, following her down into the garden.

The shadow sizzles as the dew in the overgrowth mists against her burning skin. She crosses the courtyard and starts to slip farther down the hill away from Chapel House, into the trees that edge the property. I charge through the prickly bushes and dry grass, burrs and thorns catching in my clothes and ripping at my skin.

I know where she's going now.

The rushing water is getting closer.

As I launch over a fallen tree speckled with lichen, I remember scrambling across it last time I ran this path. I remember it all as I retrace my steps. I tripped over the roots here. I skidded down a slope there. I was running and someone was chasing. I was bleeding. I was afraid.

Then I reached the river. Just like I do now.

There was nowhere to run. It was too late to hide.

Tears are sticky on my cheeks. I was crying that night, too.

This is where I died.

I grab at my stomach. I remember the feeling of the knife pushing under my rib cage. When I look down at my shaking hands there's blood slicking my palms, but when I blink it's all gone. My hands are clean and dry. I look up from them and out at the water.

There's a body in the river.

Bare feet sway in the current. A hand bobs up from under the water, chipped red nail polish bright against blue skin. Swirling tendrils of black hair writhe through the current, obscuring the corpse's face from my view.

I know anyway.

I know.

I know it's my body.

FOURTEEN

I REMEMBER SOMEONE'S weight holding me down as I clawed against wet dirt. I remember the thrust of the knife and the swell of water that rushed down my throat when I tried to scream.

I look at my body, roped against a fallen tree in the river, then bend forward and throw up water, spitting it back into the river I drowned in.

I tug off my boots and leave them at the roots of a tree. The water is a sixty-foot black gap and the moon hangs over it like a sad blue spotlight. I wade into the water. The river is cold and dark, and the silence feels like being forgotten as I pull my feet off the rocky riverbed and swim out to my body.

It's not easy to look at myself like this. It's not just that I'm sentimental about my old skin; it's also that I've been in the water for a few days now. Hungry creatures and water rot have done their work on me. I can't tell what's postmortem and what's not. I probe at the place above my right hip where I remember the knife going in, and I find myself drawn to reach in farther.

I shift back inside my body like shrugging on a cozy old coat, and I can feel all the tears in the fabric.

The stab wound in my belly wasn't the first. The first was the gouge in my shin where a knife bit deep into muscle. I still ran after that, but I couldn't run fast enough.

I let my body tell me the story of being wrestled to the ground and stabbed in the gut. Of being held underwater as my blood swam away with the current.

There was a moment of surrender when I knew that I was going to die, when all I could do was hope it would be quick. That total loss of autonomy sears worse than my skewered guts, and I jump back out of my dead skin to shiver in the dark water.

I try to find the knot in the wiry rope that ties my corpse to the fallen tree, but it's too dark to make sense of the bindings, so I give up and swim back to the shore. Water pours off my flannel as I yank my shoes back on. I pound my wet boots against the ground and climb the hill up to Chapel House.

"Sam!" I start screaming as soon as I step through the doors to the Ark.

I let my boots fall wet and loud on the hardwood floors. My clothes are still dripping steadily, leaving puddles where I stomp. I yell as I rampage through the house, banging on walls and slamming on doors.

"Where the fuck is everyone?!"

I reach the main staircase and start to climb, pounding my fist on the ornate banister the whole way up. "Hellooo. Somebody better come out or I'm calling an exorcist!" I get to the second floor and scream down the hall toward Dear's and Fern's rooms. "Hey! You hear me? Hey!"

"Child, you've been heard," a voice growls.

I spin around. Virgil is peering at me from the stairs below, his eyes slitted and sleepy. He's shirtless, blue moonlight shining on his tattooed skin. Even groggy and sleep rumpled he seems sharp and vaguely menacing, but I don't let him scare me into silence.

"Where is Sam?" I demand.

Virgil leans an inked elbow against the newel post beside him. "I don't know; where are your manners?" he says.

"Maybe I left them in *the fucking corpse I just found in the river*, asswipe."

Virgil huffs out a breath, but then he arches off the post and takes a step up the stairs. "Come on," he says. He skims a plum-stained hand along the banister and glances down at the puddles of water I left as he steps over them.

There are so many questions choking my mind that I can't help spitting one out. "If we're dead, how come we're still . . . here?"

"If you're expecting me to explain the complexities of our non-existence to you right now, you're going to be disappointed," Virgil bites.

"*Dude*, I've had everything I know about the way the universe works pulled out from under me. You can't tell me *anything*?"

"I'll tell you how arrogant you are to think you ever understood how the universe works," Virgil offers. As he passes through a patch of light from the window at the top of the stairs, the black snake tattooed around his arm coils and twists. I see its forked tongue flick out on the back of Virgil's hand before he draws it away from the banister and starts past me down the hall. He stops under a hatch in the ceiling and grabs an old wooden cane leaning against the wall. He thuds the cane against the pull-down door above our heads, but in the silence that follows I don't hear anything stirring.

"Are you sure he's up there?" I ask.

Virgil growls under his breath and pounds harder on the hatch. He doesn't stop this time, drumming the cane against the wood incessantly until the door finally shifts and drops open.

"Hey, witch, you lookin' to get burnt at the stake or something?"

Sam says, bracing his arm against the frame of the hatch to lean down and glare at Virgil.

"Don't take this out on *me*," Virgil says, throwing the cane down on the floor. "Your girl finally admitted she's worm food."

I stalk right past Virgil and yank the ladder down. I scrabble up the rungs, and when I reach the top, Sam is backing up like he's trying to get out of my way.

But I don't let him get far.

I get the confusion. I *am* barreling toward him like a drenched wrecking ball. But when I finally collide with him, my arms lash around his neck and I crush my wet chest to his. My hold is clutching, needy and desperate. My fingers claw at his shirt collar, at the hair that curls at the nape of his neck, at anything I can touch.

His arms close around me, a crushing X across my back, pressing us tighter together.

And then, finally, I break.

It's my mom's cruel recriminations. The careless reactions to the bloody scene in the kitchen. The faceless crowd finding entertainment in my leaked nudes. It's the memories that cling to me, the pain, the fear, the *helplessness*. It's Gun laughing, Owen judging, Maura missing, and Grady forsaking me.

It's the sight of my body, left to rot in the lonely river.

Sam holds me like I need to be held, an unyielding squeeze that wrings me out like a wet towel, all the shock and hurt pouring out of me in big rattling sobs. I bet I could turn to a sad, cold puddle and drip between the floorboards, running down the walls in rivulets until there's nothing left of this agony, nothing left of *me* at all. For a moment Sam's arms are the only thing holding me together, his grip binding me until I can stuff the drain plug back into my metaphysical bathtub.

When I can finally stand without spilling my whole self out on the floor, I ease my hold just enough to see Sam's face. His black eyes gleam beneath his glasses, tears caught in his eyelashes. I drag my nails against the back of his neck and murmur, "A ghost in the attic. Isn't that a little cliché?"

"You say cliché. I say classic," he returns.

I hiccup a little laugh and sniffle through my soggy nose. The blue-black sky is bright through the windows, and strands of glowing lights with fat multicolored bulbs weave around the eaves overhead. They cast Sam in warm jewel light, his hair wet and messed from my fingers, his soaked shirt glued to his chest.

I look down and lift one boot, then the other, splashing in the puddle pooled beneath me. "Sorry about the flooding. I just found my body in the river," I say. "Also, I'm finally ready to admit it: I'm a mermaid."

Sam huffs like he's stuck somewhere between anguish and laughter. He yanks me back to his chest, and I lift on my toes to hug his neck fiercely. Against my ear he says, "It's gotta take the lowest form of deplorable nonentity to try and knock off a nonpareil like you. You're the meanest gem I ever met. Nothing like this should've ever happened to you."

"I'm not sure anyone would agree with you," I say. "Seems like everyone would think I got what's coming to me."

"If there's one thing I've learned about a square, baby, it's that they sure can grudge you your lack of right angles," Sam says. He pulls back and his hands lift, palms framing my cheeks, thumbs smearing the trails of mascara. "Don't let small minds put shame in your heart. You didn't deserve this."

I sigh and close my eyes. I nod, my head bobbing in his hands, and then I mutter, "I can't believe I'm fucking *dead*."

"Yeah. You're ripe for the lilies. So are we," Sam says. His thumb swipes once more at my cheek before his hands drop away. "I'm sorry I didn't tell you. I still don't know if it was the right choice, trying to let you come to it on your own, but we were scared you'd start breaking up if we just dumped it all on you."

"I don't know, either," I tell him. Without him near I feel wet and cold. I cross my arms around my stomach, wrist pressing where the knife went in. "I don't know why I can't remember what happened that night, but I knew *something* was wrong with me, and with all of you—I mean, I was working on some pretty farfetched theories, but this is . . . I just thought maybe you guys were vampires or something. Not, like, the *Twilight* kind. More like *The Lost Boys* with less misogyny."

Sam is squinting at me the same way he does whenever I make a pop-culture joke or use a bit of trendy slang. Like he has no idea what I'm talking about but he likes the way I'm saying it. There's a smirk on his lips and an arch to his brow, and I think I finally understand what that look really means.

"Holy shit. How long have you been *dead*?" I ask.

"Ah." Sam leans back and looks up at the bare beams crossing the peaked ceiling. "Sixty-six years now, I guess."

"Shit," I say. "Are we *ghosts*?"

"You know, the lines are kind of blurred."

"What the hell does that mean?"

Sam shrugs and says, "As long as your body stays on this mountain, you never die."

"But I *am* dead." I dig my nails into my palms. It hurts, but not the way it should. "I feel . . . weird. But I don't feel *dead*. And we *eat*. We eat and we can just . . . walk around. You carry *cash*. People *see* us. That's not how ghosts *work*."

"Who are you, the mythology police?"

"Sam."

"We're *corporeal*," Sam says. "Yeah, we can scarf slop and rub elbows with the cubes, but we can't get out of town. We get too far from the mountain, and we start to get scrambled. Look, I . . . I can't tell you exactly *what* we are. Vengeful spirits or revenants or ghosts. It doesn't really matter."

Sam paces away from me to a dresser against the wall, and I take in the rest of the attic. The walls tuck into various sides of the house, creating shadowy nooks here and there. Round windows with panes like spiderwebs let the moonlight in.

The attic is more like a loft than a bedroom, stacked with bookcases, a sitting area with a record player, a desk, even a hammock in one corner. The multicolored lights in the eaves cast a hazy glow on the sun-bleached beige wood, and there's a smoky pine smell in the air. I squint at the titles of some of the books on the shelves, noting a distinctly sci-fi bent.

"Are we *always* corporeal?" I ask Sam.

"When we want to be. Sometimes you might find it serves you better to be unseen."

"So, like, could I just . . . keep living my life, if I wanted to?"

"You can." Sam nods, handing me a towel. I take it, fingers rubbing at the shabby terry cloth, worn and soft and definitely tangible. "I mean, you couldn't go on forever—it's gonna catch attention if you never age a day—but while you can get away with it, I think you should."

I can't say I really *want* to go on with my shitty life in Hagley, but considering that's the life someone tried to *take* from me . . . maybe I will.

"What about the dogs?" I say as I wring my wet hair with the towel.

"They come at night," Sam says. "They can only find you when you're out on the town. They don't come up here, they can't get inside houses or buildings, and they don't cross water. You can never let 'em catch you, all right? Those mutts are a one-way ride, Crazy. No one comes back from where they take you."

"Because we aren't supposed to be here," I say, echoing what he told me earlier in the night.

"Doesn't that make it even better?" Sam says, a smirk on his lips and fire in his eyes. "Who cares whose rules we're breaking. How many people get a chance to avenge their own deaths?"

At his words, a current of energy surges through me. I *do* want vengeance. I'm starved for it, with a hunger that burns and gnaws. I rub the towel over my face to mop up the mascara on my cheeks. My voice muffled by the cloth, I tell him, "I've *done* things. I think I cracked the kitchen ceiling *with my mind*. I stuck my fingers in Trevor's head and saw his memories. I, like, *teleported*. Like, if Carrie and the Hulk had a baby, that would be me."

When I pull the towel away from my face, Sam is taking off his shirt. His skin is splashed with watercolor glows from the rainbow of lights roping the beams. I notice two more tattoos in addition to the words that circle his wrist: on his forearm a rat wearing a crown, and over his heart a grinning skull and crossbones.

And I notice a lot more besides that—smooth skin, lean muscle, hard lines, and soft dips my fingers long to trace.

Oblivious to my staring eyes, Sam says, "Yeah, sometimes when we get worked up, we go full ghoul. You can control it if you just remember you can make them see you the way you see yourself. And that's not some self-help-life-coach bullshit. I mean if you think you have claws, you'll have claws."

"Hm. I keep hoarking up water. Please tell me *that's* gonna stop soon," I say.

Sam shakes his head regretfully while he tugs on a dry shirt. "We all have some quirks. Death echoes, I guess."

"There's a whole cemetery full of bodies up here. Are you guys really the only ones?"

"There *are* others, but they're not like us. They're fogged, you know? Just ghosts, in the classic sense. They're missing the glue. Can't keep themselves together," Sam explains. "What we are, it's not just about being dead. It has something to do with the *way* we died. Unjust. Unfair. Unavenged."

Murdered.

Someone *murdered* me.

What would have happened if I hadn't been killed and left on Resurrection Peak? If I had died and stayed dead, the way that most people do—would anyone even have noticed? How long would it have taken them to find my body roped beneath the swell of the wide black river?

No one was even *looking* for me.

Sam is right. I didn't deserve this.

And even if I can go on living my life for the time being, I'll never do the things I wanted to do. There will be no apartment with Maura in Princeton next year, no more summers prowling the boardwalk with sunburned skin, no wandering New York hunting for thrift store scores, no chance I'll ever see anything but *Hagley* ever again. I really am stuck here . . . *forever.*

My eyelids feel bruised and heavy. Dawn light streaks across the orange treetops outside the windows, and I am tired of crying.

"Do you want a change of clothes?" Sam asks me.

I nod. As he gathers clothes for me, I notice a weird abstract sculpture on one of his dressers, his bongo drum by the record player, a modish kidney-shaped coffee table with a few colorful pulp sci-fi magazines spread across it. I don't think any of Sam's furniture—or many of his belongings—postdate his death by very long. His attic is a time capsule. I wonder if someday I'll be stuck in a bygone era, too.

Sam hands me clothes and turns his back to give me some privacy. I toe off my boots and work open the buttons of my flannel. While Sam selects a record and sets it on the turntable, I say, "When I caught Trevor in the corn maze and shoved my fingers in his head, I saw him waiting behind my house that night. It was him, Gun, and Darren. I don't know what they were doing, but it seemed like they were planning something."

"Hm," Sam hums. He sets the needle on the vinyl, and velvet jazz croons through the attic. "We should have chilled them when we had the chance."

"You really think it was them?" I ask as I put on the shirt he gave me. It's big enough to skim my thighs, soft white and worn thin. Fern must have embroidered it for him. In red thread on the breast pocket it reads: *What in the Sam Hill?*

"Sure," he says. "Don't you?"

"I mean. I know they did *something*." I shrug, pulling woolly socks onto my feet. I forgo the flannel pants he gave me out of spite. I've caught Sam looking at my legs, and after what watching him change his shirt did to me, I'd like to return the favor. "And I know Gun's a bastard, but somebody chased me out here and straight-up *overkilled* me. My body is *tied to a tree* in the river. That seems kind of . . . advanced for him."

"What about the one with the . . ." Sam points to his eyebrow. "The supraorbital dead lifter."

"Trevor?" I say as Sam's terminology draws a smirk from my lips. "Maybe. I'm just . . . not sure yet." I reach out and curl my icy fingers around his wrist. "I'm tired. Can we crash?"

Sam closes his hand around mine and leads me to the hammock in the corner. I fall in first and he pulls the wrinkled navy blanket off the floor and drags it over us as he climbs in beside me. Gravity slings us close together. I press my face into the curve of his throat. He smells like scorched evergreen and his skin feels hot, throwing warmth like a lit fire. I close my eyes and let it toast my damp cheeks.

"When we wake up, we'll bury you," he murmurs.

"Bury me?" I open my eyes to look at him. The knowledge that I'm rotting in a watery grave is bad enough; I hate the idea of being trapped beneath the dirt even more.

"We can't risk anyone finding you. If your body gets moved off the mountain, you're gone for good," Sam says. His head rolls to the side, his eyes finding mine in the shadow between our faces. "You want to stay, don't you?"

My fingers twitch greedily on his arm. "Yeah. I want to stay."

"Then get some sleep, Annie. Tomorrow's your funeral."

FIFTEEN

IN MY DREAMS I float through Hagley, scrawling messages for my killer in the bloodred that coats my palms.

On the big wooden pumpkin sign out in front of Decker Orchards, I streak with my red fingers: *I CAME BACK FOR YOU.*

Slashed across the shiny steel side of the diner: *YOU CAN'T GET RID OF ME.*

On the weathered stone alongside the bridge over the Paulinskill: *LET'S MEET AGAIN BY THE RIVER.*

Down the obelisk monument by the old mill:

> *THIS*
> *TIME*
> *I'LL*
> *BE*
> *THE*
> *KNIFE.*

I wake up late in the day and roll over in the hammock to blink past the tangerine sunlight pouring through the windows, reflected brightly off the tops of the autumn trees outside. I hold up my hands and stare at the peeling paint that sticks to the lines of my palms, scarlet as it was in my dream.

Sam is no longer at my side, but there's soft music humming

from the record player, and I'm not alone in the attic. Fern and Dear sit opposite each other with a very vintage game of Battleship spread out on the coffee table, talking quietly.

"C-three," Fern declares.

"You know," Dear says as he jams a peg into one of his plastic ships, "you ain't even supposed to be playing this game."

"Why not?"

"Well, look at the box," Dear says.

Fern glances over to the weathered cardboard box on the shag rug beside her. "What about it?" she asks.

"I'm just sayin', the instructions only show cartoon *men* playing this game."

"Oh." Fern reaches for the box top and flips it over to inspect it. After some consideration she says, "Not only are they all men, they're all *white* men."

"Well, you're really showin' them what you think of those game-playin' qualifications now, ain't you?" Dear says. After a pause he announces, "F-five."

"Miss."

"What the hell, woman! You playin' with submarines?"

I laugh. I can't help it. They look over at the sound, and Fern starts to twist at the braided bracelet on her wrist. I swing my legs over the edge of the hammock and set my feet against the floor, toes warm in Sam's wool socks.

"Hey," I say.

"Mornin', darlin'," Dear says. "You all right?"

I shrug. "I'm fine." I look down at my palms, streaked with phantom red, and I think of blood on my palms in the moonlight. "I had a weird dream, though."

A dream that didn't feel like a dream.

A dream that is on my hands still, like I woke up in the middle of vandalizing my hometown with taunting messages for my killer.

I look up at them, holding my palms up as evidence. "Is this, like, a *thing?*"

"No rest for the wicked, sweetheart," Dear says.

Fern cuts him a look, but she sits forward and puts her elbows on her knees to tell me, "The dead don't dream. Dreaming pierces the veil, and we're locked here on this side of eternity. So, when we rest, we wander as vapor instead."

"Good news is, dogs can't get you when you're nothin' but mist," Dear adds.

"It's no fun, though," Fern says. "I always feel like a balloon someone let loose the string to, floating around all alone out there."

I sigh and say, "So, you're telling me I really did graffiti Hagley last night?"

"You sure did paint the town red," Dear says, and drums out a little badum-tshh on his knees.

I roll my eyes and stand up, combing my fingers through my hair and finding twigs and pine muck still tangled there. "Sorry about last night, by the way."

"Dying is a pretty good excuse for a bad attitude," Fern says. She looks cozy in jeans and an oatmeal sweater, suede mules on her feet, and a silk scarf wrapping her hair.

"And you oughta know we're sorry, too," Dear says. His rugged brow is drawn, and he avoids my gaze by digging a pencil from his pocket and taking it to the Battleship box. As he speaks he doodles winged eyeliner and curly hair on one of the cartoon game-players on the cover. "We weren't meaning to hide nothin' from you. But if you couldn't see it, nobody thought it was smart to make you. It went to a vote, and we all had to abide by that."

"It wasn't a unanimous vote." Fern sighs. "Are you sure you're up for this thing?"

"What thing?" I say.

"Sam told you, didn't he? About the funeral?" Fern asks.

"Oh." I frown. "I thought he was joking."

"That happens a lot with Sam," Fern says, ruby eyes rolling.

"Yeah," Dear agrees. "He told me they made that fella from *G.E. Theater* president of the United States, and I thought it was true for the longest time."

I purse my lips, but whatever Dear is referencing goes right over my head. I look back to Fern and pick at a twist of my mucky hair. "I'll probably feel more up to it after a shower," I tell her.

"Oh, of course we're gonna get sharped up and threaded down, baby," Fern says, standing and patting Dear's broad shoulder as she steps around the coffee table. "A funeral's a formal affair."

"Hold up," Dear says, setting the Battleship lid aside. "I been instructed to get a gist of where your meatsuit's chillin'."

I give him the best directions I can to the spot where my body is tethered in the water, then Fern and I descend the rickety pull-down ladder from the attic and head to her room. I shower fast under the cold water that coughs from the rusted nozzle in Fern's private bath. After I scrub the mud off, I wrap myself in a towel and dash into Fern's boudoir.

She's lit the fireplace in her bedroom and the heat has spread to the dressing room, but my teeth still chatter as I pick clothes from Fern's collection. I choose a black velvet wrap dress that I can cinch tight on my waist, and once we're dressed, Fern and I plant ourselves side by side on the cushioned bench in front of her vanity.

I stare at my reflection while I smudge eyeliner across my lids. I look the same as I did before I died. My eyes are still green as sour apples. My knee is still marked with the raised white scar I got when I fell off Maura's trampoline. My right brow still arches higher than the left, and when I part my lips to swipe on red lipstick, my big front teeth still peek out beneath my upper lip. I drag a comb through my hair, and it still gets caught in dense black tangles and shorn split ends.

Everything is the same, but what I am now is something else. Something both more and less than what I used to be.

Fern has changed into a somber black cocktail dress with a high collar, her hair swept into an updo save for a twist of curly bangs on her forehead.

As she brushes dusty-pink powder over her speckled cheeks, I turn to her and ask, "Why doesn't *everyone* come back? Why is it just you guys? Why is it just this town?"

Fern's brows raise, and she pops her brush against the apple of her cheek a few more times before she lowers it and turns to me, our knees pressing together. "There's a certain recipe that makes a monster like us. It takes all the right ingredients. First, you need an unfair end. Helpful if it's bloody. Then you need the body to be *here*, on Resurrection Peak. But then, there's a third thing that's harder to account for. . . . Something in your constitution that makes you dig your heels in and refuse to pass on through those pearly gates."

It makes sense, but it still feels a bit too open-ended. I press, "What if it wears off someday?"

"Sometimes it does," Fern admits. "Not everyone sticks it out. It wasn't always just us few. Everything we know, we learned by losing someone."

"What, like, to the dogs?"

"To the dogs. To the sunrise on All Saints' Day. To loose threads that come undone," Fern says. She turns back to her mirror and takes up her pot of eyeliner. She licks her brush and then starts to draw her wings, long and straight and knife-sharp. "The first we ever lost was the hardest. Baby Betsy. She was only nine, and she died right beside me. But when she came through, she didn't remember dying at all, not till we told her. It was too much for her. Now she's just a shadow you can see sometimes in the field behind the churchyard. That's why they were so scared of telling you the truth."

"Damn," I mutter. Sam *had* told me they lost someone that way, but the details are enlightening. It's impossible for me to begrudge them the secret if all their laws are made from losses. But . . . "*You* wanted to tell me, though. How did you know I wouldn't lose it?"

"Oh, baby, I know you got the spirit," Fern says, a faint smirk on her lips. She sits back, her eyeliner slick, jabbing toward the sky. She looks at my reflection in the mirror and asks, "Are you ready for this thing?"

"Well, I'm not getting any fresher."

I don't know where this funeral is taking place. So I let Fern lead the way, holding her cold hand as we march downstairs and out through the front door.

The sun is setting over the summit, and for just a moment the sky is bloodshot orange, but the road away from Chapel House is shrouded in hazy blue shade. As we pass through the front gate, I grab a snarl of the poison ivy roped around the iron arch and wind the vine into my hair, weaving myself a venomous crown.

We walk down the unpaved roads of Resurrection Peak, and I feel eyes watching us through shattered windows, shadowy figures crouched within the ruined houses along the way. Soft wisps of music play from one butter-yellow house, where there's a flickering glow in the kitchen window. For an instant, I see the outline of a man raking leaves on his dusky lawn, but when I try to look directly at him, he's gone.

There are ghosts everywhere up here.

Eventually the faded, whitewashed steeple of the town's church comes into view, perched atop a hill studded with gravestones. There are lights on inside the church, glowing through the dust and grime that clouds the stained-glass windows.

"You know, there's a reason people don't usually attend their own funerals," I say as dread wrings my watery guts.

"We're unusual." Fern shrugs.

We climb the church steps and the heavy door groans on its hinges as we step into the cavernous nave. There are candles throwing glimmering light across the aisles and hanging lanterns overhead. Sparkling garlands and Halloween-themed bunting adorn the pews. There's a table heavy with food and a punch bowl filled with Virgil's dark purple-red potion. All the religious iconography in the chapel has been desecrated, the crucifixes affixed to the walls turned upside down.

Past a pair of saintly statues with broken faces, a cobwebbed old coffin sits on a raised dais. The lid is closed and there's an evergreen wreath resting on top. Above the coffin hangs a banner that exclaims *Congratulations!* in glittery letters. It's in bad taste, and I feel my unease leave me in a flood as I take in the irreverent little ceremony they've set up for me.

No matter how nervous I was, the attitude inside the church is infectious. Nothing feels that serious.

"It's about time," Sam says. He's standing just behind my coffin, keeping watch over it like some tousle-haired bird of prey. He looks grim in a suit and skinny tie as black as his eyes. Eyes that are on me now, shining in the warm light from the candles. I think he's trying to decide if I'm all right, if I'm less shaken by the thought of being buried than I was when he brought it up the first time. I smirk to reassure him, and a dimple sinks into one of his cheeks as he steps around my coffin.

"Figures you'd be late to your own funeral," he says.

"Figures you'd open the eulogy by talking shit," I say. He grins and I feel the water in my chest turn to hot steam.

Sam's not the only one dressed up for the occasion. The twins are crawling out from under a pew in matching tweed suits with dapper little daisies pinned to their lapels. Virgil looks at home in an emerald velvet blazer with his sharp black undercut slicked back. Even Dear has polished up, dressing in brown corduroy slacks and a charcoal sweater.

I'm pretty sure every scrap of clothing on them is an antique, and I'm glad for the cup of dark wine that Dear brings me from the punch bowl—thinking about how long they've all been dead up here makes me feel like I need a drink.

"You guys didn't have to do all this, you know," I say, gesturing to the decorations strung up around the chapel.

"Oh, it was no trouble. We were already decking the halls. We just borrowed some frippery from the Ark," Fern says.

I recall the decorations that were half-hung in the ballroom last night, streamers and lights and balloons. I ask, "Yeah, are you guys throwing a Halloween party or something?"

"Oh, it's *the* Halloween party," Fern says. "It's truly the mezz. *Everyone* comes."

"The house is happening on Allhallows," Virgil agrees. "Haven't you heard? Halloween night marks a liminal time when the dead can travel the world of the living. And when the dead folks around here get up out of their graves, they *really* like to party."

I try to imagine the ballroom packed with ghosts from every time period, and it seems bizarre—but I guess not any more bizarre than the fact that my body is currently sitting in a box at the front of this abandoned church.

Everyone takes a seat in the pews while Sam slinks over to the elaborately carved harpsichord in the corner of the pulpit. The bench creaks in the quiet of the chapel. His fingers stretch across the yellowed keys and start to move, smooth and synchronized as the legs of a spider. The strings of the harpsichord pluck an eerie tune that echoes in the rafters.

I sit and stare at the box that contains my remains.

I don't know where they got a coffin to put my body in. Maybe it belonged to someone else before me. I'm not sure it matters.

The twins are the first to rise. They step up to my coffin arm in arm, and judging from the solemn set to their sharp mouths, I suspect they may be taking this funeral more seriously than anyone else is. They lift their hands and pluck the daisies from each other's jackets.

"It's a funny thing," Hunt says.

"To plant the dead," Howl replies.

"To tuck the bones..."

"Like babes to bed."

"In the ground..."

"Like seeds to sow."

"In the ground..."

"As if they'll grow."

"But be careful where you dig..."

"Oh, be careful what you do."

"When you bury a bad seed . . ."

"She might come back for you."

They finish by tucking the daisies into the wreath on my coffin. After they step down from the dais, there are a few moments where the only sound comes from the chilling pluck of the harpsichord keys under Sam's fingers.

Virgil gets up next.

He swaggers on his skinny legs to the front of the chapel and stops behind my casket where the twins stood before. But unlike them he doesn't gaze at the box in front of him. Instead he lifts his eyes to mine and holds up a bottle of jewel-green liquor to toast as he declares, "I'm glad you're dead."

I spit out a laugh, and Virgil seems satisfied. He descends from the pulpit and hands me the bottle. As I take it, he bends his long body to brush a kiss against my cheek, and I murmur thanks in response. I bring the bottle to my lips, and the bright pine burn punches me in the nose as I knock back a swig.

Fern squeezes my arm before she heads up to my casket. With her back to us, she stands over my coffin and slips a little red rose into the wreath, next to the daisies the twins left.

I barely hear her over the *thunk* of the harpsichord, but to my coffin she whispers, "I grieve you, even though you aren't gone."

When she comes back to her seat, I offer her the bottle Virgil handed me, and she indulges in a sip while I scoot a little closer and rest my head on her shoulder.

Sam's fingers drift away from the keys when Dear stands and picks up his old guitar, the marbled pick guard rubbed raw with age. He steps up to the pulpit and shrugs the frayed leather guitar strap over his shoulder, settling his hands on the strings.

159

He's about to start playing when he catches himself, claps his mouth shut, and reaches up to snatch the gray flat cap off his head. He sets it down on the corner of my coffin and then clears his throat contritely. His thick fingers slip over the strings, twanging out a few notes before he bows his head and begins.

He picks a trilling melody, and when he sings, his voice is a low dry rasp.

"There ain't no grave gonna hold my body down . . ."

I don't know the song, but he sings it like a hymn. He sings it like only a dead man could.

When he's done, he grips the neck of his guitar with one hand and slides the other into his pocket to take out a coil of rope. He knots it around the wreath and exits the dais, but before he makes it halfway to the pews he twists on his heel and doubles back to swipe his hat off the casket.

Sam is the last to approach my coffin. He traces his fingertips along the beveled edge, then sets his palm down flat on the lid. Goose bumps prickle all over my skin.

"Whoever did this is only gonna live long enough to realize the mistake they made, thinking they could ever end you for good."

His gaze drops. He bows his head as he draws a cigarette out from behind his ear, his hair falling forward to curl over his forehead. He tucks the cigarette into the wreath on my coffin and says, "Some girls never rest in peace."

His words seem to release the others from their decorum. The twins shoot out of their seats to dive over the pew in front of them for the food. Virgil lights a black cigarette that smells like incense. Dear starts to pick at his guitar, and Fern twists around to watch him.

Sam just stares at me.

I stand, feeling like a ghost to everyone but him. Maybe they're giving me a moment. Maybe I need it. I step up to the pulpit, to the coffin that rests there on top of a draped pedestal. I reach out and touch my fingers to the lacquered wood. Rushing water hums in my ears.

I need to know who did this to me.

SIXTEEN

IN THE END my burial is not as well executed as my funeral.

It probably has a lot to do with the fact that my pallbearers are all hammered by the time they carry my coffin out to my grave. After the twins nearly cause a casket rollover, they get kicked off pallbearing duty, so Dear, Virgil, and Sam finish the journey on their own. A place has been dug for me beneath an illegible old headstone in the cemetery, and after my remains are lowered into the ground, I help bury them.

In stark red paint borrowed from Hunt and Howl's cupboard under the stairs, I scrawl my own epitaph:

HERE LIES A VENGEFUL BITCH.

Eventually the party moves back to the ballroom at Chapel House, where everyone continues decorating for the Halloween party. Fern strings glittering streamers up over the bandstand while Dear keeps hold of her ladder. Virgil weaves rough twine around bundles of dry branches and autumn-brown foliage. The twins start setting the table in the dining room, but they're soon diverted from their mission, instead attempting to pop candy corn in a cast-iron skillet over the fireplace.

Meanwhile all I can think about is my murder.

Maura's super into true crime, so I know the statistics. Most murdered women are killed by someone they know. And in my case, the culprit seems like a no-brainer. Gun has an obvious motive—I not only dumped him once and for all that night, but I humiliated him by posting the video of him begging me not to. And the memory I stole out of Trevor's mind incriminates them further, proving that they followed me home from the show and were clearly planning *something*. . . .

But when I close my eyes and imagine the dark figure that held me under the water that night, I just can't fit Gun into the shape of it. Trying to paint his face and form onto the black void of my killer's shadow feels like jamming your foot into a too-small shoe or stretching for something you just can't reach.

He doesn't fit.

Neither does Trevor or Darren or even Maura—though I don't have to try to press her into the shape of my killer to know she couldn't have done it.

Because here's the thing: Whoever killed me hunted me through the woods that night. They tracked me like a wild animal, and after they did it, they left me where the water would obscure the evidence of what they'd done to me.

Morgan Donovan couldn't even get away with cheating on his high school girlfriend.

So, what if whoever did this knew what they were doing?

What if I wasn't their first kill?

While everyone else drinks and laughs and hangs spooky decorations, I curl up in a dark corner of the ballroom with the phone I stole from Faith. I pull up the browser and search first for *murder Sussex County*, but after I click on an article and realize it's from a Sussex County in Delaware I backtrack and refine my search. *murder Sussex County NJ* gets me closer, but a lot of results focus on a recent incident involving a man who murdered his former landlord. When I finally search *unsolved murder Sussex County NJ*, I find what I've been looking for.

"Death of Sussex County Teen Still Unsolved Twenty Years Later."

The article details the 1999 disappearance of eighteen-year-old Katie Brideswell, a J.P. High student who was last seen at a house party in Hagley. The county police considered Katie a likely runaway, and no search was ever conducted for her.

A decade passed before deer hunters found her bones washed up on a creek bed in Stokes State Forest.

When asked about Katie's cause of death, the detective quoted in the article said Katie could have overdosed at the party or wandered off and succumbed to the elements. The water washed away any evidence that might have proven otherwise, and the case was closed as far as the cops were concerned.

But some people quoted in the article didn't believe Katie's death was an accident.

When I put Katie's name into the search bar, more articles come up. I discover that Katie was seen arguing with her boyfriend at the party that night, and that her friends have always insisted that Katie didn't just run away. But without anyone looking for her in the aftermath of her disappearance, the details of that night are muddled and vague—and by the time Katie's body was found, her bones weren't saying much about the night she died.

I find some pictures of her, too.

In yellowing Polaroids and harsh snapshots, she always seems a little blurred, like she was constantly in motion. She had honey-brown hair and arms toned by the breaststroke—the articles say she was on the swim team. I can't tell if her eyes were brown or green in the stark contrast of the grainy photographs. She doesn't look like me, not really, but . . . as I stare at a picture of her, beaming on the hood of her candy-red Trans Am, I recognize something wild in her eyes that feels like a fresh twist to the knife in my guts.

Maybe I *wasn't* my killer's first victim.

Maybe I wasn't the last, either.

Where are you, Maura?

"What's rattling your cage, Crazy?"

I look up from the screen and blink until my eyes adjust to the shadowy ballroom. Sam's jacket scrapes against the peeling wallpaper as he sinks down and sits beside me on the floor. He has a beat-up paperback book in his hands, and he rubs his thumb against a worn corner as he looks at me through his tortoiseshell glasses.

I suck in a shuddery breath and say to him, "Just wondering if my ex killed me or some total rando who dumps a girl in the river every twenty-five years."

I don't wait for his response. I reach across the space between us, and my fingers drag against his cheek as I swipe the cigarette from behind his ear. I put it between my lips, and he strikes a match to give me a light. I lean in and touch the cigarette to the flame cupped in his hand.

When I sit back up, he's not looking at me. His eyes are on the phone cradled in my hand, the screen beaming blue light up at our faces. I glance down at the photo of Katie Brideswell on her Trans Am, then return my gaze to Sam's face as I breathe out smoke.

"There was another girl murdered in Hagley in 1999. Left in the river, like me. But I have no idea if that actually means something or not."

I scroll back through the other photos of Katie that came up on the image search. As I do, Sam watches me. He takes out his Lucite cigarette case and lights a smoke of his own, his eyes never leaving the screen in my hand.

That's when I realize he's probably never seen a smartphone up close.

"By the way," I tell him, leaning closer so he can better see the screen, "nowadays, *this* is a phone."

"That's a *phone?*" Sam chuckles, drawing on his cigarette.

I'm not sure how to explain a smartphone to a boy who died before the first moon landing, but I try my best. "Yeah, but it rarely gets used for, like, actual phone calls. Mostly people text these days. It's kind of funny, this thing can send messages instantly to anyone in the world and access pretty much the entirety of human knowledge, but people mostly use them to watch porn and argue with strangers."

"You're pulling me dead to the curb," Sam says. He reaches out and taps his thumb on the screen, causing Faith's Starbucks app to open. I snicker as his glasses reflect the pumpkin spice latte glowing between us. "What else can this beastly gadget do?"

"It can kind of do anything," I say. "What's something you've always wondered about?"

"Hm," Sam hums, pursing his lips. He tucks his book into his jacket pocket and shifts, lifting his arm to drape it around my shoulders. With his elbow hooked behind my neck and his jaw resting against the top of my head, all coherent thought is blasted out of my mind like dry leaves in a breeze. It's lucky I hear what he says next over the pounding in my ears. "Cosmic AC, how may entropy be reversed?"

"How— What?" I balk.

"Just ask it the question," Sam says.

I shake my head, but I type the words into Google anyway. In an instant, Sam's question is revealed to be a quote from an Isaac Asimov story printed in *Science Fiction Quarterly* in 1956. "Holy shit, *nerd alert*," I say, and his laugh rumbles against my side.

"I guess there's sufficient data for a meaningful answer after all," he says. He sounds pretty impressed that my "beastly gadget" managed to place his reference so quickly. "The future's far out."

Maybe it's the heat of his nearness and the smoky smell of his evergreen, or maybe it's the fact that I just attended my own funeral, and thinking about Katie Brideswell's bones in the river is making me feel more dead than alive. Suddenly I want nothing more than to be alone with Sam. I tuck Faith's phone down the front of my dress and slide out from under his arm, hauling myself off the floor.

"You wanna get out of here?" I say with a nod toward the door.

Sam gets up, too. As he starts to follow me, he says, "Are we just taking the air, or are we up to something?"

"I'm always up to something," I say. I weave around the flicker-ing candles on the floor and head for the glass doors onto the portico behind Chapel House.

"Baby, you're a first-class hell-raising sister of Satan," Sam says, placing a hand over his heart. "I didn't mean to impugn your pen-chant for troublemaking. I'm just curious what felony we're peram-bulating toward this time."

"Murder, if you don't shut up," I say, and Sam chuckles as we pass through the doors and step out beneath a big yellow moon in a purple velvet sky.

"With threats like that, who needs sweet talk?"

I twist around to look at him in the moonlight, the mansion looming behind him, all dark bloody brick and glimmering black windows. I walk backward and he follows, a smirk on his lips to match mine.

I reach out, trailing my fingers along the collar of his leather jacket. His brows shoot up over his glasses. My hand dives inside his jacket and I snatch the book he tucked away, bringing it out into the moonlight so I can see the cover.

"*1984?*" I laugh, reading the title off the red cover emblazoned with a staring blue eye.

"Indeed, comrade." Sam nods. "It's doubleplusgood prolefeed for a simple Ingsoc like me."

"Are you Newspeaking me right now?" I demand, recognizing the fictional language from the book, which I *did* read in ninth grade English, though I nearly flunked the class anyway because Mr. Harris didn't like how I called him out for only including books written by men in the curriculum.

Sam blinks at me and says, "Oldspeak is crimethink."

I smack him on the arm with the book, which causes his candy-wrapper bookmark to fly out of the page he had it tucked into. His jaw drops in exaggerated shock, and he snatches the book from my hand.

"Listen, buster, what gives you the right to lose a man's place like that?" he says while stowing the book inside his jacket like precious contraband.

"Get bent, nerd," I say, followed by a squeal as Sam lunges for me.

I take off running down the road away from Chapel House. The moon is high over the summit, lighting my way as I scamper through the ghost town. My laughter is breathy and wild, echoing on the empty mountain while Sam chases me.

The abandoned main street is equipped with the bare necessities to make a town. I run past a post office, the front door standing open to show ancient mail piles covered in dust on a buckled old counter.

A grocer, windows hung with meat decayed down to the bone and baskets full of cobwebs. And when I pass the general store, for a moment I think I see a pair of glasses floating above the counter, like some invisible clerk is still keeping shop, but when my steps falter and I stare into the dingy old windows, there's no one there.

I take off running again, headed for the graveyard at the end of the road.

I stumble through the gate into the unkempt cemetery, burrs and branches tearing at my tights. Near my freshly dug grave, I twist to scope out the field of jagged headstones and the iron arch I entered through.

Sam's not there.

He *should be*, of course, he was right behind me, but all I see are orange leaves and blue headstones jutting from the ground.

I roll my eyes and kick the ground. "Dude, are you ghosting me?" I say.

Then I turn around and slam into his chest.

His arms go around me, lashing tight to keep me from tripping. I huff in surprise, tense for only an instant before I ease into his hold, glad as a cat in the sun. He catches my momentum and sweeps me in a spin-and-dip. My back arches and my head dangles toward the ground as he bends over me. I cackle and release my hold on his jacket, going limp as a corpse in his grip. I spread out my arms and tilt my face to the sky while he spins me until the stars are blurry streaks overhead.

He swings me so long that when he stops, my head keeps spinning and the graveyard whirls at the edges of my vision, a kaleidoscope of crooked stones. He holds on to help me stay upright, but the ground beneath my feet seems to rock and buck.

"Check this out," he says, pulling me along. I stumble, still recovering my equilibrium as we trek across the graveyard to a slate mausoleum. Sam presses a hand to the diamond-webbed window on the door and leans in to peer through the glass.

"What is it?" I ask.

I can't see through the glare of the moon on the glass, but Sam raps his knuckles against the door. Dust billows from its frame as he knocks a syncopated rhythm on the wood. I don't recognize the tune, but I hear music in my head that rises up to meet the beat he pounds out—first the trill of a blue saxophone and the booming vibrato of a double bass, then the clink of a bony xylophone and the tinkering chords of a guitar. The thud of drums joins in, and it's only then that I realize none of it is in my head. The music is coming from inside the tomb, and when I open my eyes, there's a violet light glowing through the beveled glass.

"Killer-diller," Sam says as his hand drops from the door. His beat isn't needed anymore—the band has taken it and run.

"What the hell?" I lean forward and try to squint through the cloudy window. For a moment I catch a glimpse of a skeleton band that seems to glow in the misty light. I try to get a closer look, but Sam sweeps me away from the window and swings me into a dance.

"Come on, Crazy, shake it till the meat comes off your bones," Sam says.

Maybe I could deny the draw of his dimple-cheeked charm, but I don't bother to try.

What's one more mystery, anyway?

I find my feet and start to move.

The music tumbles and rolls in waves. Our steps rip up dried vines as we dance. Sam is fast on his feet, and though the rhythm is strange and unpredictable I match his pace. One of his hands knots with mine while the other grips my waist. I hold tight to his shoulder when he isn't flinging me in dizzy circles or sweeping dips, grasping the taut line of muscle beneath the rough of his jacket.

"Hell, baby, you really swing like a noose," Sam praises after I surface from a shimmying spin around a cracked headstone. "I've stomped my boots at a couple of dime grinds, but I never had a barbecue as gone as you."

"God—seriously, Sam, *barbecue?*" I laugh. The rapid pace of our dancing eases as the music winds down to something more lilting. Sam pulls me closer. I coil my arms around his neck, breathing in ash and earth and evergreen.

"I mean it, you know?" Sam tells me. His low voice makes chills nibble across my skin. "You're totally elevated. You're weird and wild and way far out. Other gals run on gas, but you're all electric."

"This is the weirdest flirting I've ever experienced," I inform him.

"Sorry," he says, a frustrated stitch forming between his brows. His body is flush against mine and we move together to the music, but I can tell he's got something on his mind.

When I look up into the black of his eyes and see the way he's staring at me, I think I know what it is.

I've been wanted before, but never like this. Other boys always seem to think of me like their favorite dish off a menu—desirable, preferred, but still meant to be consumed.

Sam is different.

I stretch up toward him as the saxophone howls a plaintive note. My hand travels from his shoulder to his jaw. I rise up on my toes and tip my face to his. I feel his little inhale of breath against my lips, and shock stiffens his mouth for a moment before he returns my kiss. He makes up for hesitating by crossing his arms behind my back and kissing me with such hungry intensity that he arches my spine over the fold of his arms. My nails bite into the leather at his collar. His kiss rambles on like our conversations, and my chills don't stop when he draws away.

The last sad blow of the saxophone echoes in my ears. I feel like I'm glowing as bright as the waxing moon overhead, but my happy haze ends when I open my eyes to look at him.

His hair is on fire.

"Holy shit!" I exclaim, reaching up to smack at the lick of flame near his temple. He recoils from my swatting palm, but he brings his own hand up and finds the errant blaze burning on his head. He scrubs it out, and when his hand comes away, there's a streak of ash on his forehead.

I think I already know, but I still ask, "What the hell was that?"

"I told you we all had our quirks," Sam grumbles.

It's his death echo, just like the water that fills up my chest. Was it fire that killed him? Just another question I've yet to ask. I reach up again and this time he doesn't flinch. I brush the ash from his temple and take one more kiss.

The ghost band has stopped playing. I wonder if they've crawled back inside their coffins. I shiver, but it's more from the creepiness of that thought than the cold breeze blowing down the hill.

Sam shrugs off his jacket anyway. "C'mere," he murmurs. He sits down against a mossy headstone and holds out the jacket beside him. I crouch and curl up against his side while he wraps the jacket around my shoulders. It's still warm. My body hasn't been warm since the night I died, but Sam always radiates heat like a lit stove. I press my cheek to his chest, and he rests his chin on my head.

"Well, Crazy, you just destroyed about five thousand of my corpuscles," he says, and I can hear the smirk on his mouth. I close my eyes and feel my lips curve to match his.

"Yeah, I like you, too," I mumble.

SEVENTEEN

I DREAM OF FIRE that moves like a live thing, crawling up walls and punching through windows. I wake with my brain blazing, staring into the smoldering face of a girl on fire.

"Come and see."

Her voice sizzles. I blink the sleep from my eyes, but she's still crouched before me in the tall grass, smoking in the moonlight.

"What do you want?" I whisper, my fingers curling in the fabric of Sam's shirt. He doesn't stir.

"Come and see," she says again. She sinks down and twists through the grass like a snake made of burning shadow. I have some reservations about following the creepy hellfire ghost into the night, but I can't deny that she's been helpful before. How long would it have taken me to find my body in the river if she hadn't led me there?

So, I slip out from under Sam's arm and trot across the graveyard to catch up with her. She slithers between the headstones and through the cracks in the stone wall at the edge of the cemetery. I hop over the wall and follow her down the street, where she crawls on her toes and fingers up to the general store I passed earlier.

"Where are we *going*?" I demand, but the burning girl doesn't answer. I only hear the faint hiss of the fire simmering beneath her blackened skin as she skitters inside the shop.

I stop on the road, watching the firelight fissures on her skin glimmer through the dusty windows. Watery dread roils in my guts as I step up onto the general store's porch. The floorboards groan under my boots as I cross the threshold into the darkened shop.

With the moonlight through the grimy glass and the fire burning under the corpse's skin, there's just enough light to make out my surroundings. Cobwebs drift in the breeze from the open door. Dust gathers on shelves frozen in time. She's standing just a few feet from the doorway, facing me, her edges blurring as smoke wafts off her.

"What do you want?" I croak, gripping the door like I might just turn and run.

"Come and see," she hisses. Her arm snaps out to point one blackened finger at the wall.

There's something there, hanging on the decaying wood, but I stay just inside the doorway, bright moonlight at my back.

"Who *are* you?" I ask.

She wisps and crackles. *"Who is he?"*

"What do you know about him?"

"Come and see," she repeats, her head rolling as she turns her face toward the wall she's pointing at.

I creep closer.

So close I can feel the heat of the fire burning her. The smell of wet wood and old smoke fills my nostrils. When I get close enough, the sizzle of her crackling skin sounds more like screams.

I look at what she's showing me.

There's a poster nailed to the wall, paper yellowed with age, mold spots blooming here and there. Up top, in thick block letters, it reads THE DEVIL IS HERE!

And underneath, visible even through the rot, I recognize the boy pictured in black-and-white.

Sam.

Two mug shots, side by side, one facing forward and one in profile. His chin tipped up in defiance, cowlick curl on his forehead, a mottled bruise circling one ink-black eye. A letter board chained around his neck, reading: NYPD 6-18-57 ACKERSON, BYRON.

And beneath the photos, in more bold screaming letters:

BYRON ACKERSON

FOUND GUILTY OF THE MURDER OF FIVE INNOCENT GIRLS. EXECUTED BY THE GRACE OF GOD, RESURRECTED BY THE HAND OF EVIL.

REPORT ANY SIGHTINGS AND ANYONE SUSPECTED OF CONSORTING WITH BYRON ACKERSON IMMEDIATELY. ALL WHO AID IN THE DEVIL'S WORK WILL BE PUNISHED BY GOD'S WRATH.

With effort I turn from the poster to the smoldering shadow beside me. In the empty sockets of her eyes, two flames flicker like angry pupils. Her nearness makes water steam on my clammy skin.

"Is that *Sam?*" I ask.

"*Sam,*" she huffs, ash puffing from her dry mouth. It sounds like a curse, scornful and mocking.

I shake my head, glancing back at the poster. All that shit about God and the devil means nothing to me—it reads like superstitious hysteria, like something straight out of the Puritan era. What matters to me is the verdict printed just below Sam's mug shots: FOUND GUILTY OF THE MURDER OF FIVE INNOCENT GIRLS.

"Is that... Did he really..." I look back to the burning girl, whose smile shows broken black teeth in her twisted jaw.

I don't finish my question. Her grin is all the answer I need.

I tear out of the empty store, stumbling out into the cold blue night. My heart writhes in my flooded chest.

On the dirt road outside, I twist around and stare into the graveyard.

Sam is no longer asleep against the headstone where I left him.

I turn fast and dash for the cover of trees and overgrown yards, cutting through the woods toward Chapel House.

There's still music humming from inside the Ark as I creep along the edge of the garden to where my Cutlass is parked.

Virgil's laugh hisses from the dance hall as I wrench the door handle. The twins scream and it reverberates off the domed ceiling of the ballroom. I scramble into the driver's seat and wrap my fist around the screwdriver Sam left in the ignition. I jam the clutch and twist the makeshift key and Bathory roars to life.

I have no doubt the sound will draw *someone's* attention, so I shift into reverse and tear away from the house with an overzealous stomp on the gas. I flick on the headlights and they sweep across the mansion, highlighting the silhouette of someone standing on the peaked roof over the dining room, staring down at me as I make my escape.

The set of his sturdy shoulders and the rumpled outline of his dark hair seem both familiar and strange to me.

I know it's Sam.

It's just that now I know he might be a killer.

EIGHTEEN

I'D NEARLY FORGOTTEN what the burning girl said to me that first day in Chapel House.

They're not going to tell you the truth. They follow him. The king of lies. There is no truth in him.

At the time those words meant nothing to me. Just another riddle to add to the pile of unknowns. But the more I know about what happened to *me*, the less I feel I know about Resurrection Peak—and the other ghosts who haunt the mountain.

What if all the stories I heard about an axe murderer stalking the town were true?

What if all the stories were really about . . . Sam?

It's hard to believe Sam could have killed five girls. I might not know everything there is to know about Sam, but I do *trust* him.

Though, considering the fact that someone I trusted might have killed me, I'm not sure that accounts for much.

Maybe I'm an idiot for trusting Sam, for trusting *all* of them. By not telling me I was dead, they let me walk into town clueless. For all they know, I could have delivered my killer the perfect warning, a chance to get away entirely before I even knew what to look for. Sam said he was afraid I'd lose what keeps me here if he told me the truth, but I *know* I wouldn't have.

I know what keeps me here.

Vengeance.

The only thing that telling me the truth would have given me is an advantage over my murderer. Knowing I was dead sooner would have put half the puzzle together for me.

So maybe he just didn't *want* me to know.

I mean, whoever killed Katie Brideswell totally got away with it. And wouldn't it be easy for a ghost to leave no clues?

What if Sam is some kind of phantom serial killer?

What if the continued corporeality of the ghosts of Chapel House requires a quarterly human sacrifice?

What if they murdered me so I could join them, like some kind of killer ghost frat hazing?

After the week I've had, I'm ready to consider any theory, no matter how much some of them sound like *American Horror Story* subplots.

And what about the burning girl? The twins said she wasn't a friend, but she's done nothing except help me so far. She brought me my jacket. She led me to my body in the water. Has she also been trying to warn me about Sam? Does she believe he did something terrible—or does she have her own agenda?

In the face of all this unknown, I think of the best mystery solver I know: Maura.

I dig Faith's phone from inside my dress and glance between the road and the screen as I thumb Maura's number into the keypad. It's the only number I know by heart. I press the phone to my ear and listen to the hollow rings.

"Please... Maura..." I whisper into the line.

But she doesn't answer.

Where is she?

I dial again. Each ring feels like a fresh twist to the knife in my guts. When her voicemail picks up a second time, I chew my lip as I listen to her recorded voice say, "Maura Harker. Leave a message."

As the tone blares, I choke out a watery gasp. Into the silence, I say, "Maura . . . where are you? They said we were together, but you're not . . . you weren't in the river. . . ." My wet hand slides along the steering wheel as my speeding Cutlass winds a curve in the road. "I need you, Maura. I'm so fucking lost. I can't do this without you."

I end the call and drop the phone into my lap as sobs rattle my rib cage.

I drive for hours, but I have nowhere to go. I'm a dead girl with no mourners, and my murderer could be anywhere, any*one*.

Tears blur the road before me, but I keep driving in circles around Hagley until just before dawn. Neon shines across the windshield as I pull into the parking lot of the Die.

My headlights flash on the dripping red letters streaked across the silver siding, a message left for my killer: *YOU CAN'T GET RID OF ME.*

Fern and Dear told me ghosts don't dream, but I'm still surprised to see the graffiti I painted in my sleep. I park in sight of the hazy window full of sparse diners sipping their coffee, and I stare at the message on the siding as I smoke a few cigarettes from the dented pack on the dashboard.

My eyes close.

When they open, I'm not in the diner parking lot anymore.

I'm in the Evil Dead Shed with Maura, sitting knee-to-knee on the woven rug with a Ouija board between us. We're thirteen, brimming with giddy energy after the eighth-grade dance we went to earlier in the night. Our eyelids shimmer with pearly shadow, and light from the battery-powered lantern on the floor beside us sparks on the glitter that clings to our hair as we bow our heads together. Our fingers rest on the teardrop planchette between us, our sun and moon rings opposite each other's, our nails painted a matching shade of electric blue.

"I hope we get Marilyn Monroe again," I say as we push the planchette in a slow circle around the board.

"That was *not* Marilyn Monroe," Maura insists.

"She said she was!"

"You believe everything the board says?"

"Ghosts can't lie through the spirit board, M'ra," I declare. "I read so on the website."

"What website?" Maura scoffs.

"Just shut up and chant," I say. Maura sighs, but when I start, she does, too.

"Spirits of the underworld, gather now around this board. We have come to seek the truth; enter, spirits, we call to you."

When we finish the third iteration of our cheesy mantra, we allow the planchette to still on the board. Our fingertips hover against the edges of the plastic oracle.

"Hello? Are there any spirits here with us now?" I ask.

Maura and I hold still, waiting for an answer that doesn't come. All I hear is the rustle of wind through the trees around our little cabin. After a minute of breathy silence, Maura says, "Hello? Is there anyone who wishes to speak with us?"

The planchette gives a sudden jiggle under our fingertips.

"Was that you?" Maura hisses.

"No, it wasn't you?"

"No—"

We stare as the planchette begins to slide across the board. I look at Maura's fingertips to see if she's pushing, but her fingers are poised lightly on the edge of the pointer.

"Is there someone here with us?" I question. The felt under the plastic pegs sweeps against the cardboard surface as the planchette slides to YES.

"Cool. I have some questions," Maura announces. "Like, are Jason and Kira still dating?"

This is where Maura and I differ. While I prefer to pry for details about the spirit's life and death when we make contact with an entity, she just wants to reach across the veil for juicy gossip. I roll my eyes, but I let her ask her question.

The planchette slides to NO.

"Sweet." Maura smirks. When she glances up at me and sees the sourpuss look on my face, she huffs and asks the board, "Why is Annie such a biatch?"

"Shut up, M'ra," I growl.

"I kid, I kid," Maura insists. "Okay, spirit . . . Where is my mom?"

I look up at her, surprised by the question. Maura doesn't talk about her mom much. She always says she can't remember her. But I watch pain flicker across Maura's face as the board spells out an answer: V-I-R-G-I-N-I-A.

And I wonder if Maura secretly *does* miss her mom. If it's possible that there are parts of Maura I don't know.

"Virginia," she says aloud, voice husky on a sigh. "Is she happy there?"

The planchette slides to NO.

"Good," I spit out like a wad of gum. "I hope the deserting bitch is miserable."

"Right," Maura says. She nods, takes a deep breath, then pivots with, "Is Dad gonna make sheriff next year?"

YES.

"Awesome. We're *so* gonna be able to get away with robbing a bank," I say.

"Will me and Annie rob a bank together someday?" Maura asks the board.

NO.

"What *are* we gonna do, then?" she demands.

The circular window on the planchette hovers over the letters D-I-E.

"We're gonna *die* together?" I laugh.

"Yeah, sure. As two old widow witches in a Park Slope brownstone full of cats. Right?" Maura looks down at the board, arching her amber brows.

The planchette says NO.

"All right, then . . . How will we die?" I ask.

"Oh, don't ask it that," Maura groans, but the planchette is already moving.

M-U-R-D-E-R.

"Rabbit," Maura whines, wiggling her knees against mine. "This ghost is being a *creep*."

"Just relax," I murmur. I ask the board, "All right, creep. Who are you? What is your name?"

The planchette slides to M.

Then to A.

U-R-A.

A sudden crack snaps through the quiet. The bulb inside the lantern goes out, throwing the room into darkness. Maura shrieks, jerking her hands away from the planchette.

"Okay, screw this," she says. The only light in the cabin comes from the glow-in-the-dark surface of the board, and in the phosphorescent glow I see the fear on Maura's face. I know I should be afraid, too, but as I listen to the pitch of her quickening breath I just feel . . . *hungry.*

"Put your hands back on the planchette," I snarl.

"Annie—"

"Put your hands on the planchette, Maura."

"Annie, you're scaring me—"

"*Now!*"

Maura's hands shoot to the planchette as if my voice has curled around her wrists and yanked them back. Maybe it has. She looks surprised, staring at her hands as if they've betrayed her.

"What the f—"

The planchette starts flying across the board, pulling Maura's trembling hands with it.

"Maura," I say to the board, "Maura, where are you?"

R-I-G-H-T H-E-R-E, it says.

"Yeah," the Maura across from me whimpers. "Annie, I'm right here."

"Shh," I hiss. "Look."

The planchette is moving faster now, darting from letter to letter, whipping us back and forth across the board as if we're playing tug-of-war with it.

G-E-T H-I-M.

G-E-T H-I-M.

G-E-T H-I-M.

"Get *who*?" I scream at the board.

Our bodies jerk from side to side while the planchette spins through the letters. It moves faster with each rotation, until the pointer is a blur and our arms ache from its breakneck pull. Finally Maura manages to wrench her hands free, and she flies back from the board, kicking it over with her flailing feet. It slaps into my lap, the planchette bouncing across the rug.

My body goes limp.

I stir to the smell of evergreen and ash. Someone is tapping on the window, and I jolt awake, but my tension eases when I see Leo holding up a steaming cup of coffee on the other side of the glass.

I reach for the crank and lower the window. I take the cup Leo offers, and the coffee burns my fingertips through the cardboard.

"You know, I'm not running a motel here."

"Sorry," I mutter, digging into the pocket of Sam's jacket. "Hold on, there's gotta be a couple bucks somewhere in here—"

"Stop. Forget about it," Leo commands, propping his elbow against the door as he leans through the window.

"Thanks," I mumble as I bring the coffee up for a sip.

"Were you here all night?"

"No, just a little while," I say.

I look at Leo—*really* look at him. I haven't forgotten what I saw on his Instagram feed. The girls scrolling by, one after the other, all around my age.

Around Katie Brideswell's age, the night she died.

I drop my coffee into the cupholder. "Hey, did you know Katie Brideswell?"

"Huh?" Leo frowns. He rubs his hand through his hair, locks already greasy from hours behind the deep fryer. "Who's that?"

"Katie Brideswell. She was a senior at J.P. in ninety-nine," I say.

Leo blows air through his teeth and shakes his head. "Nah, I didn't go to school out here. Hell, before I bought this shithole ten years ago, I never even *heard* of this bumfuck town."

Right. Leo grew up in Philly, and he bought the diner to escape the grind of working as a line cook in the city's toxic restaurant scene. He told me that once, but the information barely stuck. I really didn't give a shit at the time. Now it matters, though, because it means that he wouldn't have been here when Katie was murdered.

I sigh and flop back against my seat. I reach for the screwdriver in the ignition, ready to start the Cutlass, when Leo's eyes flash wide and he seems to remember something. "Wait—is that the girl who was murdered?"

I freeze, turning back to the window. "Yeah. You know about it?"

"No—no, not really," Leo says. "But Red Hot asked me about it, too, a couple months back. Said she was doing an article on it."

Rotten muck creeps up my throat. I twist the screwdriver and Bathory's engine snarls. I knew Maura was researching an unsolved murder, but I had no idea the case she was investigating was Katie Brideswell's. Maybe she told me, but Maura's *always* jumping down true crime rabbit holes, and to be honest, I usually just zone out while she regales me with all the confounding details she finds so fascinating.

If Maura told me about Katie before, I wasn't listening. It didn't mean anything to me then because I hadn't yet died the same way as Katie Brideswell.

"I gotta go," I say, my voice a whisper of steam. "Thanks for the coffee."

"Sure thing," Leo says, patting the side of the Cutlass. "Look, don't be so weird next time. Just come inside. I got a bottle in the back with your name on it."

He winks at me, and disgust turns my stomach. I stomp the gas and pull away from him.

As I swing my Cutlass out of the diner parking lot, I pick up Faith's phone from my lap. Maura hasn't called back. I dial her number again, but when it goes to voicemail, I shriek in frustration and throw the phone into the back seat.

I don't know where Maura is, or why she's not answering me. It does seem uncanny that she was investigating a murder so similar to mine, but I don't know for sure that there's any connection, and there's something major I'm missing.

How did I go from being accosted on my back patio by Gun and his shitty sidekicks to potentially being hunted by a *serial killer*?

What the hell happened in my kitchen once they shoved Maura and me inside?

Well. I know exactly who to ask.

And, as usual, I know exactly where to find him.

NINETEEN

HAGLEY'S HARVEST PARADE.

It's a town tradition, one so old and archaic that it will never die, like boat shoes or capitalism. Folks from all over the backwoods of Sussex County come to gawk at giant pumpkins on wheelbarrows and floats adorned with corn and marching cops with bagpipes or whatever. It's generally agreed that the parade is tragically uncool, but they close school for the day and usually set up a few rides and food trucks in the parking lot of the antique mall, so everyone shows up anyway.

As I whip my Cutlass down Route 15, I switch tapes in the vintage stereo and blast L7. I drum my palms on the steering wheel as my tires whip leaves across the winding wooded road to the center of town.

I avoid the congestion by parking at Village Market, the aptly named only grocery store in town. Everyone from Hagley knows this Harvest Parade hack—the lot is nearly filled with the cars of locals—and I cut off Frank Leona's dirt-spattered Jeep to swerve into one of the last remaining spots.

As I climb out of my Cutlass, Frank hangs out his window to scream at me.

"Hey! What the hell! Hey, Annie Lane, you dumb skank!" Frank yells.

As I pass Frank's window, my eyes flash livid black, and I lift my middle finger. Frank's mouth claps shut in startled horror, and a smile creeps across my red lips.

For a moment, I think this might be kind of fun.

But as I stalk through the crowds choking the parade route, I find something unexpected.

Sure, a lot of it is *exactly* what I expected. Giant pumpkins, apple barrels, kids in costumes, cider stands. The local VFW riding by on a *Frankenstein*-themed float. J.P. High's football team tossing beaded necklaces at the crowds on the sidelines like it's fucking Mardi Gras.

One of the players, Kev Ford, spots me as the team marches by. I couldn't tell you what position he plays—I don't give a shit about football—but I know he's not the worst guy on the team. He's never called me a slut to my face, anyway.

He throws a necklace at me, and I catch it instinctively.

I look down at the shiny beads in my palm, gleaming orange and black.

And the unexpected thing I find is that it *hurts*.

It hurts, watching life go on without me. People laughing, shouting, celebrating, unaware that the water running beneath the bridge at the center of town is tainted with my blood.

I sling the beads around my neck and shove through the crowd.

As I reach the gristmill parking lot, a familiar laugh shoots through the water in my ears, and I twist like a striking snake.

Trevor's hyena yowl sounds from above. I cast my gaze up to the platform of the Gravitron, one of several ramshackle rides thrown up in the gravel lot.

I expect to see Gun there, surrounded as usual by his shit-heel friends, but when I search the platform there's only Trevor and Darren, climbing the neon-green steps up to the ride. The flashing

THRILLER sign glares above their heads as they disappear through the open portal into the Gravitron.

If I can't find Gun, his dickbag friends will do.

I march across the parking lot and jump the handrail to skip the line. Nobody notices me, because I don't want them to. I slip up the wobbly stairs to the platform and step onto the ride, settling in a spot on the wall directly across from Trevor and Darren.

The diamond lights on the wall douse the whole space in red as the ride kicks on and starts to turn.

I stare at Trevor across the spinning vortex. He's busy watching the centrifugal force on Elizabeth Gomez's tits and doesn't notice me watching.

But Darren does.

His elbow thumps Trevor's side. It takes a second, harder jab before Trevor peels his slimy eyes off Elizabeth and turns to Darren.

And then Darren nods over at *me*.

Trevor looks, and I could eat up the fear on his face like toffee, sweet and sticky enough to get caught in my teeth.

I show him a smile full of river rot across the flashing red whirl as the Gravitron picks up speed, pinning him tighter against the padded wall. I wait until the ride reaches its maximum speed, the rickety wheel spinning like an out-of-control top. And I watch his face as he realizes he is nailed in place by inertia.

Then I rise off the wall, hair swirling behind me, caught in the current that propels me.

I float across the Graviton. Trevor and Darren squirm like mice in a glue trap, but there's no way out for them.

No one else sees me.

Even in this crowded capsule, the two of them are still all alone in their terror.

"What's the matter, Trevor?" I whisper. "Never seen the consequences of your own actions before?"

"Fuck off, demon bitch!" Trevor shrieks, hateful and shrill.

I slam my hands against the wall on either side of his shoulders and crash over him like rushing water.

"Did you do it?" I hiss, letting blackness swallow my sour eyes. "Did you do it, Trevor?"

"She *is* a demon," Darren says, horrified, rambling under his breath. "She really *is* a demon—"

"I *told* you, God damn it," Trevor wheezes.

"Right. I'm a demon," I say, droll and flat. "And if you don't tell me what you did, I'm going to make you puke pea soup out of your dickhole for the rest of eternity."

"I didn't do anything to you! *You're* the reason all this happened!" Trevor yells.

"Hey, bro, are you good?" a guy from the grade below ours pinned to the wall beside Trevor asks.

Trevor's eyes go wider.

"Can't you see her?" he says. "Can't you fucking see her?"

"See *who*?"

"Trevor," I snap, grabbing him by his wormy chin, wrenching his face back to me. "Where is Maura?"

"How should I know?" he whimpers. "I didn't do anything, okay? I just gave Gun the K. It was all his idea."

"The *K*? As in *ketamine*? You drugged us?!" Cold water rises in my chest, churning behind my ribs. "Did you touch her? What did you do to her?"

"Nothing! We didn't do anything! You two bitches started fighting and then she *left*, all right? If something happened to her, it's *your* fault for chasing her away!"

His words hit me like a kick to the chest, knocking the rage right out of me. My arms go limp. Gravity flings me across the whirling ride, throwing me into the opposite wall, where I land like a spitball, just a chewed-up wad of wet ghost muck on the side of a flying metal wheel.

My fault.

It *is* my fault.

I remember that night when Maura picked me up from Boondocks.

I remember sitting in the passenger seat of her Crown Vic, rubbing the mascara stains from under my eyes in the visor mirror. Loretta Lynn was playing through the speakers, and Maura was laughing in response to my recollection of the night's events.

"*What* is his *thing* with Riley?" Maura marveled. "I mean, she is like a heartbeat above a blowup doll, but he just can't quit her, can he?"

"You know, I don't even hate her this time," I said with a sigh, flipping the sun visor shut.

"Oh? So, we don't get to do a remake of *Invasion of the Boyfriend Snatchers*?" Maura said.

After I first broke up with Gun in May, Maura had known just the thing to cure me of my wallowing rage: She'd drawn crude stick-figure renditions of Riley on scraps of paper and hung them up on trees in the woods behind her house. We spent the afternoon running through the forest with Nerf guns, waging war against an army of crayon Riley Cassidys, until the ground was littered with Styrofoam bullets and I had laughed out all of my heartbreak.

"Honestly, this time I'm just mad at *myself*," I said.

"Don't do that." Maura sighed. "Self-flagellation is *not* your style."

"I'm really the biggest asshole in this situation, though," I insisted. "He played me one dumb song, and I stuck on a big red nose and hopped right in my clown car for another ride. Besides, how can you defend me after the way I treated you earlier?"

"Oh, I'm not defending the Annie Lane from earlier," Maura said. "Fuck her. She's a bitch. But I'm talking to *right-now* Annie, and I'm telling her I love her, and I will literally *die* before I let Morgan Donovan leave even *one* bad feeling between us."

With burning eyes and tears caught in my throat, I reached across the center console and wound my fingers with hers. I tipped my temple against the headrest, watching her profile in the dark of the car.

"I love you, too, M'ra," I whispered.

I was so glad she came for me.

I had no idea the danger I was putting her in.

TWENTY

WHEN I OPEN my eyes, the ride is empty.

I'm just a leggy spill of wet hair and dripping clothes on the metal floor, wishy-washy and groggy with sorrow. I scramble to my feet just as the next batch of riders starts to march in, pushing past a boy in the doorway to stumble down the stairs and out into the crowd.

I look around for Trevor, but he's long gone.

I let him get away—*again*. But at least he admitted to *something*. I've heard Trevor brag about his ketamine stash before, like it somehow makes him cool to take advantage of drugged girls.

I don't know what Gun would want to drug me for, but I sincerely hope it's not *that*.

I'm wandering the parade route aimlessly, mopping up the splashes under my eyes, when I spot Riley Cassidy sitting on the front steps of her mom's antique shop. She's got her chin on her hand as she puffs on a vape pen, blowing candy-scented clouds from her glossy lips while she watches the parade go by.

The dizzy guilt swirling in my guts turns to ice, hard and sharp and unforgiving.

Riley *fucking* Cassidy.

If it wasn't for her hooking up with Gun that night, I never would have left Boondocks. I wouldn't have called Maura to come get me. We wouldn't have been drugged by my heinous ex and his slimeball friends. Maybe I'd still be *alive*, if it wasn't for Riley fucking Cassidy screwing my ex in the back of his Mustang.

She doesn't notice me coming until I'm standing right over her, boots nearly crashing into her dirty purple platform sneakers.

Her head jerks up, eyes going a little wide when she sees me there, all streaky mascara and river-tumbled hair. She shifts on the stair, uncrossing her legs, planting both feet on the ground. Like she's ready for a fight.

Good. She might get one.

"Annie, what the f—"

"Tell me, Riley, what'd you get up to when you were done fucking my ex that night?"

Riley's eyes go even wider, blue irises so pale they're nearly translucent, her lids smudged with mint-green shadow. She's really too pretty to be throwing herself at Gun the way she does, but I'm not about to tell her that.

"Huh?" She huffs on an exhale of vape smoke.

"That night at Boondocks. After you and Gun hooked up in his car. What did you do?"

Riley snorts, sitting back to prop her elbows on the step behind her. "Are you seriously still coming at me like this? About *him*? After what he did to you?"

My pupils expand, black swallowing sour green. "Do you know what he did to me?" I ask her.

"Of course I do. It's my fucking fault," she says, her tone defiant despite the apparent confession.

"*What?*" I hiss.

Riley sighs and rubs her hand roughly across her freckled face, scrubbing at her upturned nose. She keeps her eyes closed as she mumbles, "Look, I'm really sorry, okay? I had no idea he'd do *that*. I mean, I know he's a piece of shit, but that's just *so* messed up—"

"Riley, what did you *do*?"

Riley's hand drops away from her face. She shakes back her white-blond hair with bangs streaked electric blue and looks into my eyes. "I'm the one who reposted that video. *I'm* the reason he dropped your nudes."

Fury seethes in me, vengeful and hungry.

I'm not sure if I'm mad that she's to blame for my nudes getting leaked or that *this*—just this—is the revelation she was getting at. For a second I thought she was about to tell me everything. I thought the search for my killer was finally at an end, and that Riley Cassidy—of all people, right?—was about to close the case for me.

This isn't the confession I was expecting.

But that doesn't make me any less pissed off.

I lunge, grabbing her by the collar of her patched denim jacket. She shrieks and her platform slams into my shin. I fall forward, landing on her, driving her into the worn wooden step she's sitting on.

And then her fist crashes into my face.

Shouts sound around us, and spectators gather with phones out to record. I yank Riley forward and then shove her back down, smacking her head against the step. She lurches up and throws an elbow into my chin. I punch her in the ribs. She grabs the back of my knee and throws me over, both of us falling off the stairs. People howl and gasp when my back hits the sidewalk, Riley landing with a knee dug into my hip, but she's only on top of me for a second.

Our movements are fast and frenzied like brawling rats. We roll across the pavement, tearing at each other. I bounce her head against the ground. She uppercuts my jaw so hard that my teeth snap against my tongue, and then she grabs a handful of my hair and yanks my face down close to hers.

As blood wells from a split in her lip, she locks her eyes with mine and whispers, "I'm *sorry*, you bitch."

"I don't *care*," I spit back.

"I found your shit in his car!" she shouts, blurting it out fast before I can start swinging again. "Listen, I swear, I had no idea he was going to do that! I just— Before the corn maze, he asked me to roll a blunt for him, and I was sitting in his car and I dropped the paper and I—I found your bag under the passenger seat. It was there, with your phone and everything."

I'm frozen above her, looking down, seeing the hysterical sincerity in her pale eyes. I think she understands the gravity of what she's telling me. My phone and bag being in Gun's car is a big deal. I still had both when I left Boondocks.

Did I end up back in Gun's car that night?

I ease my hold on Riley and she continues.

"The whole time he'd been telling me what he told the cops. He said you took off from Boondocks and he didn't see you again, and you set up this whole fake crime scene to make him feel bad for you. But while you were gone, people kept talking about this video you posted, this video from Boondocks that was only up for an hour, and I . . . I was curious about it. So I turned on your phone and I looked for it. And once I saw it . . . I knew. He'd been lying to us *both*. He kept telling me you were up his ass, that you kept following him around everywhere, that you were *crazy* and wouldn't let him go. And I guess he was probably telling you the same thing about me. So, I thought, Fuck him, you know? Fuck him. I reposted the video. But I had no idea he would retaliate like *that*. . . . I'm *sorry*, Annie."

I remember Riley in the corn maze, distant and disinterested in Gun's antics as she hunched over a phone screen with her friend. How did I not recognize how *done* with him she was then?

I hold out my hand to her, helping her sit up. She's got blood dripping down her chin, soaking into her striped halter top. "Did you . . . find anything else?" I whisper. "Anything of Maura's?"

But my question is only met with a confused look as she answers, "Maura's? No. It was just your bag in there."

I blow out a breath. Maybe Trevor *was* telling the truth. Maybe Maura really did get away before shit got homicidal. I ask, "Where is it now?"

"I put it back where I found it," she says, scarlet slicking her teeth. She reaches out, fingers groping for her purse, hooking the strap to drag it off the step she'd been sitting on. She digs inside, crumpled receipts and lipstick tubes and empty vape cartridges falling out before she draws a cracked phone from her bag. "But I kept your phone. So he couldn't take the video back down."

I close my hands around the phone, but my eyes are locked on hers. "Thanks," I whisper.

"I saw his car at Village Market," Riley says. "If you want your bag back."

I nod, gathering my legs beneath me.

"Tit for tat, bitch!" some boy whoops from the crowd around us. Cackles swirl behind my back.

I stuff my phone into the pocket of the too-big jacket I'm wearing—Sam's jacket, painted skull on the back grinning at all the cameras still recording me, I'm sure.

I plant my boots on the ground and take off toward the Village Market parking lot.

It's not that I don't believe Riley. On the contrary. I'm certain she's telling the truth, and my purse is under the passenger seat of Gun's stupid Mustang, and if I have to wait until the sun sets and the Hellhounds come out before I find him and make him tell me what the fuck it's doing there, I will.

It isn't hard to spot Gun's car in the lot—the ostentatious color stands out, shimmery emerald under the gold autumn sun. My feet clip across the pavement until my hands collide with the passenger-side door.

I lean in and press my face against the darkly tinted glass. But there is no vantage point from which I can spot my bag beneath the seat, the window tinted too dark, the bag too well concealed.

Just as I'm pulling away from the glass, someone grabs me by the elbow and turns me around.

Even if I'd lost most of my senses, I'd know who it is before I even see his face.

If I had only my sense of smell, I'd know him by the cozy musk in the fabric of his clothes, the same eau de old house that permeates the tartan sofa in the Harkers' den.

If I could only hear, I'd know the buzz of the radio clipped over his heart.

If I could only feel, I'd know the squeeze of his hand on my arm.

All that is to say, I know the sheriff has found me long before he whips me around to face him and I meet his basset-hound eyes.

"Have you absolutely lost your mind?" he grits out between teeth so tightly clenched I think his jaw might crack.

His intensity stuns me. It feels like when you pick up a box expecting it to be heavy, but it's empty—that off-balance gut-drop shock. I know I sometimes piss off Grady, but the fury lining his weathered red face seems so unfamiliar . . . and yet, *not*.

I actually *have* seen this look on his face before, I realize. Like when Maura and me tried to give each other tattoos with a sewing needle and marker ink, and he caught us hunched over with bloody little skulls etched on our wrists. We did a terrible job—the lopsided little skulls mostly disappeared as the tattoos healed, leaving only a few blots of ink under our skin—but the way Grady raged left a mark of its own.

It's more than disapproval. It's disgust. I've seen it other times, too. I remember them like scars.

"What the hell is it gonna take to keep you away from him? A goddamn hole in the head?"

My mouth is full of pine needles. My eyes are wet with tears. I shake my head, pulling weakly against the hand encircling my arm. But he only yanks me back in, and I wobble on my legs from the force.

"I'm not here with him. I'm not," I say.

"Come on, Annabel, I know this is his little douchebag mobile," Grady says, gesturing at the Mustang behind me.

"He has my stuff!" I shout. "My bag, he has it in his car, he's been *lying* to everyone! Look, you're the sheriff, can't you just smash his windows? Look inside, you'll see. Please, Grady, please, *please*—"

My pleading gives him pause. He glances at the nearly black windows of the Mustang, then returns his gaze to me. "How do you know it's in there?"

"Riley told me," I say.

Grady, who picked up enough of the saga of my doomed romance with Gun to know Riley Cassidy had something to do with our breakup, arches his rusty brows. "And you believe her?"

"Yes! Grady, please, he's been *lying*, he saw me again after Boondocks—"

"Ay, Sheriff," someone interrupts, "there's no key to this car, I think."

I look over at the deputy, some rookie dweeb named Kinney who tried asking Maura out once and now owes her his life for not telling Grady. My eyes slice past him to my Cutlass, parked a few rows down with a squad car blocking it in.

"What the hell is this?" I snarl.

"Dawn reported it stolen." Grady sighs. "Where's the key, Annie?"

"Why don't you ask *Dawn*?" I say.

"Nah, Sheriff..." Kinney pulls up his duty belt nervously. "I mean she's been starting it with a screwdriver."

Grady huffs. "Damn, you really MacGyvered the hell out of that grand theft auto, didn't you?" he grumbles at me. To Kinney, he says, "You can't take it out of the ignition now, she's probably screwed the whole thing. Just start it that way and get it back to Dawn's."

"Grady, that's *my* car—"

"Yes, sir." Kinney nods, trotting off back to my Cutlass.

"Grady, she can't report *my car* stolen—"

"Annie, *I'm* the one who told her to keep that car on lockdown. You clearly can't be trusted," Grady says, glancing pointedly at the Mustang again.

"I *told* you, I'm not with him; he has my stuff!" My Cutlass starts without me, wormy Kinney at the wheel, sitting in *my* velvet seat, driving *my* car. Anger snaps through me, a whipcrack of energy that fractures the tinted window behind me. Grady flinches in surprise, jerking my arm so hard I lose my footing.

He catches me when I fall forward. His arm thuds my ribs, and I cough up cold water and river muck. "Annie, hey—Rabbit—"

He turns me to him, smoothing my hair back from my forehead. My clammy hands come up, encircling his wrist, pressing the heel of his palm against my temple.

"Grady. Please. He's lying. He was with me that night. He did something. He did something to me."

"*What?* What did he do to you, Rabbit?" Grady presses, clutching me tight.

But I can't tell him the truth. I can't tell him I'm dead, and Gun might have murdered me. Grady has no tolerance for the supernatural—it's why we always played Ouija board in the Dead Shed, safe from his judgmental huffs.

So instead I mumble, "He drugged me. I can't remember."

"Jesus, Rabbit . . ." Grady wraps his arm around me, folding me in against his chest. I shrink there like a withered leaf, wet cheek soaking his musty uniform. He looks past me, eyeing the spiderweb crack in the passenger-window glass of Gun's Mustang. "You really think your stuff is in there?"

I nod, and Grady reaches a hand out to run his fingers along the crack in the glass. He sighs and says, "Look, let's do this on the books, then. Let me get a warrant. If you're right, we need to be able to prove chain of custody."

"I'd rather handle this mys—"

"You're not *handling it yourself*, Annie, that's ridiculous. Let me do this. Let me help you."

Maybe he's right. How am I supposed to solve my own murder? I'm the same idiot who took half a year to figure out Gun was cheating on her. I'd probably never have caught him if Maura hadn't gotten the idea to snoop on Riley's Finsta with a decoy account. There's a moment of temptation to just let Grady take over for me—but it's followed by a feeling like my fingers slipping off a ledge.

I can feel myself fade like drying mist, like a radio losing signal. I grip Grady's sleeve and whisper, "No... It's why I'm here—"

I'm not sure what he sees when he looks at me, if I'm flickering like a burned-out bulb, but he squeezes me tight and says, "Rabbit, hey, hey, are you okay? *Rabbit?*"

"I am literally... the furthest thing possible from okay...."

"Rabbit, what's going *on?*"

If someone is going to make Gun pay for what he did, it has to be me. I can't let Grady take this from me. But I know he wants to help, so I'll give him something. I pull back enough to look up at his worried face, strands of cinnamon and silver on his scruffy chin. "I'm... I'm just hungry. Can we get some food?" I say.

He melts like butter, any remaining chill disintegrating from his hold as he looks down at my pleading face in the circle of his arms. He nods, just like I know he will.

When nothing else is certain, I can always count on Grady.

TWENTY-ONE

AS WE CROSS the Village Market lot and cut through the parade route, Grady keeps a hand pressed between my shoulder blades, steering me along the wave he makes in the scattering crowd. Wherever Grady goes, it's always like this—no one wants to get caught in his path. It's not fear, exactly, though in his capacity as sheriff he does tend to make folks afraid of him. Really, it's just the force of his presence, the authority in his stride, his every move unflinching and resolute.

All that never scared *me*.

I always found it comforting how Grady seems so *sure* about everything. He's not like my mom, whose every move feels like pulling a brick from a Jenga tower. Grady is always a steady hand. But with him, the game isn't even Jenga. It's more like follow-the-leader. Grady's in charge, and I'm stumbling along beside him, a barnacle clinging to the bow of his steamship.

"Grady," I say, small and watery, "have you . . . Have you talked to Maura?"

Grady looks over at me, a frown pulling at the corner of his mouth. "She's really not been with you?"

I shake my head. "I'm worried about her. She came to meet me that night, and . . . I found her ring in my kitchen." I hold out my hand so he can see the silver sun circling my finger. When anxiety starts to etch itself into the lines of Grady's forehead, I add, "But she posted on Instagram, like, two days ago. So, she must be alive."

Grady's brows lift at that statement. "Jesus, Annie, did you think she was *dead?*"

"It's more possible than you think," I mumble.

"And wait—she posted something?" Grady stops on the curb in front of Hagley Café and turns me to face him. Both his hands squeezing my shoulders, he asks, "*When?* What did she post?"

"It's this picture of us in New York. Me and her." I realize that the photo was taken on a day when Maura and I snuck into the city on the pretense of babysitting my cousins in Union—an alibi we chose because Union's exactly the same distance from here as Newark Penn Station—just in case her dad checked the mileage on her Crown Vic when we got home.

Deciding to be vague, I go on, "I think the caption was a message for me. It said 'check my rabbit' and I . . . I'm her Rabbit, you know."

"Hm." Grady nods. "She's been mad at me. I think I put too much pressure on her to pick Princeton. So . . . I don't know, a picture of you two together in New York . . . maybe it's a message for *me.*"

Maura never explained why she chose Princeton over Columbia. It was weird, since she's been talking about Columbia since seventh grade. But in seventh grade I thought I was gonna be a Hollywood stunt driver, so I figured sometimes plans change.

"Did you not want her to go to Columbia?" I ask.

"It's just . . . you girls aren't prepared for the city, you know? You've been *here* your whole lives, you never learned any street smarts, you never *had* to. New York would chew you up and spit you out."

Grady has no idea how many times Maura and I have hung out in New York since he gave her the Crown Vic last year. How we'd walk for hours through the city, browsing shops of oddities and antiques and used clothes, eating at restaurants with the most hyper-specific niche cuisine imaginable, befriending bodega cats and wandering any museum we could afford admission to. The city was exhilarating, vast and full of potential, but we never felt like we were in *danger* there.

Meanwhile, here in harmless old Hagley, I was brutally murdered.

So maybe Grady has no idea what the fuck he's talking about.

He goes on to say, "I was just trying to keep her close. And I ended up pushing her away. Did she tell you she's been talking to her mother?"

His words are cold stones dropping into my gut. I narrow my eyes at Grady and shake my head. "She didn't tell me that," I murmur. As far as I'm aware, Maura hasn't had any contact with her mom since she was a baby. When did that change? And how could she keep it from me?

Maura feels so far away, the distance between us the black span of a raging river. And I have no idea what hides beneath the swell.

Maybe we stopped knowing each other a long time ago.

"Could be she went to stay with her mom," Grady tells me. "Maybe we just pushed her too far."

It makes sense, in a way that's as painful as it is reassuring. Riley said there was nothing of Maura's in Gun's car, so maybe she really did ditch me that night. She posted on Instagram, so she can't be dead, not unless her body is on Resurrection Peak like mine—and in that case, I would have found her ghost by now.

But if she's gone, if she *left*, maybe it's *still* my fault.

Maybe she'd really, truly just had enough of me.

Grady drapes his arm behind my shoulders, and his hold is like a cozy sweater enfolding me in protective warmth. We walk up to the lot across from the former gristmill, where Hagley Café is open to diners despite the parade grinding along on the street outside. The hand-painted sign that dangles between the gingerbread-trimmed porch posts swings in the breeze.

By the time we walk through the screen door into the café, I've mostly rubbed the tears off my face. The waitress behind the counter smiles and says, "Afternoon, Sheriff," like she doesn't notice my puffy eyes at all. Her pin says her name is Josie, and I recognize her as another long-time resident of Hagley. Grady gives her a little salute, his usual wordless greeting.

Like everywhere else in town, Hagley Café is a little bit of everything it's ever been. The paneled walls and wide floorboards are coated in creamy white paint to hide the signs of their age, but the embellished bronze cash register on the front counter has probably been sitting there since this place was a general store for the mill workers in the 1800s. The mismatched tables and chairs make it seem like this is where all the dining room sets in town come to die.

Shock jumps through my watery limbs when I glance around the café. Sam's there, sitting at one of the tables along the wall with a view of the river. He's lounging in his seat, his boots propped on the chair opposite him as he reads a newspaper through the lenses of his tortoiseshell glasses. He glances up after I notice him, and when our eyes meet, I feel goose bumps drip down my arms.

FOUND GUILTY OF THE MURDER OF FIVE INNOCENT GIRLS.

I watch him warily as I walk at Grady's side toward a table. I see the way his inkblot eyes trail across the leather jacket I'm still wearing—*his* leather jacket. Sam folds his paper and sets it down, standing up when we near his table, his smile friendly but deliberately drawn. The usual rakish hook to his mouth is missing.

"Hey, nosebleed, what gives seein' you in this drag-and-eat pad?" Sam says to me.

"I don't know. I'm pretty sure *you're* the one out of your element," I say, eyeing Sam's rumpled brown pomp, the little silver skull with aqua gemstone teeth pinned near the collar of his striped sweater, and the cigarette tucked behind his ear.

He doesn't *look* like a homicidal maniac, but that doesn't mean he's not one.

I turn to Grady and tell him, "This is Sam. He's trying out for an off-Broadway production of *Grease*. And he's a method actor."

"Ah." Grady nods, in the stiff way that tells me he's not sure if I'm kidding. I am, but somehow, that joke is actually *less* weird than the truth. Grady looks at Sam like he's still trying to decide how serious I am while he says, "Well, best of luck to ya."

"Much obliged," Sam returns, but his narrowed eyes don't leave mine. "You in some kind of trouble, Crazy?"

I guess I kind of *am*. Grady is doing his best, but he's going to be a terrible third wheel on my hunt for vengeance. I have to lose him, a mission made harder by the fact that he's had his deputy confiscate my car.

As loath as I am to admit it, I need Sam's help getting out of here.

I give my head a tiny shake, one I hope he perceives as unconvincing, while I gesture at the sheriff behind me. "This is my U-Thor," I say.

"Gotcha. How do, Sheriff?" Sam holds out his hand, his fingers smudged with newspaper ink, and Grady takes it for a brief shake.

The faintest tremor runs through Grady when his palm clasps Sam's. After he drops the handshake, Grady curls his fingers to a fist.

I pull out a chair and drop into a seat across the table from Sam's. I snatch a menu off the windowsill and flip it open, but Sam and Grady remain locked in a literal standoff.

I glance up from a list of sandwich options to glare at both of them. "Can you *sit?*"

"Here?" Grady grunts.

"Please, be my guest," Sam urges, gesturing across the table at the other empty chair. Grady hesitates, but eventually he takes a seat beside me, wooden legs groaning beneath his weight.

Sam sits down, too, and I eye him over the menu as I ask, "So, what brought you crawling out from your crypt?"

Sam lifts his chipped coffee mug and says, "I heard they got a brew to wake the dead." He takes a sip and then asks me, "How'd you wind up with your own police escort?"

"Grady thinks buying me lunch will make up for the fact that he's *stealing my car.*"

"I'm under no such misconception," Grady says, gaze on the chalkboard menu over the front counter. "I know how long you can hold a grudge, Annie Lane."

"True. I still haven't forgiven you for eating the last Baby Ruth out of my Halloween candy ten years ago," I say.

"Whoa, baby, you're ruthless," Sam says, and to my great surprise, Grady grunts out a laugh. I'm pretty sure no boy I've ever liked has been able to make the sheriff laugh, but Sam's corny joke seems to have done the trick.

Of course, just my luck, the only boy on earth who could win over my father figure *would* turn out to be a serial killer.

When the waitress arrives, Grady orders a turkey sandwich, and

I feel a little guilty following his modest order up with a request for fries, three eggs over easy, well-done bacon, rye toast, and a slice of pumpkin pie. When I complete my list of demands, Sam grins at the waitress and slides his cup forward.

"Just draw me another, doll."

Josie simpers and refills his cup. She brings two more for Grady and me before she disappears into the kitchen. I start to dump sugar into my coffee while Grady turns his attention to Sam.

"So, Sam, are you from around here?" he asks.

"I'm docked pretty close," Sam says. "But it's not my port of origin."

"Yeah? And where is?"

"Coney Island," Sam answers. It's news to me, but then again, I never asked.

"I have a cousin in Brooklyn," Grady says. "How old are you?"

"Eighteen," Sam says.

"You in college or something?"

"No, sir," Sam says.

"Why not?"

"I'm not much for institutions."

"What the heck does that mean?"

"*Grady*," I snip, flicking a mostly empty sugar packet at him. Grains of sugar scatter across the tabletop, and the little paper projectile hits him on the back of his freckle-spotted hand. "What's up with the interrogation? Is he being detained?"

"It's just conversation, Annie," Grady assures me. I know he's trying to Dad me. I could curl up in that fact like a warm bath, but it doesn't mean I can let him ask so many questions. The longer Sam talks, the more suspicious his manner of speech and evasive answers are going to look to Grady.

And once Grady's guard is up, it'll be impossible for me to lose him.

"That's not conversation, Grady, it's an inquisition," I say.

"Well, what would *you* like to talk about?"

"I don't know." I shrug. "If somebody in Hagley was a murderer, who would it be?"

"Excuse me?" Grady snaps, droopy gaze narrowing on me.

"I mean, like, who in town do you think probably has a collection of human heads in their freezer, you know what I mean?"

"Christ, Rabbit, that's not funny," Grady huffs as he clunks his mug down on the table. Black coffee splashes over the rim and spatters on Sam's newspaper. Grady grimaces and snatches a napkin to dab at the brown droplets.

"I'm not *joking*," I assure him. "It's totally my right as a citizen of this jurisdiction to know if there are any, like, drifters or vagrants or dudes with wire-rimmed glasses and mommy issues I should look out for."

Grady shakes his head and adjusts his Stetson over his sweaty cinnamon hair. "This isn't conversation, Annie, it's an inquisition."

"Fine." I sigh. I roll my eyes toward Sam. "Why don't *you* pick the topic?"

Sam's brows lift when I put him on the spot, but he pushes his glasses up his nose and nods at Grady. "That's some lightning artillery, Chief. Don't see many revolvers in service these days."

"No, you don't," Grady agrees, patting the gun holstered at his hip. It's the same revolver he used to teach Maura and me to shoot, before he let us try out any of the other guns in his safe, and in all the years I've known him I've hardly ever seen him without that revolver fastened to his side.

"Smith and Wesson?" Sam asks.

"Sure is," Grady nods.

"You a quick load or a sure shot?"

"Both," Grady says, and his stubborn mouth actually cracks a small smirk.

"I thought you were more of an axe man," I say to Sam. It lands like a slap, stunning him into silence as he turns his dark eyes on me.

When he finally recovers enough to speak, he grinds out, "Yeah? And where'd you hear that from?"

"You're not the only friend I've made up there, you know."

"Three eggs?" Josie interrupts, suddenly standing over us with a tray full of food.

I hold up my hands to claim my plate, but Grady takes it from Josie, saying, "I got it, Rabbit. It's hot."

"Considering your own history with grapevines, I'd think you might be a little more wary of hearsay," Sam says to me.

"Fries," Josie says, and Grady grabs *that* plate, too, setting it down in front of me.

"Grady, I can get my own plate," I huff.

"What's all this about?" Grady asks, looking back and forth between me and Sam.

"Nothing, Grady, I just have the worst taste in men," I say.

"Turkey for the sheriff," Josie coos.

Sam grabs it before Grady can, dropping the plate down onto the table in front of him hard enough to make the lettuce slide off the pile of gray lunch meat.

"You believe it? Just like that?" Sam snaps at me. "Is that really what you think of me?"

"Pie?" Josie squeaks.

I take the plate and set it beside the others in front of me. "I don't really even *know* you," I say.

"That's rich. You got more needles than a Christmas tree, Crazy, you know that?"

"Can I get you guys anything else?" Josie asks.

"We're good, Jo," Grady says. He turns to me, concern stitched across his rusty brow. "Is there some kind of problem here?"

"*No*, Grady." I sigh, rolling my eyes to the ceiling. "It's nothing. We're just rehearsing. For *Grease*."

"I don't remember none of that being in *Grease*, Rabbit."

"It's a gritty reboot," I say, and I kick Sam's shin under the table just in case he has a mind to contradict me.

"Right," he chimes in, sitting up in his chair and adjusting his glasses. "Let's not spoil the show, baby. We'll save the rest for the stage."

The conversation continues awkwardly while I scarf my lunch, and when we're done, I sense my window of opportunity is about to open. Of course Grady insists on paying the check, and though Sam protests and tries to hand him some "folding green" for his coffee, Grady gets his way.

I lean in toward Sam while Grady goes to pay at the counter. "Look. Since he's confiscating my car, I'm gonna need you to get me out of here."

"Wow, first you accuse me of murder, then you ask for a ride? You're one mixed-up chick."

"Are you going to help me or not?"

Sam gives a heavy sigh and scrapes his hand through his tousled hair. When that one curl escapes to brush his forehead, I think of the mug shots on the poster. But his voice sounds so gentle when he says to me, "Yeah, of course I am." He glances at Grady, still chatting with Josie at the counter, and then brings his inkblot eyes back to mine. "Say you need to use the girls' room, then slip out through the back. I'll meet you there."

I nod, and as Sam moves to stand, I get up, too. I peel off the jacket I've been wearing all day, the leather worn soft, smelling like smoke and evergreen. My thumb rubs against the collar as I hold it out to him.

He's careful when he takes it, not allowing his fingers to brush mine. He shrugs it on, and the worn skull painted on the back grins at me as he makes his way to the screen door.

"See ya, Sheriff. Thanks for the coffee," he calls to Grady, who sends a dismissive salute Sam's way.

I move in the opposite direction, toward the bathrooms at the back—and the rear exit. "Gotta pee. I'll be right back, Grady," I lie.

And I slip away like an autumn breeze, gone before he even turns around.

TWENTY-TWO

WHEN I STEP through the back door to Hagley Café, the chugging rumble of a vintage engine draws my attention to a cream-and-chrome motorcycle idling nearby.

"Hop on, Crazy. Let's dissipate," Sam calls over the snarl of his bike.

I'm annoyed enough by how good he looks with his windswept curls and his boot on the jockey shift of his cream dream bike that it's easy to maintain a resting bitch face as I approach. I swing my leg over the motorcycle and straddle the smooth brown leather behind Sam.

I've ridden in all the fastest cars in Hagley, but I've never been on a motorcycle before. Sam's Triumph is mean and gleaming milk-white, and when I put my arms around his middle, I feel like my heart's RPM might exceed his engine's. Sam's foot hits the clutch and the bike kicks up gravel as it swings out from behind the café and heads for the road.

Sam deftly weaves through the wandering masses while I curl my fingers into the leather of his jacket and hold on tight.

As we swing onto Route 15, red on the obelisk catches my eye—red as a kiss, red as blood.

THIS
TIME
I'LL

BE
THE
KNIFE.

Each word following the other down the worn granite, just how it looked in my dream.

To me, the obelisk has always just been another reminder of Hagley's boring history—standing on the corner by the gristmill, a monument to a bunch of Continental soldiers who died on Resurrection Peak during the winter of 1778. But now it's something else.

Now it bears another message to my killer, dripping red and loud as a scream.

A message I painted in a dream that wasn't a dream, because according to Fern, *the dead don't dream.*

Which means I wasn't dreaming when I remembered playing Ouija board in the Dead Shed with Maura, either.

The Dead Shed.

It all rushes into my mind, cold and quick as a current. Maura's message in the caption below her Instagram post—*check my rabbit.*

She wasn't talking *about* me, she was talking *to* me. She meant the stuffed rabbit from Grady's Easter-egg hunt, the one she has that matches my own, both secret stashes for our favorite form of contraband.

Only Maura can't get away with smoking weed in the sheriff's house, so she keeps her stash rabbit in the Dead Shed.

I slap my palm on Sam's chest insistently, and he turns to look at me over his shoulder. I unravel one arm from around him, spinning my finger in the air, wordlessly commanding him to turn around.

He nods dutifully and whips his bike across Route 15, swinging it to speed in the opposite direction.

The Harkers don't live along the single square mile of suburban civilization around Hagley's main street. Their 1870s farmhouse hides at the end of a long dirt drive on a wooded stretch of Route 15, an unmarked turnoff that's distinguishable from all the other unmarked turnoffs only if you've lived in this backwoods no-man's-land your whole boring life.

When we reach it, I point it out to Sam, and he shoots his bike up the driveway while the sinking sun burns over the treetops.

I know Grady's still on duty—and probably still looking for *me*—so he won't be around. If Maura left a message for me here, I need to find it. Maybe it will tell me something about what happened that night . . . or maybe it will prove she didn't run off because of me.

Honestly, I'm not sure which I want more.

We pull out of the trees and up to the house, all weathered white siding and dark windows with green shutters. I've always found the sight of the Harkers' farmhouse so comforting, but now when I look at it, I just wonder what secrets Maura's been keeping here.

Sam kills his bike at the top of the empty driveway, planting a boot on the ground to steady it. He squints up at the house, the darkened windows reflecting on his glasses, black as his eyes.

"This your best bacon's abode?" he guesses, and I nod as I swing off the back of his bike.

Squirrels have gnawed the pumpkins we put out on the porch. The plastic skeleton we propped on the old wooden swing still sits in front of the bay window, but it's pitched over against the armrest, lap full of leaves.

My boots leave wet footprints on the wood as I climb the porch steps.

If she was here, Grady would have told me. I believe that, but still—I press my face to the bottle-glass window on the front door and stare into the foyer. Dusky sunlight glints on dust motes and pours over the oval rug rumpled on the floor and the shoes tossed under the wooden bench by the stairs.

My eyes stop on the yellow Chuck Taylors flopped on the ground, half-shaded but still visible.

Those shoes are ubiquitous in Maura's wardrobe. One toe is patterned with doodles I drew in Sharpie while Maura sat with her feet in my lap during a house party over the summer. I remember how the smell of the marker mixed with the smell of the dried chlorine in our hair. Mosquitoes were biting us, and Maura was singing along with the Fleetwood Mac song playing on her phone. I wrote WHEN THE RAIN WASHES YOU CLEAN, YOU'LL KNOW between swirling blue raindrops on her toe, and I can still hear her singing the words in her husky voice as I stare at the doodles on her favorite shoes.

Just like her ring on my kitchen floor, those shoes feel like another sign of her leaving me behind.

Maybe I'm totally wrong about that caption under her post. Maybe there's nothing for me here. No hidden message, no secret code meant to reunite us. Maybe Maura left me here like an old pair of shoes, and that post was just a final "fuck you."

Maybe . . . but I have to check the Dead Shed anyway.

I push off the window as I turn around, jumping off the porch. I stalk past Sam and hike across the leaf-strewn lawn toward the tree line.

Sam follows a few steps behind me as I slip between two raspberry bushes, barreling into the murky forest. The early evening is gathering darkness between the dense trees, but I don't need to see to know where I'm going. I know the way by heart.

I step out into the small clearing where the Evil Dead Shed stands, mossy roof turned brown with autumn's rot.

When we first found it, it was just an old shed that probably once housed tools or winter provisions back when the farmhouse had an actual farm. But now it's our place—refurbished by Grady into a cabin fort for Maura and me, complete with a tiny porch and two cushy old camp chairs out front.

We named it the Evil Dead Shed because of its creepy cabin-in-the-woods vibes. We'd spend half our summers out here, staying up all night telling scary stories and sharing the futon by the diamond-paned window when we got too scared to sit on the porch any longer.

I step onto the little porch, the boards Grady laid down a decade ago creaking under my boots. There's always been a latch on the door and a place for a padlock to hang, but they were just a remnant of the property's farming days. I've never actually seen a lock on the Dead Shed before.

Not until now, anyway.

I touch the padlock that hangs on the door, heavy steel with a thick shackle. Why would Grady or Maura lock up the Dead Shed? Maura and I slept here not even a week ago . . . and it's not like there's anything worth stealing in there. Or anyone dumb enough to trespass on the sheriff's property, for that matter.

No one except me, I guess.

I drop the padlock and kick the door in frustration, boot thudding hard against the wood. If Maura hid something in her rabbit, I'm not going to find it now. It's just another dead end, another unanswered question, another thread I can't follow.

Maybe I'll never know the truth. Maybe my killer is just going to *get away with it.*

Sam takes a step up onto the porch, shoulders tensely bunched.

"Hey, Crazy, you solid?" he asks, reaching out a hand that stops short of my shoulder when I twist around to glare at him.

"Shut *up*, Sam!" I snap, all my anger spilling forth like a flood. "God, I'm so sick of you and all your cryptic bullshit! Just tell me the truth, did you kill those girls or not?"

"*No*, of course I didn't!"

Maybe, once upon a time, I would have seen the bare desperation on his face and taken it for sincerity.

But I can't trust anything anymore—not even my own judgment.

I take a step away from him, backing up on the shady porch. His voice ashy with despair, he goes on: "Look, baby, that town was twisted. The folks up there were totally bughouse. They all followed this priggish preacher-man like he was the Second Coming, and when I got in and shook 'em up, he made me out to be the devil."

"So you *killed* them?"

"I didn't *do it*, Annabel!" Sam shouts.

Just then, a low snarl rumbles in the dark behind me.

I leap off the porch just as a toothy black beast bursts from the shadows, fangs tearing at the air where I was standing seconds ago. I scream as another massive hellhound jumps up from the ground by my feet, snapping at my ankles as I take off for the trees.

I don't run back to the Harkers' house, where Sam's bike waits to carry us off to safety.

Instead I run through the trees like a watery blur, ghosting through the dusk. I may never know what happened on Resurrection Peak all those decades ago, but nothing Sam can say will convince me that he's innocent. After all, if Maura could keep secrets from me, *anyone* can.

I think I'd rather stick with the devil I know.

So I run through the woods, all the way to the blue shake house at the end of Quarry Road.

It's a last resort. The hellhounds are hot on my trail, and I have nowhere else to go. Still, I feel the cold churn in my chest as I break through the trees at the edge of the yard.

The house I grew up in doesn't really look that different from some of the houses on Resurrection Peak. The neglected landscape grows thick and disorderly, bushes crowding against windows and grass growing through the walkway. Part of the gutter has been hanging off since last September, and the siding hasn't been painted in so long that mold has started to bloom between the sun-worn shingles. The roof is balding in patches. When my brother Neil was around, he did his best to keep the place in order, but he never asked to be the man of this house. There's only so much a twenty-year-old boy can do. Sometimes I wonder if he joined the army just to get away from this house and everyone in it.

Not that I can blame him.

The key hidden in the pot of dead ivy unlocks the door for me, and a whirlwind of smell and sound assaults me from the dim wood-paneled kitchen. Cooper is eating burned pizza bagels and watching TikToks on his phone at full volume. Owen is blocking it out with a pair of headphones while he munches on cheese curls, head back and eyes on the crack in the ceiling.

For them, this is the usual dinner fare. Meals are a fend-for-yourself free-for-all in our house. Dawn is almost never home, and on the rare occasions she *is* here, it's not like she'd wake from her benzo stupor long enough to cook a meal for her ungrateful progeny.

Cooper shrieks when he notices me. It's not a shriek of horror, or joy, or any genuine emotion really. My littlest brother just has no chill. The scream does get Owen's attention, though—he nearly falls off his tipped-back chair in his rush to yank down his headphones and identify the reason for the scream.

His sour eyes narrow on me, standing just inside the doorway.

"Jesus. You still look like shit," Owen says. I can hear Black Sabbath playing through the headphones around his neck. My chest churns as I cross the kitchen and yank open the fridge to survey the bleak offerings inside.

"Missed you, too, dear brother," I say.

I glance back at Owen. He's chewing his lip, knee bouncing as he eyes me. Behind him, Cooper's phone is blasting what frankly sounds like a car-crash video.

"I'm serious, Annie. You look more fucked up than the ending of an M. Night Shyamalan movie," Owen says.

I snort and say, "Worse than *The Village*? Worse than *Old*?"

"Worse than *The Happening*," Owen says.

"Oh, damn. Angry plantpocalypse bad, really?" I pat the top of my head like that could smooth my untamed hair and grab an expired jug of orange juice from the fridge. "I'm ashamed to show my face."

Owen huffs like he's in pain. He reaches over to wave a hand over Cooper's phone screen. "Coop, shut that shit off," he commands.

"Shut *your* shit off," my ten-year-old brother responds as he flips to the next video. Owen snatches the phone out of his hand, thumbing it into silence. "Heeey!" Cooper protests, but Owen isn't even looking at him.

He stands and takes a step toward me.

"Are you really okay, Annie?" Owen says.

I swallow a mouthful of rancid orange juice and turn to face him, half-drowned in refrigerator light. I nod and say, "If you're disappointed, join the club. Maybe Mom will let you be treasurer."

"She does always trust me with the pizza money," Owen says.

"She thinks I'll buy drugs with it," I say, slamming the juice back into the fridge. "As if *she* wasn't gonna buy drugs with it."

"Yeah, Annie, um—I'm sorry," Owen blurts like the words have been stuck in his throat, like getting them out is some kind of verbal Heimlich maneuver. "I came downstairs at the wrong time. I should have checked on you again. I had no idea you were actually . . . in danger."

My hands start leaking river water, cool droplets running down my fingers. The fridge blows cold air through me, and it rustles at Owen's long, wild hair.

"Owen . . . what happened that night? Did you see anything?" I ask him.

"Yeah, I . . . When you guys first got here, I came down. But when I saw *he* was here, it pissed me off so much . . . I went back upstairs and put my headphones on. I just ignored you guys. I should have made sure you and Maura were okay."

"It's not your fault," I say, shutting the fridge so I can turn to him fully. "And anyway, I'm fine."

"You're not fine," Owen says, small but fierce. "I know you aren't *fine*, Annie."

Behind him, Cooper gets up to stand on his chair. He's munching on a bite of pizza bagel, and there's sauce stuck between his teeth.

"I came down to get soda and I saw you *kissing!*" Cooper announces in his too-loud voice.

"Kissing *who?*" I hiss.

Cooper giggles and stuffs another burned pizza bagel in his mouth. "Your *boyfriend,* stupid," he crows.

I press the heel of my palm against the place where the knife went under my ribs. My vision is blurring with tears, and it reminds me of being underwater, trying to see through the thrashing river.

I would never have kissed Morgan Donovan of my own free will that night. *Never.*

"Annabel."

My mom's voice is a cold snap from the kitchen doorway. I turn to her with my jaw slack and eyes bloodshot with tears. She's standing there in the shadowy hall, her hair a garish tumbleweed and her face gray as old lunch meat. She looks more like a ghost than I do.

"What are you even doing here?" she asks me.

"I kind of live here," I say, squeezing every drop of sarcasm I can through my tight throat.

My mom strides forward, a gust of stale cigarette smoke and sandalwood perfume, and her bony fingers clutch my arm with a steel grip. "You don't *live* in this house, Annabel," she snarls. "You *infect* it."

"Mom," Owen squeaks. "Um. I thought we agreed on a calm and assertive approach—"

"I didn't agree to anything, Owen," Dawn snaps at my brother. She leans in closer to me. "Don't you see what you're doing to your brothers? Cooper said someone in his class had a *naked picture of you.* Now, how the hell does a ten-year-old get a naked picture of *you?*"

I take a step back and my spine thuds against the kitchen counter. "Mom, it's not my fault—"

"Bullshit," Dawn says. "You're always passing the blame; you never take responsibility for *anything*—"

"Gun *posted those pictures*, Mom!" I shout. "I pissed him off and he *posted my nudes*, it's not my fucking *fault!*"

"God, don't you hear yourself, Annie?" My mom laughs. "You

just breeze right over *your* role in everything. What did you do to him, huh? You think you can treat everyone like shit, and they'll just *take it* and *take it* forever? Don't tell me this isn't *your fault*. Hell, why would you even *take* those pictures in the first place?"

"Mom," Owen snaps, closing in behind her. "That's really unfair to say—"

"What's *unfair* is how she treats us. I can't take it anymore, Annie, you hear me? It's over. I want you *out* of this house," my mom says. She finally releases my arm, but only to swing her hand and point to the door. "Out!"

I wonder if it would have been as easy for her to let me go if I had stayed dead.

Would she have kept waiting for me to come home until the river finally washed my bones into some hunter's path?

Or would she have long since stopped leaving the key in the hanging pot outside for me?

I gag on a sob. I press my fingertips against my eyes and curl in on myself. Cold water leaks down my cheeks. I gasp against the flood in my lungs a few times before my brother wraps his gangly arms around me and presses me tight to his chest.

"Leave her alone," Owen says. "You're being super fucked up right now."

"I'm tired of dealing with her shit," my mom grumbles.

"I think you need a better grasp on how much shit we take from *you* before you make a judgment like that," Owen tells her.

I'd laugh if I could, but I can barely stand. My mom tells Owen, "Fine, *you* handle her, then," and she crawls back to the darkness from whence she came.

My brother guides me into a chair at the kitchen table. He fills a glass with tap water for me and gives me the dish towel to dry my teary face. He sends Cooper away to his room, and he rummages through the cabinets for something I can eat. Eventually he comes up with a pack of stale Pop-Tarts, and I obligingly pick at them. But I know they won't satisfy my hunger—at this point, only one thing will.

I haven't forgotten what Cooper said. *He saw me kissing Gun.* It's hard to imagine, even though I know I was drugged. Is that really what Gun wanted the ketamine for—to hook up with me while I was too impaired to tell him no? My guts heave and I put down the Pop-Tart, pressing my wrist to my lips to stifle a gag.

I look across the kitchen, trying to recall the details of the "crime scene" Grady showed me on his phone. The broken glass. The bloody handprint streaked on the cabinet door. The spill of blood on the floor.

What happened after that kiss?

Did Gun drug me to hook up with me, or did he want to incapacitate me for another reason? When they were waiting for me on the patio that night, had they already made up their minds to murder me?

And if that's the case, did they really just let Maura leave?

I grope for my phone, but I left it in the jacket I gave back to Sam, so I ask Owen if I can borrow his.

I log into my Instagram and ignore the screaming triple-digit notification bubble as I open the messenger.

My fingers leave damp prints on the phone screen.

I need to see you.

I type out the message and send it to Gun.

TWENTY-THREE

I KNEW HE WOULD fall for my DM. His response comes almost immediately.

Where are you?

I streak water across the screen as I type back, Home. I can sneak out.

Is your bf going to jump me or something?

He's not my boyfriend. Pick me up at the end of the block.

Sure omw

What an opportunistic little scumbag. He's actually vain enough to believe I might still want him. It nearly makes me laugh, but then it makes me too angry to laugh.

I hand Owen his phone back and fetch my backpack from Bathory before stalking upstairs to change my clothes. I put on Gun's old Venom T-shirt, pull torn black stockings up my legs, and lace up my boots. I swipe red across my lips and leave a kiss on my mirror.

I dig my jacket out of my backpack. It's still stiff with patches of blood—*my* blood—but I shrug it on anyway.

And then I walk out of my house, ready for revenge.

The cold October air stirs my tangled hair. I wrap my jacket around myself and start to walk.

I can hear the Mustang idling at the end of the block as I get closer. There's music growling from the speakers, but Gun at least had the sense to turn it moderately low. I approach the muted riot of whatever bullshit he's playing and swing around to the passenger side.

I eye him the whole way. It feels surreal to reach for the door to his car, to yank it open and climb inside. It feels surreal to smell his overload of Axe and the burned leather of the Mustang's bucket seats. It feels surreal to look over and meet his blue eyes in the dark of his car and know that I might kill him tonight.

"That's my shirt," he says.

I want to say, *I think I left my virginity in your backseat, so call us even.*

Instead I purr, "It's mine now."

He flashes the arrogant grin that used to make me swoon. Now it makes me sick. I gnash my teeth in return, but he doesn't even register my disgust as he pulls away from the curb.

"What the hell is up, Annie? You are truly the stuff of legend lately," he says.

"Am I?" I ask.

"Totally. Your bitchfight with Riley was like the livestream of the century."

"I bet," I mutter.

"Well, it was really hot," he says.

The fight between Riley and me was no sexy bikini mud wrestle. There was nothing *hot* about how I banged Riley's head against the concrete. That "bitchfight" was a *brawl*, and I cannot imagine the breadth of his disconnect with reality if he thinks otherwise.

So, I snarl, "Is violence typically appealing to you?"

His grin falters for a moment. As usual, I'm straying off script. I'm not surprised when he decides to change the subject. "Uh . . . so where are we going, anyway?"

"Just keep driving," I murmur.

He obliges with a shrug and for a few minutes the only sound between us is the music thrashing through the speakers. I eye the crack in the glass I made with just a snap of energy and feel a little smile pull at my lips.

"Do you want to go get food or something?" Gun asks.

"With you? Not really."

"What the hell's the difference between talking here and talking at the Die?"

"I'm afraid if I have to look at your face in a well-lit area, I'll end up lobotomizing you with a butter knife," I say.

"All right," Gun snaps as he jerks the steering wheel and slams on the brakes. His tires scrape through mud at the edge of the road as he pulls over. "This is how it's going to be? What the hell did you message me for, Annie?"

I stare out the window at the tree line we're parked against. My eyes reflect the shadowy spaces between crowded trunks while I tick away the seconds following his outburst. I don't look at him. I can feel his squirming impatience mounting the longer he is ignored. Finally I say, "Just drive, Morgan."

"I'll drive you straight home if this is how you're gonna—"

"*Drive.*"

The word is sharp on my lips as I snap my head to face him. His hand takes the wheel without his consent. He shifts out of park and pulls away from the shoulder. Fearful confusion twists his face.

"Faster," I hiss.

His foot sinks down on the gas. "Annie. Annie, what the hell—"

"Shh." I pull my knees up onto the seat and crawl across the center console into Gun's lap. I straddle his thighs and face him, blocking his view of the road. He strains to see around me, and every time he struggles the car accelerates more. The engine screams as the Mustang rips around curves, gaining speed. I know that his terrified face is mirrored back at him in the black that swallows my eyes.

"Did you do it?" I demand.

"Do *what*? Annie, holy shit, get *off*, what *is wrong with you*—"

His eyes are wide and his face is slick with sweat. He's still gripping the steering wheel like he's in control, but I'm steering the car and I set the speed. The needle climbs the dashes on the speedometer. My hands claw up Gun's shoulders and grasp him by the jaw, forcing him to look at me and only me.

"Did you do it?" I ask again, my voice a ghoulish snarl.

"I warned you!" Gun says. "You shouldn't have put the video back up!"

"Did you murder me over a fucking *Instagram* post, Morgan?"

The whites widen around his frantic blue eyes. *"What?"*

"Just admit what you did!" I yell.

"I—I did it, I posted the pictures! But you seriously— I mean, what did you expect? After *you* put the video back up—"

"Shut *up*," I say, dropping his chin. That is not the confession I'm looking for. My knees squeak against the leather seat as the Mustang bucks over a dip in the road. "How'd you even manage to make me take it down in the first place?"

"I didn't *make* you do anything; we *agreed* it should come down!"

"Morgan, I have never agreed with you in my *life*," I say.

"You *did*," Gun insists.

A rattling surge blares through the car's speakers, the sound of rapids crashing against rock. The static rushes and bubbles around us.

"Tell me what *really* happened," I say, my voice a watery snarl. "Tell me what you did."

"Annie, come on, I'm sorry, I just wanted you to forget!"

"Forget *what?*"

"I thought—if you forgot about me and Riley—"

"Is *that* why you drugged me?" I laugh, harsh as a hiss. "Seriously, Morgan?"

"You—you know about that?" Gun whispers.

"Oh, did Trevor not mention our little conversation?"

"No, he—" Gun shakes his head. "I don't know what he told you, Annie, but I didn't do it to be *creepy*, okay? I just wanted you to forget what you saw so we could . . . so we could really start over, you know? But when we saw you were with Maura, I knew she had to take it, too, because you *for sure* had already told her everything."

"There's a remarkable amount of victim blaming in this confession, Morgan," I say. Headlights glare through the windshield behind me. A horn wails as the Mustang drifts across the road. Gun tenses, cringing until the other car veers around us.

"No! I didn't—I didn't *do* anything to you, all right? I just needed you to forget, that's all! But once it hit you guys, you both got super weird. You started kissing me, and Maura—she totally flipped out."

"Did you do anything to her? Did any of you touch her?"

Gun whimpers and bangs his head back against his headrest. "*No*, we didn't touch her! She just *left!*"

"That's it? You just let her leave like that?"

"Look, we had our hands full trying to keep *you* from hurting yourself!"

"Me? What was *I* doing?"

"After you fought with Maura, you started acting *crazy*, Annie." The Mustang swerves around a sharp curve in the road. My fingers dig deeper into Gun's shoulders. "You were yelling and climbing on the cabinets and stuff, real *Jackass* shit. Then you started knocking stuff off the shelves and you cut yourself on some glass, like, really bad— Annie, please, stop, just *stop*, how are you *doing* this—"

"Shut *up*." The needle pushes to the top of the speedometer on the dashboard behind me. The headlights flicker out and leave us plummeting through pitch-darkness. "What. Did. You. Do."

"You puked a little, so we thought . . . we thought maybe you needed to eat something, but there was no food in your house. We took you to the Die and we ordered you some food, but you wouldn't eat it. God, Annie, you were so fucked up . . . I'm sorry, I'm *sorry*, we just . . . You went in the bathroom, and you wouldn't come out and we thought you . . . you passed out in there, so we . . . so we left, we left you there."

Water drips down my tangled hair as I stare at him. There's a sincerity in his eyes that was lacking in the video I took of him at Boondocks, something bare and candid. This is probably the only time he's ever told me the truth.

And I do believe him.

I recall the pink bathroom from my disjointed memories of that night, and I realize it must be the bathroom at the diner—I just didn't recognize the view from the floor in front of the toilet, where I bent over the rust-stained bowl.

It wasn't him.

Gun didn't kill me. Not really, not intentionally.

He and his bumbling shithead friends meant only to save themselves. They thought they could make me forget what I saw, they thought they could reshape the truth once I sobered up with no recollection of what happened at the show. Strangely enough, I probably would have been safer if I had stayed with Gun that night. Instead he left me drugged and disoriented, all alone in the bathroom of the Die.

"Who was there?" I hiss, shaking him. He winces back against the seat. "How many people were in the diner when you left me?"

"No one!" Gun insists. "Nobody, I swear, just—just Leo."

Leo.

I should have known. Even before I saw his perversely curated Instagram feed, I should have realized how weird it was that Leo gave Maura and me sexy pet names, that he never hesitated to feed us liquor and weed in the back of his restaurant. Gun had even made some bitter comments about Leo wanting to fuck me from time to time. But he still left me there with him. He still let this happen.

He shares the blame.

"Do you want to know what happened to me after you left?" I whisper. My nails drag against Gun's jaw. "He went into that bathroom and found me. He put me in his car. He drove me to the woods."

I can feel Gun start to tremble. There are tears pooling in his blue eyes. I've never seen him cry before. I touch my fingertips to the crease beneath his eye, soaking up the tears he sheds.

"I'm sorry," he whimpers.

"No. You're not sorry. But you will be." The Mustang clips the edge of the road and tears up a streak of grass from somebody's lawn. The wheel jerks to correct the car's trajectory. "Do you want to know what happened next?"

He doesn't answer. He doesn't even look at me. His eyes are squeezed shut, but he can still hear me.

"After you left me there alone. After he took me into the woods. Do you know what he did to me, Morgan?"

I slide my hand down and wrap my fingers around Gun's throat.

His Adam's apple bobs beneath the press of my palm. I curl in close and whisper against his ear.

"He stabbed me. He drowned me. He killed me."

"I'm so sorry, Annie," Gun sobs. "I'm so sorry, I'm so sorry."

He knows it's true. He knows whatever I am now is not what I was before, and I believe he understands the role he played in my death. He probably *is* sorry for it. He is stupid and selfish, but he's not evil. He couldn't foresee the horrific outcome of his careless actions. He didn't know that I would die.

But I can't forgive him.

"Do you want to know what it felt like?" I hiss.

Gun opens his eyes in time to see the crossed beams of the wooden guardrails on the narrow bridge over the Paulinskill—right before the car plows through them.

The Mustang plunges into the icy river. Glass shatters and metal twists. I wish I could swallow his scream before the water does, but it rushes in too fast. I grasp the dashboard and kick against the seat. As the car sinks to the bottom of the river, I float out through the smashed window.

I glance back and watch Gun as he struggles to free himself from the crumpled steering wheel pinning him in his seat. Then I stretch my arm through the broken window. Gun is reaching out to me in a desperate plea for help, but I don't take his hand.

I grope beneath the passenger seat and tug out my purse.

I sling it over my shoulder. And I leave him. Just like he left me.

I don't bother to surface. I move through the murky dark and my body flows in the current. I swim far from the bridge and the mangled Mustang, following the river as it snakes through town. When I've gone far enough, I claw up out of the water to stand among the trees. From the riverbank I follow the neon glow, leaving a trail of wet leaves behind me.

When I emerge from the woods, I'm standing behind the diner.

My boots leave puddles on the rickety steps as I climb them. I push through the screen door and slip inside the kitchen.

Leo doesn't know I'm here. He has his back to me, his attention focused on whatever he's frying up on the stove. He doesn't hear the creak of the door over the snapping grease in the pan and the Nirvana tape blaring from his stereo.

I close my fingers around the handle of a knife and draw it from the block on the counter.

I stop when I'm standing right behind him with the point of the knife leveled at his gut.

"Leo," I say, and he turns around.

TWENTY-FOUR

LEO RECOILS WHEN he sees me. He knocks into the stove, and as his elbow bumps a sizzling pan, he yelps and jerks away from the range. But that puts him a little closer to *me*. He flinches away from the knife pointed at his belly, holds up his hands, and freezes where he stands.

"Whoa, shit, Annie, what the hell?" His eyes dart from the knife in my hand, to the river water puddling around my shoes, to my black eyes. I can't tell what scares him the most. "Annie, Cherry, hey, what's going on? Annabel. Are you okay?"

I stab the knife into the carving board beside him. The point splits the wood, sinking deep into the grain. I draw my finger along the grip and then drop my hand with a shrug. "I'm fine. You said you had a bottle with my name on it."

"Uh." Leo blinks a few times and then reaches for the half-empty bottle of tequila next to the stove. He glances at the label before he holds it out to me. "Your name is Jose, right?"

I snatch the bottle from his hand and spin the cap with my thumb. I let it fall to the tile and roll under the counter as I tip the bottle back for a gulp. I keep my eyes on him while I drink, and I'm ready to reach for the knife with my free hand, but he doesn't move a muscle. There's a smear of red on the lip of the bottle when I hand it back to him.

"Are those contacts?" His voice is strained and anxious. He takes the bottle back, but he doesn't drink.

I'm shaking my head when I hear the clink of cup against saucer from the diner beyond the swinging door to my left. My eyes snap to the round window, head turning so I can scan the view it allows of the diner counter. A waitress named Lori is on duty tonight. She shouldn't be a problem for me. I turn back to Leo.

"Hey, Cherry, what's going on?" he asks me.

My lip curls and I snarl, "What kind of forty-year-old man calls teenage girls things like Cherry and Red Hot?"

"Don't make it like that," Leo huffs, setting the bottle down on the counter.

"What kind of forty-year-old man only follows girls my age on Instagram?"

"That's not fair. I'm not doing anything. *They* post those pictures on there," Leo protests.

"What kind of forty-year-old man gives teenage girls liquor in the back of his restaurant?"

"Cut it out. I didn't throw a net over your head and drag you back here. If you're uncomfortable, you can leave."

"I'm not uncomfortable," I say. My hand drifts up, and I run my fingertip along the handle of the knife. "Are you?"

"A little. Can you— That knife is not a joke, Annabel."

"I'm not joking."

"What the hell *is* this? Are you high on bath salts or something? What's wrong with you?"

"Stop asking me what's *wrong*!"

My voice goes shrill, and my fingers coil around the handle of the knife. I yank the blade from the carving board. Leo makes a break for it, darting sideways down the counter without turning his back to me. He scuttles around the steel prep table, gripping its greasy edge like he's ready to upend it and use it as a shield.

"Stop asking. Stop asking like you don't *know*."

"Cut it out, Annie!"

"Annie is *dead*." I push my hand down against the table between us, and my body feels like soft clay around me. I mold my own image. As I draw my legs up to crouch on top of the table, my skin sinks to sallow gray. Mottled rot spots appear, and river muck crawls up my hair. Waterlogged bloat mangles my face beyond recognition. While Leo is petrified by shock, I crawl across the table and lurch for him, knocking him off his feet.

I land on top of him on the floor and press the knife to his throat. He struggles and tries to scream, but his arms are pinned by the steel grip of my legs, and his thrashing just slices a jagged cut across his neck. He whimpers and stills, blinking against the water that drips from my hair onto his sweaty face.

"What... what..." He doesn't finish his question. Maybe he already knows the answer.

"Why? *Why?* Why did you do it?"

"Do what? *Do what?*"

"You. *You* killed me. They left me here with *you* and you *killed me*."

"No! *What?* Are you talking about that night—" Leo inhales sharply. I see revelation explode behind his eyes. "Oh my god, no... No, no, no, *Annie*. Your dirtbag boyfriend and his shitty little friends, they... they brought you here and I knew something was wrong. They kept telling me you were just drunk, but I knew better. I called... I called Grady. I called Sheriff Harker. I thought they were going to... I wanted to help you. I wanted to help. They dumped you and took off before he got here, but... But, Annie, Grady took you. *Grady* took you."

I pull the knife away from his throat, his words dredging up my memories from the murky deep. They crash over me like a freezing tide.

I remember Grady busting through the door to the bathroom stall and scooping me up from the floor. I remember being glad he was there. He carried me out and set me down in the passenger seat of Maura's car. I didn't ask him why he was driving Maura's car instead of his Bronco. I didn't ask him where she was. I just held on to his sleeve like a scared little girl while we drove away.

I remember.

I remember everything.

I scramble away from Leo. My shaking hands can't keep hold of the knife, and it clatters to the sticky tile. Leo keeps trying to say he's sorry through the sobs stealing his breath. I get up and back away, not saying a word and certainly not apologizing. I am beyond the capacity to feel remorse for attacking him. The numb shock I feel is the pause between a trigger pulled and a bullet making impact.

There's only one thought screaming through my mind.

Maura.

Grady was driving *Maura's car.*

Maura's car, with the same winter tires he bought me. Their tread identical to the one I saw carved into the mud on Resurrection Peak.

I dash out the back door and run to the river. Somewhere behind me I hear toothy snarls and the pounding of paws against the forest floor, but I am in the water long before they can catch me.

When I hit the surface, I splatter against it like a raindrop. I am scattered, shapeless and formless in the rushing current that carries me to the Harkers' little farmhouse at the edge of town.

As I draw closer, I think I might not be able to pull myself back together when I reach it. Maybe I'll be like the burning girl, amorphous and incorporeal, trapped forever in the rush of the river. I am about to settle into the rocks and stay there when I remember why I went into the water in the first place.

Maura.

I know where to find her.

I re-form and slither out of the river in the shape of a girl, but I don't move like one. I run too fast, I jump too far, my boots barely touch the ground as I shoot through the trees.

That night we played Ouija board in the Evil Dead Shed after the eighth-grade dance. I asked, "Where are you, Maura?"

R-I-G-H-T H-E-R-E.

And Maura, thirteen and wide-eyed with terror, looked up at me across the board and said, "Yeah, Annie, I'm right here."

But the dead don't dream, and that wasn't the only version of Maura I was talking to that night.

Moss spatters the roof of the Evil Dead Shed like blood. Tall dry weeds snatch at my wet stockings. I slap my hands against the door, the padlock clattering against the latch. I drive my shoulder into the door, hinges shrieking as I loosen them.

"Maura?" I whine.

Maybe she'll answer.

Maybe she's just locked away inside.

"Maura, please!" I wail, hammering the door with both wet palms.

But when I hear her voice, soft and muffled by wood, I know she's not just held captive.

"Right here, Annie."

The door caves in, hinges popping as I fall through and tumble to the wide pine floor.

I splash like a sponge hitting a wall, landing flat on my belly with my cheek turned to the wood. I cough up a little water and push against the floor, slowly twisting my head to look around the dark shed.

The moon shines through the diamond window on a bundle of blankets bound with rope.

A spiral of red hair spills through a fold.

I crawl across the floor to her, her body laid out on the green rug in front of the futon we used to share. The quilt from the Harkers' couch is covering her face. I pull it away with shaking hands, a whole river's worth of tears pouring from my eyes.

She's washed pale beneath her ruddy freckles. There's a black-red bullet hole just above her right eye, dry blood trailing down to her temple. My fingers comb at her frizz-chewed hair, and I trace her cold cheek. I whisper her name again and again, but she isn't here.

She didn't die on the mountain.

She won't come back.

For a long time I lie curled up beside her, my fingers playing through the frayed ends of her cinnamon hair. I separate her sun from my moon, and I find her hand, cold and stiff, and gently push her ring back onto her finger. Tears drench the rug under my cheek. I feel her near and distant. I heard her voice when I busted through the door, but it was so far away, muffled and weak. I whisper her name and it escapes my lips like vapor and dissipates. I know she can hear it on the other side, but she can't answer me. She's gone.

Something falls off the futon with a soft *thump*.

I sit up, one hand on Maura's still shoulder. There, fallen on the bloodstained rug, is Maura's stuffed rabbit.

"Right," I murmur. The message from her post—*check my rabbit.*

I grab the rabbit, turning it over in my lap. I find the hole in the rabbit's stitching and dig into the stuffing, probing until my fingers touch something solid.

I draw out a folded piece of paper. I can feel something tucked inside, and when I open the note, a little silver key falls out and clinks on the floor.

The message on the note is written in Maura's messy script.

It says: *If I go missing, Dad killed Katie Brideswell. All evidence in lockbox inside pillow.*

I pick up the key that fell to the floor, rubbing my thumb over the flat metal as I look around the shed. There are tons of pillows on the futon, cluttered all around the wall, collected over the years to enhance the coziness of our clubhouse cocoon. I carefully crawl over Maura's body, still shivering with icy tears as I get up onto the futon and start squeezing at some of the random cushions lining the wall.

Eventually I find one that is decidedly not squishy.

The lockbox is well disguised inside of a zipped corduroy pillow. I drag it out of its sheath and sit it on the futon, where the moonlight through the diamond-paned window is a bright blue beam. The key turns the lock and the latch pops open.

Maura wasn't kidding about *evidence.* There's a lot of it here.

There's a page ripped out of a yearbook with a grainy photo of Katie dressed up as Trinity, posing beside freckle-faced Grady dressed up as Neo. Above the photo, the commendation: Best Couple's Costume.

Grady was the boyfriend who was arguing with Katie that night.

I rifle through more of what Maura uncovered. There's a USB

drive I can't check now, but there's plenty of other stuff in here, too. Katie's silver charm bracelet, which an article I read mentioned was never found. A list of all the guns in Grady's safe and their serial numbers, with a footnote that marks the date and an explanation that this serves as an official log "should any of these guns be unaccounted for in the future." There's a letter, addressed to Grady from Katie, telling him she's going to school at FIT the next year whether he likes it or not.

There's stuff about Maura's mom in here, too.

Photocopies held together with paper clips. A copy of a domestic violence incident report from 2002, Grady listed as the perpetrator, her mom the victim. The report adds that the victim did not want to press charges.

I guess it wouldn't have mattered if she did. Grady became a cop right out of high school, so he always had the law on his side.

Flipping further, I see incident reports, restraining orders, and court documents. A custody battle that ended with Maura's mom being denied contact with her daughter.

Another police report, this one about Natalie Harker accusing her husband of murdering his high school girlfriend. *No evidence of foul play in Katie Brideswell's disappearance*, the cop taking the report notes.

A tear of crumpled paper with a Virginia address on it, jotted down by Maura.

I throw the papers back into the lockbox, looking over at Maura's body on the floor. Tears drip off my cheeks as I stare at her slack, lifeless face.

No wonder she never asked me what was going on with me and Gun. While I was getting stoned and playing chicken with my feelings for my douchebag ex-boyfriend, Maura was in the middle of a *murder investigation*.

She knew her father was a killer.

And when he came back that morning, I bet she knew exactly what he'd done to me.

I guess that's why he had to kill her, too.

TWENTY-FIVE

I REMEMBER WHAT Grady said to me after we pulled away from the Die.

"I've had enough, Annabel."

His voice was cold. In that moment I could recall the other times I've heard him speak to me that way. Like when Maura and I were twelve, and I brought a red bikini to go swimming in the river.

When I came out of the bathroom in my bathing suit, he was in the hall, waiting just outside the door like a snake ready to strike. He grabbed me by the arm and told me to change. I didn't want to, but Grady said Maura would want a two-piece because of me and he couldn't allow that in his house. I obeyed him because the way he glared at the exposed parts of my body made me feel like I had done something wrong. He brought me one of Maura's bathing suits to change into and I had to tell her I forgot mine.

I kept my T-shirt on over my borrowed one-piece while we swam that day.

The night he killed me, I remember thinking that Grady was staring at the road the same way he had looked at me in my red bikini.

"Maura told me what you were up to with those boys."

"Yeah? What's that?" I hissed.

His fists kneaded the steering wheel of Maura's Crown Vic. "You know what you were doing."

I shook my head. Nausea kept shivering through my body in waves. I opened the window and leaned toward it, letting the muggy breeze blow against my cheeks.

"Annabel."

I didn't want to answer him. I didn't know what his fucking problem was. My stomach was heaving, and my head was spinning and I didn't have the energy to argue my case at all.

"Please just take me home," I whispered.

"No. I can't believe Dawn keeps leaving you alone in that house. I tried to warn her about you."

"You . . . what?" I rolled my head back on the seat and blinked at him. "What did you tell my mom?"

"I told her what you've been up to with that Donovan boy."

"Gun and I aren't even dating anymore."

"That's not what I heard," Grady said. "Powell saw you two in the back of his car out by the Orchards."

"That was in *May*. We haven't been together since school ended last year—"

"You realize I know everything that goes on in this town, don't you?" Grady snapped. "You can't lie to me."

"Dude, chill out. You're the sheriff, not Big Brother—"

Grady's hand sprang off the steering wheel and clamped on the back of my head. My weak body offered no resistance when he drove me forward and slammed my face against the dashboard. I shouted in pain as he dragged me upright by my neck and shoved me back into my seat. My hands clasped over my nose and blood dribbled against my palm.

"You need to stop lying, Annabel!"

"I'm not lying!" I cried.

"Powell saw Donovan's car parked out there *last week*."

"I wasn't in it!"

"He saw you!"

"No, he didn't," I whimpered. "If he said he did, he lied." The blood on my palms glittered under the passing streetlights. My head felt sluggish and hazy. I didn't want to look at Grady.

I just wanted to go home.

"Please, Grady..."

I turned to him, and I saw the hollow black eye of his favorite pistol staring me down. He glanced away from the road to look at me with resignation in the lines of his face. He had his finger on the trigger, and I knew he was ready to close the distance between the cock of the hammer and the strike of the bullet.

I knew he really meant it when he said he'd had enough.

Maybe I could have talked him out of it. Maybe if I had been cowed, if I had begged for my life and confessed remorse for my actions, he might have spared me. Maybe if I had just pretended that I was sorry, he would have lowered the pistol and taken me home.

But I wasn't sorry, and he had no right to decide I needed to be.

Rage burned away my weakness, and my muscles all shocked to life at once. I twisted away from the aim of his gun and pulled my legs up to my chest. As I drove my feet forward, one boot collided with his wrist while the other bashed against the side of his head. I gritted my teeth and kicked again, crushing his head between the stomp of my boot and the glass of the window. The brim of his Stetson got stuck in the grooves on the sole of my shoe, crumpling on top of his head. My other foot had knocked the gun out of his hand, but I wasn't sure where it had fallen. I didn't want to give him a chance to find it.

The car was spinning, and I kept kicking. Grady snatched for my ankle while we swerved down the dark highway. I saw a glint of metal and realized that the revolver wasn't the only weapon on his duty belt.

I felt the blade of his hunting knife sink into my shin.

I screamed and smashed the back of my head on the dashboard in my rush to get away from the thrust of his knife. My boot knocked against the steering wheel and the car veered onto the shoulder as Grady stomped on the brakes. If my back wasn't already braced against the corner of the dashboard, I would have been thrown forward, but my position steadied me through the sudden deceleration. I watched the momentum fling Grady against the steering wheel and crush the breath from his lungs.

The tires sliced tracks through the mud before the car slammed into the embankment at the side of the road.

Grady looked dazed from the impact with the steering wheel, but I didn't know how long that would last. I grappled for the door and fell out as it swung open, landing on my side in the mud. I scrambled to my feet and searched under my seat for the gun Grady dropped, but I gave up when he started to stir. I turned around and stumbled up the incline at the edge of the road.

I thought I could outrun him in the dark. I thought I could lose him in the thick of the woods around Resurrection Peak.

I thought he'd never catch me, but he did.

I wonder if he knows I'm coming for him now.

When I leave the Dead Shed, I don't go back into the water. I move through the trees like a wraith—my feet barely touching the ground, my shape a scraggy blur. Whirling flashes of red guide me out of the woods right where Route 15 crosses the Paulinskill.

There's an ambulance pitched at the road's edge, police cruisers surrounding it—three, to be precise, which is almost all the cruisers Hagley has. Standing at the tree line, letting water mangle my face and my hair writhe like it's caught in a current, I watch as a stretcher is loaded into the ambulance.

Gun's head lolls to the side as the stretcher lifts.

He must see me standing between the trees. Hysterical terror twists his face before it disappears from my view, the stretcher sliding into the back of the ambulance. His arms flail. The paramedics rush in to calm him down.

I prowl out into the splashing red light, the rot sinking from my face. The deputies are clustered by the water's edge, looking out at the river Gun's Mustang sank beneath. I'm not sure exactly how I look to them—probably still waterlogged, skin sallow gray, eyes as black as the river—but at least I'm not unmistakably a corpse.

There's a message in red on the old stone wall of the bridge behind me.

LET'S MEET AGAIN BY THE RIVER.

I recognize the deputy who notices me first. Kenny Powell likes to pull me over pretty much whenever he sees my Cutlass, even though he never gives me a ticket. Every time it's the same old shit, him leaning into my car window, puffing his stale breath in my face while he impotently wisecracks about my speed.

I feel bilious muck rising up my throat as he says my name.

"Annie Lane?"

Judging by the way they turn with rapt interest, the other cops know who I am, too. I glance at them, but my sunken eyes return to Powell as the ambulance doors slam shut behind us.

"Where's the sheriff?" I ask him.

"Annie, are you okay?" Powell asks, and then giggles at his own reference.

I bare my teeth at him. *"Where is Grady?"* I hiss.

"Jeez Louise," Powell groans. "You're in a mood, ain't ya."

Voices buzz from the radios on the officers around me. The dispatcher promises backup from Wantage is on the way. Another voice 10-4s her message and then adds something about the diner being "all clear."

A ripple of decay slips across my face. Drenched in red from the light of their cruisers, I ask, "Did Leo call you guys?"

"His waitress did." Powell shrugs, apparently not thinking much of the question.

"Does Grady know about it? Is he there?" I press.

"I mean, I'm sure he heard it go out on the radio, but the waitress asked for EMS, not us," Powell says.

One of the less brain-dead cops narrows his focus on me—Deputy Chazek, a young officer with a try-hard crewcut. He steps up, eclipsing Powell to stand in front of me with the heel of his palm resting against the gun at his hip.

"What's the problem here, Annie? What do you need the sheriff for?" Chazek demands.

I don't answer immediately. I tilt my head and watch Chazek, showing him his own reflection in the black of my eyes. My hair slithers in an invisible current. The ambulance carrying Gun pulls onto the road and heads off with a few blares from its siren, and in its absence the sound of the river rushing alongside us is deafening.

Finally I say, "I found a dead body." I watch Chazek's eyes sharpen as I continue. "I'll tell you where it is if you tell me where to find him."

Chazek shifts on his big tactical boots. "The sheriff's just gone out to Detweiler's, asking 'em to bring their hook and chain down to get this car outta here. He'll be back soon. What's all this about a *body*?"

Something tells me that the salvage yard was never Grady's true destination. It's one of the last stops in Hagley before the road winds on toward I-80. He's making a break for it, and if I have any hope of catching him before he leaves town, I have to run.

Already climbing up toward the road, I call back to Chazek, "Go to Grady's. Head straight into the woods past the raspberry bushes. There's a shed. The door is broken. You'll find her there."

When my boots hit the pavement, I blur into motion. I run Route 15, skimming the curves at speeds nearly as fast as I can drive. I run all the way to the edge of town, to the salvage yard, where Grady's Bronco is nowhere to be found.

I keep running.

I blink out and end up on the other side of the mountain, just like I did in Bathory a few nights ago.

A ghostly vapor, I wisp by the orchard, where my message still screams, red letters looming large on a giant wooden pumpkin propped up by the road.

I CAME BACK FOR YOU.

But as I make my way through town again, past the gristmill, past the bridge, past the red light at Mill Crossing, all the way back to the salvage yard—I know.

I know he got the message.

And I know he got away.

TWENTY-SIX

GRADY IS GONE.

I sit on the curb outside the police station, where I spent hours wrapped in a drab blanket at the dispatch desk, telling different detectives everything I know about Grady and the evidence in Maura's lockbox.

They found Grady's Bronco abandoned a few towns over and brought dogs out to search the woods, but there was no sign of Grady and the trail went cold quick. He's slithered right out from between my fingers, escaping the reach of my righteous fury.

All the attention Maura's murder is getting means nothing to me. Grady's picture has been sent to every precinct in the tristate area, and by the afternoon it will be on the news. It feels like every cop in Sussex County is crammed inside the tiny Hagley police station. They promise me they'll find Grady and bring him to justice.

But for me, there is no justice.

I feel totally unresolved, weak and wet and ready to melt away. There's no point to being here anymore. Grady will never come back to Hagley, not by choice or by force. If he's caught, his trial will happen somewhere else: county, maybe even state or federal court, depending on what else he does when he's on the run. And if he goes to prison, it certainly won't be in one of the two little holding cells at the back of the Hagley police station.

Grady's punishment shouldn't come at the hands of the law. He should have to face the horror of what he did. He should have to face *me*. My unsettled business gnaws at me like teeth sawing at an apple. I wonder if it will peel away everything and leave me just a rotten core like the shadows on Resurrection Peak. I wonder if someday this dissatisfaction will undo me.

My ride pulls into the parking lot.

The cops handed me a phone and told me to call my mom to pick me up, but I dialed the number to Chapel House instead. I had a sinking thought that another shade might answer or that the twins would pick up and start chittering riddles at me, but the phone rang twice before Sam's voice came through the speaker against my ear.

"Annabel?"

"Come pick me up," I told him. "I'm at the police station."

I didn't say anything else.

I knew he'd come.

The sun is rising and the cream of his motorcycle gleams in the amber light. I stand and cross my arms around myself in my still-damp leather jacket as he pulls up to me. He braces his boot against the ground and looks me over, a frown hooked in the corner of his mouth. I know he wants to ask me what happened, but he doesn't. He nods at the space behind him on the bike instead.

"You wanna get out of here, Crazy?" he asks me.

I reach out and grip his shoulder. I can feel the warmth of him through his leather jacket. I hook my leg over the bike and climb on behind him.

I curl my arms around his chest and bury my face in the space between his shoulders, inhaling fire and evergreen.

The bike rolls away from the curb, and I turn my head so just my cheek is pressed against his back. I watch the trees flip by as we zip down the roads toward Resurrection Peak, sunlight stabbing through the auburn branches. The sky is pink and orange. The sound of the engine is a cozy rumble that can't soothe me.

I ride with him all the way to a shed at the edge of the garden behind Chapel House, where he eases the bike in beside a workbench full of tools and equipment. By the time he kills the engine I've already unclamped my arms from around his rib cage. I climb off the bike and put some space between us.

"It's Halloween," he says.

"I don't care," I return.

"You plan on telling me what happened, or am I out of the loop?"

I turn to him. He's leaning against the seat of his bike, arms crossed over his chest.

"It was Grady," I say.

"Did you get him?"

I shake my head, lips pressed together. Sam shifts off the Triumph, stepping toward me as he asks, "What about your friend? The sheriff's daughter?"

"She's dead." The words leave my mouth tasting like muddy water. "Grady killed her, too."

Sam ducks his head and scuffs his boot against the tire of his bike. "I'm sorry," he murmurs.

"Not as sorry as I am," I say. "He's *gone*. I let him get away. Now he'll never really pay for what he did."

"Hm. Not necessarily," Sam says.

"Even if they catch him, he's not coming back *here*."

"Every rule has an exception, Crazy. Halloween is ours," Sam says.

"What the hell does that mean?" I ask.

"It's a free-for-all from dusk till dawn. We can go anywhere we want as long as we get back to the mountain before sunup."

"Seriously? So, if we can find out where he is . . ."

"We can pay him a visit," Sam confirms. "No matter where he is. We'll find a way."

I doubt I'll know where Grady is in time to go hunting for him tonight. If he's gone into hiding, he won't be so easy to nail down. But eventually he *will* be found. If I can get to him, I doubt prison bars or courtroom doors could stop me from killing him.

There's still a chance I'll get him someday.

It's not over.

I stop feeling like a rapidly evaporating puddle. My boots are solid on the ground. Sam's eyes are searching mine, but I allow no softness into my narrowed gaze. I move away from him toward the double doors of the shed.

"I'll see you later," I say.

"Yeah. Whatever you need, Crazy, baby."

I know he means it, but it doesn't change anything.

I walk away from him.

My boots leave wet prints on the dusty floors as I pick my way through the halls of Chapel House. It's been hours since I crawled out of the river, but my grief keeps me waterlogged and leaves drippy puddles everywhere I go. I walk until I find a rose-embroidered chaise in a dark sitting room and curl up with my back to the windows. I close my eyes and listen to the wind that sighs through the trees.

When I sleep, I do not dream.

I travel.

I am only energy, vapor on the breeze. Time and places have no distance from me. I could float through Hagley and see the trick-or-treaters march from door to door, kicking pumpkins, snatching candy. I could watch through windows as people go about their lives, unaware that they're haunted by my angry presence.

I can fold myself into my own memories, too. Like seeing them all again from some place outside myself, invisible but present.

I find Maura there.

When we were six years old, and I got sent to the time-out corner for throwing a fit when one of my shoes came untied, because I didn't want anyone to realize I didn't know how to retie it—no one had ever taught me, and I felt like the only kid in class who didn't know. Maura threw an eraser at the ceiling so she'd get sent to time-out, too, and while we sat hunched together in the corner of the room, she secretly and wordlessly showed me how to tie my shoe.

When we were nine, and invented bubblegum kisses—blowing elastic pink bubbles with mouthfuls of fruity gum, touching them together so they'd fuse like sticky magnets before popping in our faces.

When we were fourteen, and she was mad at me for going to a party without her while she was grounded, I tried to make it up to her by baking a cake with a frosting portrait of David Bowie on it. Only the Thin White Duke came out looking like redheaded Slenderman, and Maura laughed so hard she cried when I presented it to her while singing along to "Golden Years" playing from my phone.

When she held my hand in the car ride from Boondocks that night.

I don't want to wake up, but I do anyway.

My face is buried in an embroidered cushion, and I roll over, rubbing my hands across my damp cheeks. I feel like she's still here beside me. The smells of her patchouli perfume oil and the cozy musk of the Harker house seem to linger in my nose. Cold tears trickle down my temples into my hair. My whole body trembles with sobs so deep there's no sound, only shaking anguish.

"Annie."

Her voice in my head feels like a knife under my rib cage, slicing through me.

"Annie."

My eyes blink open. The room is dark, the sun lost below the tree line at the top of the mountain. I turn my face to the side and she's right there, crouched beside my chaise with her nails clawing up the cushion toward me.

"Maura?" I choke. I grab her hand, my chipped nails the same shade of red as hers. She never took the polish off, either. Now she never will.

I fall into her arms. On the floor next to the chaise, we entwine our limbs and press our chests tight together. Her dense marigold curls soak up my tears. I cry against her shoulder, and I feel her rattling breaths as she cries, too.

I guess I should have realized she would be here tonight. Fern did say *everyone* comes on Halloween.

"I'm so sorry," I murmur against her cheek. "Maura, I'm so sorry . . ."

"Sorry for what?" She sniffles. "There's nothing to be sorry for. Unless you're apologizing for being an insufferable bitch, in which case, I already know you're sorry."

I choke out something that's almost a laugh. I pull back enough to see her face. Lying here on the throw rug beside the chaise, it's almost like when I curled up next to her corpse inside the Dead Shed. She's even wearing the ripped Kate Bush T-shirt she died in, the one she was wearing when she picked me up that night. She smells like herself, but also like death—like the moss that leaches through the roof of the shed, like old wood and damp leaves, like the smoking gun that shot her down. The moonlight is scattered by the ivy growing across the windows, and it casts spots of blue on her freckled skin and the wild copper floss on her head. Cold water drips from my eyes as I look at her.

"No, I'm sorry I didn't stop him," I whisper. "Maybe if I just... played nice when he picked me up, none of this would have happened."

"That's not fair," Maura says. "If it was someone's fault, it'd be mine. I knew what he was capable of, but I still called him to pick me up from your house that night. Maybe it's my fault he got mad enough to... But—but I'm not sorry for that, you know? We don't need to be sorry. *He* does."

Maybe she's right, but it's hard to let go of the guilt I feel. I close my eyes and drag my cheek across the carpet to press our foreheads together. The floor beneath us tremors faintly with the thrum of music from the ballroom downstairs. I guess the party is already in full swing, lively with ghosts ready to dance the night away. By the morning they'll be gone—just like Maura.

"Do you remember everything?" I ask her.

She nods and murmurs, "Yeah. I didn't drink as much of it as you did, and... things get pretty clear from the other side."

"Can you tell me what happened? Why did you leave?"

Maura chews on the inside of her cheek. A wisp of gun smoke drifts from the corner of her eye. "I left because... you kissed Gun. I thought you were, like, relapsing, and I got so mad... I told you I was sick of it and I . . ." She looks down at her hand, her finger bare where her ring should be. "I threw my ring at you like a bitchy baby."

I laugh softly and shake my head. "I found it," I tell her. "I gave it back to you."

We both watch as silver glints across her finger, the ring materializing like it couldn't exist until she knew it was there. She whimpers softly, smoke simmering in her eyes as she cries. "I can't believe I just left you there with them," she whispers.

"Hey. Remember what you said?" I remind her, lifting a hand to her cheek so I can sweep my thumb across her freckles. "We didn't do anything wrong. We don't need to be sorry."

"I know." Maura sighs. She closes her eyes and covers my hand with hers, our rings aligned as she tucks her fingers between mine, pressing my palm to her cold cheek.

"What happened next? After you left?" I ask.

"I . . . I called my dad to come get me. I was totally out of it; I wasn't even thinking about . . . about the Katie Brideswell stuff. I just wanted him to come help me. And . . . he did. He picked me up. He brought me home. He tucked me in my bed. And then . . . he left.

"I didn't know because I fell asleep. I didn't even wake up until he came home. I heard the car door, and I looked out the window, and I saw him getting out of my car. I saw the headlight was busted. And I saw he was all wet. And I got this terrible feeling. . . .

"I called your brother. He said you weren't home. So I told him to call nine-one-one, and then I ran outside and I asked my dad . . . if he'd killed you. Like he killed Katie Brideswell."

"Holy shit," I hiss. I grip her tighter, frightened by her bravery, wishing I could protect her from the moment she's reliving for me.

She goes on: "Of course he didn't answer me. He just . . . took out his gun. I ran away, I ran to the Dead Shed, but . . . I mean, obviously he found me there."

Cold water drips from my tired green eyes. Somewhere below us there's an explosion of sound as the ghostly orchestra in the ballroom tears into a new song with a pounding beat. I'm too preoccupied to wonder what the party downstairs looks like, even though the other day I was fascinated by the concept. All I want to do is hold Maura until the sun comes up.

"I didn't even get a chance to tell him I had evidence he'd killed Katie. I thought it'd stop him, you know, at least so he could find out where I'd hid it, but—he just walked in and shot me."

I squeeze her tight, grinding my cheek against her hair as I cry icy river tears into her curls.

"He's such a sociopath," I say. "When I came back, he didn't even crack. He seemed so sure of everything, I thought you had to be somewhere safe. I didn't even realize what you meant by that post until *yesterday*. I could have caught him so much sooner. . . ."

"Oh! I forgot about that post! It worked?" Maura laughs. "I set that up as a fail-safe. I made it a scheduled post, I'd just reschedule it every couple days. . . . Sorry, I know it was a little vague, I didn't want to make it *too* on the nose, just in case I forgot to reschedule it or something . . . but I figured you'd get the message if something ever happened to me."

"Shit, M'ra . . . Were you *that* afraid of him?"

"Sometimes. In the moments when I let it sink in." She chews her lip, blinking away the smoke clouding her eyes. "And . . . and when I called my mom."

"You really talked to her? What did she say?"

"She tried to warn me about him. She said there's no way to be safe forever because there's no way to stay perfect forever. Not by his standards. And I knew it was true, because I could already see it happening, little by little. It was like the more we grew up, the less he loved us."

It stings, because some part of me still clings to the memory of him, how he loved me at a time when I felt the most unloved. And how, with each step toward adulthood and autonomy I took, he peeled that love back from me until there was nothing left at all.

I wonder how long he was waiting for an excuse to kill me.

I sigh and brush my thumb across the shadow on her forehead where the bullet hole should be. "This ghost shit is so gnarly. It doesn't seem like any of it makes sense."

"It totally does, actually," Maura says. "It's all psychic energy. Even a physiological understanding of the process of thinking can't explain the cause for *consciousness* and the complexity of the mental experience. Almost like part of it exists outside of what can be quantified."

"Okay, start over, but explain like I'm dumber than a box of Trevors, please."

Maura sighs and pokes at the spikes on the shoulder of my jacket, leaving little white indents on the tips of her fingers. "You know—" She pushes on my arm. We sit up together, her hair falling down her back and our legs entwined. "He didn't put that lock on the Dead Shed until you came back. Like he wanted to make sure I couldn't get up and come after him, too."

"I wish you had. You'd have figured it out way sooner, and you'd be so much better than me at all of this. I've only been dead a few days and my afterlife is already a total shit show."

"No, Rabbit. It had to be you. I know what he did, but I could never give him what he really deserves. Not like you will."

"But I let him get away. Now I have no idea where he is, and apparently I can only leave Hagley on Halloween. So, he might *never* have to face me."

Maura shakes her head, the shadow on her temple shifting, blooming like a little flower, or a bullet hole blossoming blood. "But it *is* Halloween. And I know where he is."

I grip her elbows as vengeful hunger growls in my gut. "*Where?*"

"Virginia," she tells me. Her voice is thin as vapor.

I scramble to my feet, legs buckling as I pull her up with me. "How do you know that?"

"Because . . . when I mentioned Katie, he said I must have been talking to my mother. And because . . ." She pauses, swaying slightly in my arms. "I can see him. He's in a motel called the Cardinal. The sign is yellow with a lit-up red bird."

"You can *see* him?" I ask as I drag her toward the door.

"Yeah, I think there's some of my blood on the Smith and Wesson," she says. "I can watch him through it."

"Okay, *Ghost Adventures* never prepared me for the possibility of turning a revolver into a possessed nanny cam," I say.

Our squeezing hands bind us together as we run through the moonlit halls of Chapel House. From the top of the steps that sweep down to the great hall, I see the front doors are open. Late guests are still arriving, meandering through on their way to the ballroom. Their faces are like lenticular prints in the flickering lanterns, shadows revealing sunken features and decayed smiles while the light gleams on flushed skin and shining eyes.

A lady in a dress the color of cast iron sits on the bottom step with an entire cake in her lap, pawing handfuls of black chocolate into her mouth. As we run past her, she shouts through the sticky frosting clotting her throat, "Slow down, you ingrates!"

Eerie green flames light the ornately carved fireplace in the dining room, fire the color of snake eyes. Candles in violet glass globes line the table, gauzed by fake spiderwebs, and down the long mahogany stretch a banquet is set on platters of silver and crystal.

Forks clink politely against china. A man with a pencil mustache and a wingtip collar glares at us over his soup spoon. When he turns back to his hushed conversation with the woman next to him, I see there are worms writhing all over the back of his suit.

The twins are at the table, sitting like little gargoyles on their tall-backed chairs. Hunt is chugging his soup straight from the bowl, while Howl is making a tower of overturned cordial glasses. He must notice the urgency on my face, because when he looks up at me rushing through the dining room, he elbows his brother to get his attention. Hunt coughs on a gulp of soup and doubles over, his knee slamming the table. The tower of cordial glasses tumbles, clattering everywhere just as Maura and I burst through the stained-glass arch into the ballroom.

A wild bray of swinging saxophones fills the painted dome of the Ark.

No one was exaggerating about the turnout at Chapel House's annual danse macabre. The ballroom is packed with well-dressed ghosts whirling beneath the dangling lanterns and streamers. Strange lights spin across the walls and sweep through the crowd. I could swear the band playing on the dais is the same skeleton band that Sam provoked to play for us in the graveyard, but I don't quite recognize them with skin on their bones.

It's hard to see through the shadows made by the orbs of colorful light, but my eyes search for familiar faces. I push through the twisting bodies, popping up on my toes to peer over the crowd. I keep hold of Maura's hand to make sure I don't lose her in the sea of gyrating ghosts.

Finally I spot him.

Sam is camped at the edge of the bandstand, his shoulders pressed to the wall and his arms crossed over his chest. There's a cigarette pinched in the corner of his mouth and a disgruntled furrow to his brow as he looks over the crowd of phantom revelers. In blue jeans and biker boots he looks like he dressed for a drag race instead of a ball.

I cut through the crowd with Maura in tow. When Sam sees me coming, he pushes off the wall and takes the cigarette from his mouth. He squints through the smoke he exhales, eyeing Maura and me.

"What's cooking, Crazy?"

"I need the keys to the Blazer," I say in a tone that's more demand than request. "Maura knows where Grady went."

I don't have to say anything else before Sam's on the move, the phantom sparks flashing across his glasses as he leads us into the crowd. His head swivels between searching and checking on us, making sure we're close behind before he pushes on.

We shove up to Virgil and Fern, who are dancing together beneath the swirling lights. Fern's hair is a waterfall of curls, and her small frame is snatched in a molten-gold sarong dress. She spins in her heels with Virgil, who is considerably less dressed—wearing only black jeans and angel wings, his snake tattoo slithering in circles around his arm as he writhes to the music.

"Virgil!" Sam shouts to get his attention. "We need the keys!"

Virgil takes his time digging the keys out of his pocket. He holds them out, but before Sam can grab them, he snatches them away from his grasp. "Where are you headed so fast?"

"Virginia," I say, putting out my own hand. "I know who killed me, and now I know where he is."

Virgil deposits the keys in my outstretched palm. "That hunk of shit will *not* make it to Virginia and back by sunrise," he declares.

"It's gonna have to," I grind out, curling my fingers around the keys.

"It tops out at, like, seventy. You won't make it," Virgil says.

"The holy spirit ain't wrong," Sam says. "We can go faster on my bike."

"We can't all fit on your *bike*, Sam," I snap, gesturing toward Maura.

"No, I— Annie, I'm not coming," Maura says, her voice a rasp in her throat. I spin around to look at her.

"Why the hell not?"

"I can't. I can't do it to him, and even if I could, I'm still just a ghost. Even tonight."

I reach out to her. I grasp her arm and she feels solid to me, but that doesn't mean she's corporeal to the living. I squeeze her arm and ask, "Are you sure you want me to do this?"

"You need to," she says.

She's right.

But before I trust Sam to take me there, there's one thing I need to know.

I twist back and grab Fern by the wrist, her bamboo bangles clattering as I do.

"Whoa—" She balks as I yank on her arm.

"Give us a second," I say to Sam.

He looks perplexed. So does Fern. But I draw her far enough from him that the racket of partying ghosts drowns out our conversation, and I swing her around so Sam won't see her expression, either.

And then I ask her.

"Did Sam kill those girls?"

Fern's sparse brows arch over her sharply lined eyes. Her lips, glossy with gold shimmer, part in shock. But my guts go cold as her shock shifts to anger, ire I've never seen before burning in her ruby eyes. I mean, I'm used to people being pissed at me, but Fern's wrath is like a solar eclipse, rare and fearsome and painful to stare into.

She doesn't answer my question. Instead she demands, "Who have you been talking to?"

"It doesn't matter—"

"*Yes*, it *does*," Fern snaps. One of her cold hands hooks behind my arm, and she steps in close to me. I've never seen her look so fierce. So furious.

So protective.

"Sam didn't kill us," she says.

I reel backward as it hits me like a sucker punch. *Holy shit.* Was Fern one of those five girls? The ones that poster declared Sam guilty of killing?

"Fern—"

"I don't know who you spoke to," Fern says, cutting me off. "But believe *me*. I died in that barn with an axe in my chest. And Sam was *not* the one swinging it."

I want to believe she's telling me the truth. It's hard enough to think that Sam could be a killer, but it's impossible to imagine him killing *Fern*.

I don't really trust my gut after everything that's happened to me the past few days, but I say to Fern, "Sorry. I had to ask. I recently found out most of the men I've ever loved are shit-heels, so I'm kind of experiencing some trust issues."

Fern nods, but she still looks guarded. "You should be careful who you're talking to up here," she says. "There are a lot of snakes in this garden."

She turns away, curls swinging down her back as she storms into the crowd. I hate the idea that I've made her angry, and there are a million morbid questions circling my mind, but I don't have time for that right now.

We have to go.

I push back over to where Sam is standing with Virgil and Maura, the three of them all varying degrees of perturbed. I wave my hand as if to dismiss any questions and toss the keys in my hand back to Virgil.

"We'll take the bike," I say.

Virgil shrugs off the angel wings he's wearing. He holds them up for me and lets me hook my arms into the straps. After he fixes them to my back, he plants a kiss on my cheek.

"Savor it," he says. "You only get to do this once."

A viper smile cuts across his lips as he draws away and holds an elbow out to Maura. Before she takes it, I throw my arms around her and squeeze tight. I know she might be gone by the time we get back.

"I'll see you again," she promises as if she knows exactly what I'm thinking. As if she's thinking it, too.

"I know," I murmur, but I don't let go right away. Before my arms finally ease their grip, she leans in and says something in my ear.

"Make him tell you why," she whispers. "I just need to know why."

She slips out of my embrace and sinks into the crowd on Virgil's arm.

TWENTY-SEVEN

SAM'S BIKE MIGHT be an antique, but it can *move*.

The brief rides we took through the roads of Hagley hardly gave me a taste of what the Triumph is truly capable of. By the time we hit Harrisburg, my thighs are numb from squeezing the vibrating seat and I've scorched my ankle at least a hundred times on the exhaust pipe, but there's no doubt that we're getting there faster than we ever could in the rusty old Blazer.

I'm thankful I left my phone in Sam's pocket, because without it I would have had to rely on the old fold-out map Sam tried to offer me from the shed where he keeps his bike. Instead I watch us as a little arrow zipping along a highlighted blue route on the GPS app, compulsively checking how many miles are left between our location and the destination.

It wasn't hard to pin down Grady's whereabouts using the information Maura gave me. A motel called the Cardinal Inn came up with a quick Google search, and by the time Sam hit the asphalt at the bottom of the road to Resurrection Peak I had already mapped our route for us. I'm surprised the arrow can keep up with us as we tear down highways and interstates at speeds I never fathomed in my wildest dreams. I peek over Sam's shoulder to watch the speedometer from time to time, the needle hovering around one hundred thirty miles per hour as we fly past cars and trucks and state lines.

Pennsylvania turns to Maryland before we have to stop for gas.

When Sam eases his bike onto the ramp for a truck stop off I-81, the sudden deceleration feels like moving in slow motion.

"Sorry, Crazy," Sam says over the chug of the engine while he pulls up to one of the pumps. "Gotta refuel."

"I figured." I wait for him to nudge the kickstand down before I slide off the seat on shaky legs. "We can't all be all-electric," I add.

He glances at me when I reference that night, that *kiss*. I notice his furrowed brow, his guarded gaze, his tensed jaw. I don't blame him for being wary, and I'm not ready to let my guard down completely, either, so instead I pace away from him and take out my phone.

While Sam heads into the rest stop to pay for the gas, I look at the 93.9 miles remaining between our stop in Maryland and the motel in Virginia. It's 1:17 a.m. At the speed Sam's been keeping it will probably only take us an hour or less to reach the Cardinal Inn. That means our trip will have taken us about three hours in total. If sunrise comes around 7:30 a.m., we need to be back on the road by 4 a.m.

That gives me plenty of time to make sure Grady fully regrets what he did.

Sam returns, chomping on a toothpick, and as he closes the tank on his Triumph, I ask him, "What exactly would happen if we didn't make it back by sunrise?"

"Beats me." Sam shrugs. "I guess we cop a permanent breeze."

"Has anyone tried it?"

"Of course somebody tried it," Sam scoffs. "I'd love to tell you what happens next, but anyone who didn't make it home by sunup never came back at all. Not even for Halloween."

"That's unnerving," I admit.

"We'll make it back," Sam promises.

"We have to leave by four. Can you keep track of time when we get to the Cardinal?"

Sam shakes back his sleeve to show me his watch. He doesn't give me any other answer, but he doesn't really need to. Still, he pauses before climbing back on the bike and looks at me, black eyes searching.

"It might be harder than you think," he tells me. "To kill someone you love."

I ask him, "Are you speaking from experience?"

"I just want you to know I'll help if you need me to," he says.

"So, you think I can't handle him on my own."

"That's not what I'm saying."

"I'll ask for your help when I need it. I won't when I don't." I pat the brown leather seat on the motorcycle between us. "Let's—as you say—*dissipate*."

He doesn't look amused. He still swings his leg over and steadies the bike while I get on behind him. I hitch myself close against his back and hook my arms around his middle. He says nothing more as he kicks the bike to life and we whip into motion. We pull away from the pump and cut off a truck whose indignant honk is lost behind us.

We leave the rest stop and blast through Maryland and West Virginia. Sam seems intent on making up for any time lost during our pit stop, pushing the bike faster and faster along the interstate. I navigate by pointing toward the upcoming exits, the wind and the engine too loud for us to speak along the way.

By the time we reach our destination, it's 2:03 a.m.

We wind up on the main road of a little town in the middle of nowhere. It's like home but flatter. Sam's bike prowls down the dark street as we get closer to the motel. And then I spot it up ahead—a squat row of green doors lit by fluorescent bulbs with moth halos. There are only four cars in the lot, and the vacancy light glows beneath the yellow sign with a lit-up red cardinal out front.

None of the cars in the lot have New Jersey plates, so if Grady stole a car after abandoning his Bronco, he probably moved to another vehicle somewhere along the way. Or maybe he hitchhiked. Maybe he took a bus. It doesn't matter, as long as he's here.

Sam rolls the Triumph into a spot at the end of the lot. He kills the engine and tosses us into silence so sharp I can hear the drone of a TV playing on the other side of the motel. I shake out my tangled hair and climb off the bike, avoiding the red-hot exhaust pipe.

"We can't just go ask what room he's in," I say. "I don't want anyone to be able to say we were here."

"Yeah. Let's give it a little gumshoe." Sam draws a pack of cigarettes from the pocket of his jacket. He bites the end of one to draw it out and then tosses the pack to me as he steps up onto the sidewalk in front of the motel. He turns to offer me a lit match, his hand cupped around the flame. I light my cigarette before we prowl on, stalking down the sidewalk to assess each room.

The first two don't appear occupied when I press my hand to the glass and peer through the crack between the curtains in the window. I can't see through the closed curtains in the third room, but there's a champagne-colored Honda parked in front of the door. The fourth, fifth, and sixth don't seem occupied. The seventh has a light on, and I crane my head to spy through the sliver of space between the curtains. There's a man alone inside, but he isn't Grady.

We skip over the office in the center of the motel and keep moving to inspect the rest of the rooms. I'm only certain that one of them is vacant—the rest are impenetrable, and I know I can't use the location of the parked cars as absolute proof of which rooms are occupied. Sam walks along beside me, eyeing the cars in their spots and the road behind us, gaze panning all over the lot. I think even a shifting blade of grass wouldn't escape his notice. His vigilance is helpful, but all I care about is finding Grady.

The room with the TV is playing late-night infomercials with the curtains drawn shut. It doesn't offer me a single clue as to who might be in the room, and at the end of the line of doors I don't feel like I've learned much at all. I turn to Sam, arching my brows at him while he draws on his cigarette.

"What a totally unhelpful exercise," I say like it's his fault.

"Look, I only have so many tricks up my sleeve. If you got a better idea, let's hear it."

I spent all the time on the way here thinking about what it would be like to finally face my killer and didn't really consider how I would get to him without alerting unwanted witnesses. I look down the row of doors and let my mind churn through absurd possibilities—setting off fire alarms, getting Sam to distract the innkeeper while I steal his logbook, crawling through vents like it's *Die Hard*. Nothing really seems ideal.

"Crazy," Sam says, catching my attention again. "Do you want to deep-six that sheriff or not?"

"Of course I do."

"Then start thinking like a *ghost*."

I stare at him for a second. I wonder if he's holding back on something, but if he is, it doesn't matter. His words are enough to inspire a half-hatched plan. I look away from him and flick my cigarette onto the sidewalk, backtracking to a room I'm certain is unoccupied. I try the handle, but the door is locked.

I glance back at Sam. "Does one of those tricks up your sleeve happen to be lock picking?"

"Baby, you're talking to a master of the degenerate arts," Sam scoffs, striding up to the door. He digs in his pocket for a tarnished silver Swiss army knife and unfolds a narrow tool that he slides into the lock on the doorknob. With his other hand he removes the toothpick he was chewing on earlier from behind his ear, and I watch as he probes with the tool and pushes the toothpick deeper into the lock. When it finally pops, the door swings open into an empty room.

I move past him and skim my fingers along the dresser that doubles as a TV stand. The furnishing is minimal and the patterns plentiful. The bedspread appears to be some kind of palm leaf print, whereas the carpet is checkered and the wallpaper flecked with small flowers. I only have a couple seconds to take it all in before the stripe of light coming in through the doorway closes behind Sam. Once the door clicks shut, all I can see is the flare on the end of his cigarette.

"What's the plan?" he asks.

"I have an idea." I hold my phone out to him, and he takes it hesitantly. I follow the wall back toward the bathroom and reach inside to switch on the light. The bulb sputters a few times before it stays on, throwing cold light over the yellow tile. "I don't know if it'll work. I'll try to signal you from Grady's room if I find it. You should wait outside and keep watch."

Sam brings up his cigarette and stares at me around the smoke he breathes out. I can see the unhappy pull to his mouth, and I know he doesn't want to walk out of here and leave me on my own, but I'm not giving him a choice.

I move into the bathroom while he lingers. I turn the handles over the tub, and water chugs from the corroded faucet. Sam asks from the doorway, "What if I don't get a signal?"

I watch the water streaming from the faucet. I feel it calling to me, like to like, the rushing in my belly becoming the hum in my veins. I run my fingers through some of the condensation gathering on the wall, and I answer Sam in a whisper.

"If I don't come back, find me in the water."

TWENTY-EIGHT

A KILLER WAKES to the sound of rushing water.

He sits up on the creaky motel bed, groggy from the bottle on his nightstand. The flicker of his TV screen casts shadows on the wall and shines across the water seeping under the bathroom door. He swings his legs over the edge of the bed, and his feet slap against soaked carpet.

"What the hell?" he grumbles. He crosses the room and throws the bathroom door open. He tries to turn on the light, but it flashes for only a second before the bulb flares and bursts. Tiny shards of glass clink against the tile. He recoils from the doorway, but it isn't because of the exploding lightbulb.

It's because of what he saw in that split-second flash.

I'm lying at the bottom of the overflowing tub. My hair is a slithering crown around my head, my eyes black pits in my water-logged skull, my fingers crawling up the sides of the bath. I know he saw me, and I know he's backing away, because I am everywhere in the water that runs over the edge of the tub and rushes across the floor.

I don't get up.

I wait.

Grady grasps for the lamp on the dresser. He rips off the shade, wielding the bare bulb like a flashlight as he edges back toward the bathroom. He extends his arm through the doorway, stretching the lamp's cord as he tries to aim the light over the edge of the tub. The glare only carves a shadow across the top of the water I'm hidden beneath.

I know what keeps him here, squinting in the dark like he's seeking a rational explanation for the flood.

He still doesn't believe I've come for him.

My fingers claw over the edge of the tub.

I rise up out of the water, river weeds stuck to my hair and skin. My black eyes reflect the lamp pointed at my decaying face.

When he sees me, he screams.

The sound of it feeds my hunger, and I remain standing in the tub, water trickling down the feathery wings strapped to my back while Grady drops the lamp with a glass-crack shatter against the tile. The bulb blinks out.

He tries to run, but he can't get away fast enough. The TV strikes flashes of blue light that blind him as he stumbles across the wet floor. He trips over the edge of the bed in his rush to the nightstand, where his favorite revolver is waiting just an arm's reach from his pillow.

He picks it up, the same gun he killed Maura with.

By the time he turns to point it at me, I'm out of the tub and standing right in front of him.

"Annie. Stay back," he commands. He's got his finger hooked around the trigger again, but this time his hand is shaking.

"What's that going to do?" I ask as I step closer. "Do you think you can kill me again?"

"I didn't kill you. You're . . . You didn't—you didn't die—"

"Is that what you thought?" I laugh. The cool metal of the barrel nudges against my forehead as his hand trembles. "When I came back, did you think it was all a dream?"

"No...No, no, no," Grady repeats, a mantra of denial. "No, Rabbit, no—"

"God, get a fucking grip," I snap. "You *know* you killed me, Grady."

"That's *enough*, Annie," he barks, thrusting the gun forward to grind the barrel against my forehead. My red lips draw a smile that shows all my teeth.

"Go on. Shoot me. See what happens."

"You think I won't do it," he says.

"Why wouldn't you? You did it to Maura."

"You know," Grady sneers, "I wasn't glad when you came back. When Arroyo called and told us you were at the school, I thought...I thought I lost my mind, but I wasn't *relieved*. I thought I got rid of you, Annie. I thought I was done with your bullshit, but you showed up and brought more bullshit, bullshit, *bullshit*."

"Wow. Cool your bitchfit, Sheriff."

Rage is turning his face splotchy red beneath his freckles. His nostrils flare as he struggles to control his breathing. His trigger finger is quivering with anticipation, but he won't shoot yet. It's not enough just to kill me. He wants me cowed and conquered. He wants to be in control.

He chooses his next words carefully.

"It was easier than I thought it'd be. No one even cared where you went."

"You made sure of that," I hiss. "I can't believe you got everyone to think I staged a crime scene."

"It wasn't hard. Nobody thinks very highly of you, Annie," Grady says.

"Ouch," I intone. "You know I totally care what people think of me."

"Do you think that's a good thing? You think it's fair to completely disregard everyone around you?"

"Are you seriously lecturing me about being insensitive to others right now? You *killed* me, Grady. Did you think *that* was fair? Did you think it was fair when you shot your own daughter in the face?"

"*That* was because of *you*," Grady snaps. "It's all because of *you!*"

"*How*, Grady?" I shout. "How am I responsible for that?"

"You think I always bought you two the same toys, the same coats, the same shoes because I thought I had two daughters? *No*, Annie. I *had* to, because Maura didn't want *anything* if you didn't have it, too. She always wanted to be the same as *you*," Grady rants.

"What's that got to do with anything?" I snarl.

"Don't you get it, Annie? Even when you were *dead*, she still wanted to be *just like you*."

I stare at him, my fury rising like the swollen river after heavy rain. The TV flashes with images of rushing water and blood seeping across the floor of the Dead Shed. A metallic ring emanates from the speakers, blasting white noise. I feel it charge me as the flood on the floor starts to pool around my ankles.

My hand flies to the gun at my forehead.

I did promise Sam a signal, and I know Grady will help me give him one. As soon as he feels the cold of my hand close around the barrel of his gun, he squeezes the trigger and fires a bullet directly into my forehead. The bullet shoots through me as if through water, and I only feel a fading ripple across my brow. The shot buries itself in the wall behind me instead, and for all I know it might have continued straight through into the vacant room adjoining. Its momentum certainly wasn't slowed by me.

I watch his eyes grow wide, and I flash a hungry smile.

I rip the revolver from his grip and throw it to the side. I should not have the strength to disarm him so easily, but tonight I am as strong as my wrath.

And I am very fucking wrathful.

I lunge at him, and we crash onto the bed behind him, my fingers sharp black claws that tear into his shoulders while I sit on his chest. My weight crushes the breath from his lungs, and I lean close to growl in his face.

"So, what? You killed us both just like you got us both snow boots for Christmas? So we'd *match?*"

"You are dead. You *are* dead."

"Holy shit, we can*not* still be on chapter one here. Yes, I'm dead; get with the program, Grady!"

A knock at the door taps out the first five beats of the rhythm Sam made against the mausoleum the night we kissed. I glance at the window to glimpse his silhouette through the curtain. Messy pomp, leather jacket, cigarette smoke. I turn back to Grady and dig my nails deeper into his flesh.

"Tell me why you killed her. Tell me why you killed Maura."

"I *told* you why."

"You told me *bullshit.*"

"I didn't want to. I didn't want to do it," Grady insists. "She could have realized what I had done was for her own good. But she chose to follow you instead."

"Are you *blaming her?*"

"I'm blaming *you.*"

"Fuck you, Grady," I spit. I'm still drenched, my hair and clothes and the feathery wings strapped to my back all dripping on Grady as I loom over him. "What about Katie? Why did you kill her?"

"Don't ask me about *her.*"

"*Tell me,* Grady."

"There isn't shit worth telling you," he says, flinching as droplets of water fall on his ruddy face. "I had nothing to do with it!"

But he's lying.

The white-noise buzz begins to take the shape of a voice whispering through the TV. I hear her hissing Grady's name as the images on the screen flip through scenes of places I've never seen. It's not just Maura's blood on the floor or the river where he drowned me, it's a crowded house party in a stranger's yard, a long empty block with no streetlights, desperate screams in the dark of the woods.

It's the night he killed Katie, and she's showing him what he did.

I can feel her. She is the current and I am a diode, and her rage resonates through me. Katie's voice grows louder through the static distortion.

"*I thought they'd never find me where you left me. My bones in the cold, cold river . . .* "

"Stop," Grady pleads, thrashing below me. "Stop it, stop this—"

"Shh," I hiss. "Listen to her."

"*The water washed it all away. My skin. My face. My name. What you did to me . . .* "

"Stop!"

"*Why? Why? Why did you do it?*"

"Why did you kill her?" I press. "Why?"

Grady looks up at me, gulping for air beneath my crushing weight.

"Same reason I killed you," he croaks. "Somebody had to teach you a fucking lesson."

A sudden pain rips through my ribs. A scream is strangled in my throat as I look down at Grady's hand curled around the grip of his hunting knife, the blade sheathed in my stomach.

It all happens so fast. He twists the knife and blood pours from the wound, rot-thick and brown black. I can't even hoarse out another scream through the press of pain and the sucking weakness I feel. The gush of blood drains me of my weight, and Grady lurches up, throwing me against the bed as he jabs the knife deeper beneath my ribs.

The images on the TV screen fizz to black. Katie stops whispering through the speakers. Grady's on top of me and I'm all alone in the dark.

Just like the night he killed me.

I feel like it's happening again. His knife in my side. The rushing water in my ears. The smell of Bushmills on his breath. I cringe away from his sneering mouth and claw at his hand.

"No," I choke. "No, no—"

He pulls the knife from my gut like a cork drawn from a bottle. I thrash against him, and when my leg falls off the bed, my boot splashes into the flood filling the room.

The water is still rising.

He balances the tip of his knife against the base of my throat and grabs me by my hair. I want to close my eyes and cower beneath his leer, but I didn't stop staring him down the night he killed me, and I won't do it now. His blade lifts, poised to drop straight through my heart.

"Ever since you showed up, I've wanted to do this again," he whispers.

His fist swings downward, gripping the carved handle of his handsome old knife. The blade glints in the faint light that squeezes through the drawn curtains, moving toward me as if in slow motion. There's a crazed hunger burning in Grady's eyes, a longing for the moment when his blade will sink into my rib cage.

He wants to hurt me. He wants to stab me. He wants to kill me. All because he can't control me.

I jerk my legs up and slam my boots against his chest. He flails backward and splashes into the water that has nearly risen to engulf the bed. He disappears under the choppy surface, lost in the flood that fills the motel room. The churning waters sweep the set of chairs by the window into the current. I scramble to the edge of the bed and dive in.

The cold water closes over me and carries me like a serpent through the shallows. When I listen, I can hear him splashing, fighting against the heaving tide. I circle him in the water. I wait for him to get to his feet before my hands close around his ankles and yank him back beneath the surface.

His shout is cut off by the water that rushes into his open mouth when I pull him under. He gurgles and tries to speak or scream, but I don't care what he has to say anymore. There's no point in asking him to explain himself and I know he isn't sorry for what he did. Every second he's alive is a second he doesn't deserve.

I'll silence him like he silenced us.

I am the weight of all his sins as I hold him down beneath the murky water. He thrashes and swings his fists, but he can't get away from me. I look into his horrified eyes, and I know he's sorry he killed me now.

Out of all the girls who might have come for him, I am the worst. I make him stare at me until his eyes roll up toward the surface.

Grady Harker drowns in a flood manifested by my wrath.

The water that pushes into his lungs in his last glassy-eyed moments is the same water that drowned me. I know this is water from the Paulinskill River, though I don't know how I brought it here. It rises like a stormy sea until the moment when Grady's eyes go slack and stare, when his limbs fall limp and his heart shudders out its final pulse.

Instantly the violent waters stop churning.

Everything is still and quiet, my hunger finally sated.

I'm not sure how long I bask in that feeling before the water starts to drain like someone pulled a plug. It lowers in a rush, and I'm left kneeling on the floor over Grady's wet corpse, my hands still knotted in his sweat-stained T-shirt.

"Annabel!"

I hear Sam's voice, but my mind is far away.

I can't believe that my life has led to this: a train wreck of an ending that is somehow also a beginning. I wonder if I should have done something differently—if I should have been better behaved, if I should have focused more on school, if I should have stayed away from bad boys with good jawlines and learned to curb my rotten attitude. Maybe I'd still be alive, maybe I would have never attracted the murderous ire of my best friend's father, if I had only tried to be a good girl.

But to be honest, I think I'd rather be dead than good.

"Annie, Crazy, baby, come on," Sam urges, reaching down to wrap his hand around my wrist. "We gotta split. Let's go."

"Wait," I say. I pull my fingers from Grady's shirt and look around the room. My eyes search the puddle-splashed carpet as Sam gives an insistent tug on my wrist.

"Annabel, come on, it's almost five o'clock."

"*Five?*" I scramble up, my boots squelching against the wet floor. "Shit, Sam, I told you to watch the time—"

"I *did.*"

"Well, then what the fuck?"

"You seemed busy." Sam shrugs.

I scoff and spin away from him to scour the floor. Sam paces restlessly toward the door and holds it open for me to let in light from the parking lot.

"Come on, Crazy. Whatever you're lookin' for, it ain't worth missing our deadline."

I ignore him and round the edge of the bed, where I spot what I've been searching for. Grady's knife lies on the floor beside the nightstand, washed clean by the flood. I snatch it and charge for the door. As we step out into the lot, I tuck the blade into my boot for safekeeping. It feels important that I hang on to the weapon that killed me, at least until I understand how it was able to hurt me now. There's an expanding pool outside the door from all the water that rushed out when Sam came in, but I bet the cops will never understand how Grady Harker drowned in his motel room.

I swing the door shut behind us and close the lid on my unfinished business.

Sam mounts his bike and I slip on behind him with an ease that's becoming practiced. Sam kicks the bike to start and takes an easy curve away from the curb before we shoot off to try to outrun the sunrise.

TWENTY-NINE

WE'RE ABOUT HALFWAY through Pennsylvania when I realize I might find out what the other side looks like much sooner than I anticipated.

The time on my phone tells me it's a half hour till sunrise, and we're still ninety-eight miles from home. Our odds are looking pretty bleak, and judging by the tension in Sam's spine, he knows it, too.

"We're so screwed," I shout into his ear over the skull-shaking roar of the bike.

His only response is to gun the engine hard enough that the front wheel rears up off the pavement for a few exhilarating seconds before it hits the ground and our speed climbs faster. The momentum isn't just pushed by the engine anymore. Something in Sam is supercharging the Triumph, the same sort of energy that manifested a flood in Grady's motel room.

I wonder what else we are capable of.

I encourage his effort by pushing my hands up his chest to clasp over his heart. It's a little positive reinforcement that goes a long way—the highway is a streaky blur around us. We're moving so fast we're invisible to the naked eye, sheering around cars operated by sleepy drivers in the pre-dawn gloom. The faster we move, the foggier things get. We're past the speed of sound and past the physical realm.

We're moving at ghost-speed.

And we're not alone here.

My grasp on Sam becomes a desperate cling when something nearly rips me off the bike. I yowl in surprise, but the sound is drowned out by the snarls of the beast that has its jaws locked around my ankle, yanking with all its hulking strength.

The bike stutters and swerves.

"Sam!" I scream.

I try to pull my leg free, but the bike is slowing and the dog is relentless. There are two more flanking it, nearly caught up with the Triumph's back wheel. I swing my head to the left and see another hellhound gaining on us, teeth bared and eyes glowing.

"Hold on!" Sam yells to me. It's a plea more than a command. I dig my fists in against his ribs, but the dog plants its paws on the asphalt and jerks so viciously on my leg that I'm finally torn from the seat.

The bike tips as I fall, tilting toward the ground, but Sam recovers as I crash against the pavement, the dog's mouth tight as a bear trap around my ankle.

Headlights blind my vision and an oncoming car swerves to avoid me, horn blaring. The other dogs are making their way toward me, but they have to scatter to dodge the car that flies into their lane. One of them jumps onto its roof and lands on the pavement behind it, but the driver doesn't react.

"Annie!" Sam is calling as the dog starts to drag me away. I dig my fingers into the dirt at the edge of the highway and scramble for purchase in the grass as we descend the embankment toward the woods. I try to kick free from the dog's grip, but every crack of my boot against its head only makes its fangs sink deeper into my other ankle.

"Sam! *Sam!*" I scream, my voice shrill. I grit my teeth and look to the hellhound dragging me through the trees. I punctuate my shouts with kicks from my free leg. "Let. Me. Go. Let me *go*, you mangy Cujo-ass devil-mutt piece of shit, let me *go*!"

The dog's head gives a sudden jerk that snaps me to the side. The wings strapped to my back are snagged on a root protruding from the base of a tree, and the beast tugs on my battered ankle.

"Crazy, hang on!"

Sam is getting closer. The other three dogs dive into a ditch and vanish underground, swallowed by the copper leaves coating the dirt. The beast that has me is sinking into the forest floor, too, trying to drag me with it. I feel the strap tethering me to my last anchor fraying.

"Sam!"

The hellhound's head is almost fully submerged. It pulls and pulls, and I watch its snout sink down, taking my boot with it. The strap on my wings pops loose, and I cling to the trunk of the tree as the beast wrenches my leg into the ground.

It's going to pull me under.

I lose my grip on the tree, and the dog drags me waist-deep into the dirt. I dig my fingers into brush and scattered leaves, but it's no use. I feel like I'm suspended through a hole in the ground. My legs kick beneath the surface, not constricted by dirt but instead treading uselessly against an empty space.

Then I look up, and Sam is on fire.

He's running through the trees with flames trailing him, igniting the dry forest. The fire that surrounds him is nothing like the lick of flame that sprouted from his temple when he kissed me—this is an angry inferno, incinerating everything in his path. The only thing his fire can't burn is me, and when he grasps my arms in his blazing hands, I twist my grip to his elbows and hold on tight.

"Pull, pull, pull, pull, pull—" I chant.

Sam tries to say something, but only dense black smoke billows from his mouth. It doesn't matter as long as he's still holding on to me, heaving against the beast that has my ankle crushed in its jaws. My hands claw up Sam's arms as he draws me out of the ground, locking around his shoulders when I'm almost out of the dirt. The dog's head rears back up, fangs gnashing on my leg as its empty white eyes glare at Sam.

He reaches for the beast.

The flames on his skin crackle and lick, throwing hot light in the hellhound's eyes. It tries to recoil while still holding on to my leg, but when Sam's burning palm presses to the dog's forehead, it yelps and withdraws. The dog releases my leg as it escapes into the dirt.

I cling tight to Sam and feel his heat surround us, catching fire to the trees.

"I don't want to go," I whisper.

"I won't let you." Sam's voice is a hissing sizzle, hoarse from smoke and flame. The fire is spreading through the trees, but the flames on Sam have died down to a faint smolder now that I'm safe in his grasp.

"Sorry," I say while he pulls at my arms. "For accusing you of murder."

Sam hauls me to my feet and shrugs, shaking the ash out of his hair. "Wasn't the first time I've been falsely accused, baby."

"Do you really think we can make it?" I ask.

"No doubt. We ain't taking the eternal checkout."

The ache in my ankle fades as we start to run. Sam's hand stays clasped on mine as we dash through the tunnel of wildfire set by his death echo. We emerge from the trees to find his bike tossed on the shoulder where he must have dropped it in his rush to reach me. He rights it quickly and I climb on behind him, squeezing with my thighs while I try to tie the torn strap of my feathered wings. I fasten the knot as the bike jerks into motion. My arms loop around Sam's middle and I squint up at the teal-streaked sky.

The sun is rising.

The mile markers and exits rip past us as Sam pushes the bike faster and faster. Before long we're a phantom blur again, flying down the highway at supernatural speeds. I try to focus my own energy on powering the motorcycle, but I feel drained and dried up. I rest my cheek against his shoulder and watch the sunlight start to glimmer at the edge of the horizon.

I want to believe he'll really get us back in time.

I close my eyes for a while. If we're driving straight into oblivion, I'm not sure I want to see it coming. Maybe if I keep my eyes closed forever, it won't feel any different from this at all. But there's no way the empty place I was almost pulled into could feel the same as speeding down the highway on a roaring cream Triumph with my arms around Sam.

When I finally open my eyes, we're on Route 15 and the sunlight is gaining on us, seeping across the tops of trees as we shoot toward the dirt road at the bottom of Resurrection Peak.

"Come on, come on," I hiss in Sam's ear, squeezing him tight. We're almost there.

The bike bucks when we dip off the asphalt onto the road to Resurrection Peak. Dust clouds the path while Sam weaves around ditches in the road. We climb the mountain with the Triumph's engine wailing, protesting the super speed Sam has been pushing it to. I mentally beg it to last a little longer, my python grip constricting tighter around Sam's ribs.

The trees break.

Derelict homes stud the path as we zip through the streets of the ghost town. Chapel House looms ahead of us, the windows already reflecting daybreak.

We tear around the shaded edge of the grounds, lurching over wild overgrowth and debris along the way. When we round the corner to face the portico behind the dance hall, I see that dawn hasn't hit this side of the mansion yet and the party is still raging inside. You might say it's reached more of a frenzy than ever, a last hurrah before the sun sends the dead back to their graves.

I don't wait for Sam's bike to stop before I launch off the seat and charge into the Ark.

The scene inside is surreal. Ghosts in period garb whip circles around the ceiling, floating above the crowd of revelers. The band on the stage beats a clamorous rhythm, winding toward a wild crescendo. The lights spin across the walls, spotlighting the spectral dancers. I push my way through the throng, looking for frizzed red hair and freckle-spotted skin.

I need to tell Maura I did it.

The tune blaring from the skeleton band climbs to a frantic climax as I stumble past a knot of twirling girls in brocade skirts. Then a purple beam of light sweeps through the crowd and illuminates Maura as she dances a wild mambo with Virgil. I cut through the dancing specters and collide with her, nearly knocking her off her feet.

"Jesus *Christ*, Annie," she squawks. Her tone is cross, but her hands grab for mine and our fingers knot together.

"I did it," I say. "He's gone. It's done."

"Oh, Rabbit," Maura says. Her big brown eyes go smoky and sad, her freckled lip trembling as she bites back tears. She winds her arms around me and presses her forehead to my jaw. Whispery, she asks, "Did he tell you? Did he tell you why?"

I squeeze her tightly. I nuzzle against the top of her head as I swallow muck in my throat and say, "He did it because our power made him feel weak."

Maura sniffles against my neck and then lifts her face, tears glittering on her freckles. "He didn't actually tell you that, did he?" she says. It's not really a question. Maybe she was hoping her father had absolved himself somehow before I slaughtered him, but I won't lie to her. She gives her head a shake and sighs. "You think there are any self-help books about what to do after you find out your dad's a murderer?"

"Nope. Maybe you should write one," I suggest.

"Oh yeah. I'm sure I'm super qualified to write an advice book."

"Come on, you could make a whole brand out of it. Become a lifestyle influencer," I say.

Maura laughs, husky and low. She lifts our joined hands and tugs me close. "I saved the last dance for you."

The skeleton band's frenzied rhythm slows, easing into a plaintive ballad that mourns the night's end. I know by the time the song is over, Maura will be gone. So, I hug my arms around her shoulders while she loops hers around my waist, and we sway in time to the lamenting lullaby.

"I'll try to reach you if you try to reach me," I promise, my cheek pressed to hers. Maura just nods.

I close my arms tight around her neck and push my face into her hair. The music is starting to fade like a radio signal going out of range. I take one last breath of her mossy, patchouli, gun-smoke scent before that starts to fade, too.

My best friend's ghost wanes in the golden light of day.

When I open my eyes, the dance hall is empty, the last blue note of the violin carrying the spirits out into the dawn. Streamers sway and lights flicker as the room comes to a rest. We're the only ones left.

I look around. Virgil is sprawled on the edge of the stage, tossing candy corn at the twins as they sit atop the swinging chandelier like birds in a nest, trying to catch the candy in their mouths. Fern and Dear are still slow-dancing to the faint strains of music ghosting through the hall, Fern's gold dress glinting as she sways in Dear's embrace.

Finally my eyes fall on Sam.

He's walking over to me, hands in the pockets of his jacket and a cigarette tucked along with that cowlick curl behind his ear. He stops at my side and surveys the trashed dance hall, draws out the cigarette, and lights it. It dangles from the corner of his mouth as he slips his matchbook back into his pocket.

For a moment we both stand still in the silence, our cheeks chilled by the breeze blowing through the open doors to the portico.

"Did anyone lamp those righteous threads on the Typhoid Lady tonight?" he finally says.

"I was like, whoa! Positively puritanical!" Fern chimes.

"Typhoid Lady?" I prompt. "I don't think I had the pleasure."

"Oh, she's a real germ," Sam says.

Fern is gazing up at Dear, and her tone toward me is a bit tight, but she still explains, "A buncha folks died 'cause she thought hand-washing was for suckers. You'll meet her next year."

"Don't look forward to it or nothin'," Dear says.

"She's always dressed like a true hymn hustler. I mean, totally togged to the bricks," Sam tells me.

"That, what you just said? Makes literally no sense to me," I declare. I reach out and steal the cigarette from between his fingers. I take a deep drag and on an exhale of smoke I say, "I guess I'll just see for myself next time."

Because there will be a next time.

Until this house falls to ruin and the mountain crumbles to dust.

We will always be here.

ACKNOWLEDGMENTS

I WROTE THIS BOOK because I'm haunted by all the girls whose names and stories are buried with their bones.

I want to thank my husband, Michal Drozd, who has walked at midnight a million times with me, listening to me talk about this story. Thank you for giving me a decade of love and spooky adventures to draw inspiration from, and for believing I would achieve my dreams even when I didn't.

My undying gratitude to my agent, Larissa Melo Pienkowski, who accepted the challenge of selling this bitchy book and crafted a pitch so masterful that no one would dare ask us to make Annie Lane more likable. I also want to thank everyone at Jill Grinberg Literary—I'm so lucky to have the support of such an incredible agency.

This book is 50 percent my harebrained ideas and 50 percent the genius work of my editor, Rachel Stark. With their help, this story became sharper and angrier and bitchier than ever before. Rachel, thank you for the hours and hours of story therapy that brought us to this final furious draft.

Thanks to Zareen Johnson for designing the beautifully creepy cover emblazoned with Annie Lane's bloodred epitaph, and to Christine Blackburne for bringing that headstone to life in all its neon-splashed glory.

I'm also so grateful for assistant editors Elanna Heda and Ashley I. Fields. Thanks to our biggest cheerleaders at acquisitions, Kim

Knueppel, Loren Godfrey, Vicki Korlishin, and Dina Sherman; copy chief Guy Cunningham and the entire copyediting team; and content packaging manager Augusta Harris. I'm sending a skeleton band's worth of fanfare to all of you and to everyone else at Hyperion who had a hand in bringing this book into the world.

Thank you to Mindy McGinnis for writing killer books about angry vengeful girls and for taking the time to read and offer a blurb for this book!

For my wicked imagination, I have my mother to thank: Thanks, Mom, for reading me books every night, and for never telling me not to be myself, even though "being myself" meant being the creepy kid who won't stop telling scary stories that torment all the other children. And thanks for being my very first example of a badass bitch!

An apology to my little sister, Kaity, for being my captive audience throughout our childhood—sorry for all the scares! Thank you for being the reason I can't watch *Practical Magic* without crying.

I'm sending big, gross, saccharine sentiments to my best friends Freddie Kölsch and Alex Russell, whose love gave me the backbone I'd been lacking all my life. Also, Freddie: Who knew when I first bummed a clove cigarette off you in the Bill & Bob's parking lot that someday we would share a debut year.

A toast to all my friends who helped and hyped along the way— Kelly Kapow, Luis & Gabe Hernandez, Brooke Sponzo, and Skyla Arndt!

To all the men I've known who were afraid that someday I might write a book about them—just know that if you recognize yourself in these pages, it's only your own reflection you're seeing.

And remember, dear reader: The next time a man asks you what your problem is, drive his fucking car off a bridge.